THE CRONE WARS

5

GAME OF CRONES

LYDIA M. HAWKE

**Published by Michem Publishing,
Canada**

GAME OF CRONES

August 2022

Cover design by Deranged Doctor Design
Interior design by AuthorTree

ISBN: 978-1-989457-10-8
MICHEM PUBLISHING

We are the granddaughters
of the witches you couldn't burn
- Tish Thawer, The Witches of BlackBrook

In This Series

CHAPTER 1

THERE WERE NO MORE CROWS.

Oh, the ordinary ones were still around. Two of them strutted around the sidewalk right now, bold and cocky as only crows could be, as they pulled apart a garbage bag they'd stolen from a trash can on the other side of the street.

But the important crows—the ones that only I could see gathered silently in trees or on rooftops, or following me like my own personal black cloud, the ones that warned me of something coming—those ones were gone.

I stared out through the half-closed blinds of the kitchen window. Half-closed, because I couldn't risk being seen. Edie's kitchen window, in Edie's house, because that was where the ley line had unceremoniously dropped me after my witch ancestors had pulled me out of the cell Morok had left me in.

Edie's house, because she'd left it to me in her will when she'd died in the fire in *my* house.

But no Edie. While I'd continued to hear her voice in my head throughout my struggles to learn my magick, my battle with the goliath, my killing of the Mages, I hadn't heard a peep from her since I'd lost my magick in the ley lines. Just like I hadn't heard the ancestors since their rescue. Or even my Claire-voice.

Like the crows, they were all gone. There was only silence. Emptiness.

And with the silence and emptiness had come paralysis.

Steam rose between me and the window, turning my view misty, and with a jolt, I remembered that the water was still running. I turned off the faucet, then looked at the soap suds and water spilling out of the sink and down the front of the dark oak cabinet to pool on the black-and-white tiled floor. My apron front was soaked. Goddess, but I was a mess—in every sense of the word.

I pulled the apron off over my head and dropped it in a soggy heap on the counter. It was a pinafore like the one I'd sewn for Keven, but in a solid blue linen rather than the pink flowers she'd requested, and without a frill on the pocket, and just thinking about it—and Keven—made me feel hollow again. Gutted.

I opened the cupboard under the sink and pulled out a cloth, then stiffly lowered myself to my knees beside the puddle. Goddess, would I ever move normally again? I was beginning to think the ley travel had inflicted more damage on me than just taking my magick. Five days I'd been back, and I still didn't trust myself to so much as leave the house. Five days in the real world and Edie's house, and I still felt like an intruder in both. As if I didn't belong.

But neither did I belong in Keven's world. Or Lucan's. Or the Crones'. Not anymore. Not without my magick. Hell, I wasn't even sure I could *access* their world anymore, and goddess knew I needed to, because I had to warn them about the traitor in their midst—Kate Abraham, police officer and midwitch, who wore the pendant she had taken from me. A pendant that marked her as the newest Crone, the Fifth Crone, except she wasn't.

She couldn't be, because she wasn't even Kate anymore.

On all fours, wet rag clutched tight, I shuddered at the memory of the body that had pinned me to the filthy mattress in the filthier cell from which Lucan and I had rescued the Earth Crone. The fingers that had pried at the pendant clutched in my hand. The god I had seen behind the familiar brown eyes, inhabiting the body of the woman to whom I had once entrusted my own family.

Morok, god of darkness and deceit and lies, immortal enemy of humanity itself.

The god I had been destined to stop, once and for all, as the

2

Fifth Crone. Until, as Morok himself had said, I'd been too weak to claim the power that had been given to me. Too inept to—

"Knock, knock!" a woman's voice sang out as the back door banged open behind me.

My head sagged between my shoulders. Not Jeanne, I thought. Not now. But I pushed aside the reaction—uncharitable in the extreme after all my old neighbor had done for me in the past few days—and sat back on my heels. Pasting on a smile, I grasped the edge of the counter above me, pulled myself upright, and turned to face my guest.

Jeanne Archambault's gaze took in the puddle I hadn't quite conquered, then the water still trickling down the cupboard front. A tiny frown twitched between her eyebrows, and she regarded me with concern from behind her red-framed glasses.

Determinedly, I broadened my smile and pointed at the casserole dish she held. "Is that for me?"

Her lips pursed, and for a moment I didn't think I'd succeeded in heading off her questions, but then she nodded. "My chicken and broccoli one," she replied. "It should feed you for a few days. Help you get back on your feet."

She held the dish toward me, but I made no move to take it. I couldn't. As legendary as Jeanne's chicken and broccoli casserole (smothered in cheddar cheese) might be in the neighborhood, the very thought of it turned my stomach and made my shoulders curl in around the omnipresent ache in my heart.

The last time I'd had the casserole, I'd shared it with my then-protector, Lucan, in the kitchen of my then-house, now a burned-out hulk sitting on the neglected lot next door to Edie's bungalow. Lucan had eaten most of it, picking out the broccoli bits, and I'd barely nibbled at my portion, too overwhelmed by the turn of events in my life—him, the house in the woods, a living gargoyle named Keven—to even pretend I had an appetite.

Much the way I felt now. Again. Still.

Jeanne slipped her shoes off, leaving them by the back door, and crossed the kitchen to open the refrigerator, where most of the baked spaghetti she'd brought me two days ago still sat. Her lips drew tighter. She closed the fridge and opened the freezer compartment above it.

"It freezes well," was her only comment as she placed the chicken casserole inside and closed the door again. Then she turned to me, her gaze assessing me in her professional nursing way. "How are you feeling?"

"I'm good," I said.

One of her brows rose above her glasses frames.

"Okay," I amended. "I'm okay."

Which was actually pretty freaking stellar, given the state she'd found me in on Edie's back porch. And not quite true, either, given the soul-deep exhaustion that had plagued me since my return.

I was *so* tired. Tired of fighting—for and against—what I didn't even really understand. Tired of trying *to* understand. And bloody tired of—not to mention irritated with—the part of me that still wouldn't give up.

Life at sixty wasn't supposed to be this complicated, damn it.

Jeanne's eyes dropped to the cloth in my hand, and mine followed. I sighed. I'd clutched the thing so tightly that the water I'd mopped up was dripping into a whole new puddle. Awesome. My neighbor held out one hand, palm up, and pointed with the other at the table. Without argument, I handed over the cloth, limped to a chair, and eased myself into it.

Limped and eased, because that was how I'd rolled since the ley line and the ancestors had dropped me here. I didn't know if it was because I'd had no pendant to protect me from the ley's magick this time, or because I'd just made one too many trips through on my own, but this last one had almost been the literal death of me, and recovery from it was ...

Unattainable. The thought slipped unbidden into my mind, and I thrust it away fiercely. Angrily. *Challenging,* I corrected myself. Because unattainable wasn't an option. And thanks to

Jeanne's intervention and nursing skills, I *was* recovering, thank you very much. Just more slowly than I would have liked.

And much more slowly than I needed to. Because if I didn't get my act together soon, Morok was going to win.

Jeanne cleared her throat, and I looked up to meet her expectant expression. I'd missed something, hadn't I? Again.

"Sorry, I ..."

"I asked if you've eaten today." She pointed accusingly at the sink of dishes I'd been doing pre-flood. "Those look like dinner dishes, not breakfast."

I considered lying in order to avoid a lecture, but my stomach grumbled its first interest in food in days, and I thought it best not to lose the advantage. I shook my head.

"I wanted to clean up first," I replied. "I was going to make eggs afterward."

She wiped her hands on a tea towel and pulled open the fridge. "Scrambled or fried?"

"I can—"

"Scrambled," she repeated, making the words sound like a threat rather than a query, "or fried."

"Scrambled," I said. "Please."

I watched her put two slices of bread into the toaster on the counter, and then take a frying pan from the cupboard beside the stove and eggs from the fridge. Bread and eggs that she'd provided for me, along with whatever other groceries were here. I honestly hadn't paid attention beyond trying to refuse them in the first place. But Jeanne had overridden my objections, along with my attempts to protest her three-times-daily visits to check up on me.

Jeanne, it turned out, wasn't quite the pushover I'd always thought her to be, despite her continued marriage to Gilbert, who had been the very definition of a crotchety old man even when I'd met him thirty years before.

I frowned at my neighbor's ample, plaid-shirted back as she expertly cracked two eggs into a bowl and whisked them together. When I thought about it, the only thing she hadn't pushed back on was my refusal to go to the hospital when she found me, despite my practically being at death's door—and my insistence than no one else could know that I was here. Which begged the question of ... why?

And for that matter, how? How had she even found me in the first place? I'd landed in Edie's enclosed but still freezing back porch, crumpled against the back door in the middle of the late October night, and—

Beside the fridge, the back door to the porch slammed open, and Jeanne and I both jerked our heads around to stare at ... nothing.

CHAPTER 2

"TABERNAC," JEANNE MUTTERED UNDER HER BREATH, planting her hands on her hips. "What now? Am I not doing enough for you already?"

My astonished gaze moved from the door to her. "I beg your pardon?"

She flapped a hand at me. "Not you. *Her.*"

I'd been referring to her use of the French-Canadian curse *tabernac*, because Jeanne had never, in all the time I'd known her, uttered any kind of profanity—and goddess knew she'd had plenty of reason to do so, married to Gilbert. But her response made me blink and swivel my gaze back to the open door and empty porch beyond.

"Um … her, who?"

My neighbor pushed the door closed, twisted the deadbolt to its locked position for good measure, and picked up the long wooden staff that had fallen over. She tucked it back into the corner between the door and the fridge. It was mine—the staff, not the fridge, although technically, I supposed that was mine, too—and had been made by Lucan from a linden tree. *The* linden tree, to be precise. The one I'd grown from a wand in order to defend my family from the Mages' first attack on the house.

All of which seemed a lifetime ago, now, especially when—

My heart contracted at the memories I didn't want to think about, and I forced my attention back to Jeanne and her answer as she returned to the stove.

"Edie, of course," she muttered.

"You can see her?" I asked, startled that the devoutly church-going Jeanne would admit to such a thing.

7

"Of course not." Jeanne dumped the eggs into the heated pan and scaped them around briskly.

"Then—"

"This is her house. Who else would it be?" Jeanne looked back over her plaid shoulder. "That's how I knew you were here, on the back porch that night. She flashed the lights to get my attention."

I wanted to question further, to know more, but Jeanne sniffed and turned back to the stove, and I knew that for her, the subject was closed. I leaned back in my chair.

Edie.

I should have known. That explained why the living room blind wouldn't stay closed, no matter how many times I pulled it down in my attempts to keep prying eyes from seeing me. From noticing that I'd returned to the neighborhood fold. Edie had been trying to get my attention. To let me know that she was here.

My heart gave a tiny leap, its first in days. My best friend, it seemed, hadn't deserted me after all.

A cupboard door, left open by Jeanne when she'd retrieved a plate, banged shut, and I winced. Edie had also improved at manipulating energy since she'd poured me that cup of tea the night Bedivere and Anne had arrived at the Earth Crone's house.

"Magick is energy, I'm energy. It's not that difficult, once you get the hang of it," echoed the memory of her voice in my head. The self-pity I'd felt at the time tried to resurface. I pushed it away. I had no time for that. I needed Jeanne to leave so I could converse with our dead friend. Or commune. Or whatever one did with a ghost when their voice no longer inhabited one's head. Because Edie's presence meant the possibility of answers and help. Both of which I desperately needed.

I considered hobbling across the floor to take over the cooking so my helpful neighbor would go home, but somehow I didn't think Jeanne would relinquish the spatula without a fight.

8

Instead, I turned my thoughts inward and tried to reach out to Edie.

"Edie? You there?" I asked in my head. Once, a scant week ago, I'd held entire conversations with her that way. But now, no answer came, and nothing moved that might indicate she'd heard me. I tried again, aloud this time, but whispering so Jeanne wouldn't hear me.

There was still no answer from Edie, and across the kitchen, Jeanne vigorously stirred the eggs in the pan, muttering something under her breath that I couldn't quite hear but suspected meant I hadn't been as quiet as I'd wanted to be. I abandoned my efforts to contact my friend for the moment and turned my attention to my living companion.

"How—" I caught back my unwise *how long has Edie been haunting you* question in the nick of time and changed it to, "How is Natalie doing? Is there any change?"

The memories I'd tried to protect my heart from slipped free, slicing it open in my chest. Natalie. Paul. Braden.

Jeanne slapped the two slices of toast onto a plate and plopped the scrambled eggs beside them. She took a fork from the drawer beside the sink. "I told you I would let you know if there was."

So that would be a no. I blinked back a sudden swell of tears.

Lips pressed together in a sour twist, she set plate and fork before me with more force than necessary. Then she softened.

"There's no change," she said gruffly. "But I check in on her every day, and I sit with her on my breaks."

"And—" My voice cracked, and I swallowed, then tried again. "And Paul? Have you seen him?" It was the first time I'd asked her about my son. The first time I'd spoken his name aloud since he had knocked my hand away from Natalie as he cradled her limp body in the clearing outside the Earth house and blamed me for her injuries. For the magickal war being

9

waged around them. The war I'd brought them into and couldn't protect them from.

Jeanne's gaze narrowed behind her glasses, and I saw her wrestle with her curiosity about what had transpired. She hadn't asked for any explanations so far. Not about how I'd come to be on Edie's back porch. Not about where I'd been for the weeks before that. Not about what had happened to Natalie. Not about any of it. That didn't change now.

"He comes in every day before he goes to work," she said, turning away to plunge her hands into the soapy water and begin scrubbing dishes, "and again before he picks Braden up from school. We don't talk much."

In other words, she hadn't asked him what had happened, either, and he hadn't volunteered the information—or mentioned me.

I tucked away a fresh stab of pain, shutting it behind the door I'd created in my mind to hold back the many others. The loss of Keven, of Lucan, of my very magick itself—the memory of my grandson's soft, sweet-smelling hair against my cheek and my son's savage voice snarling that I would never see Braden again.

My breath hitched beneath my ribs, and I expelled it shakily, poking my fork at the eggs on my plate as I pulled my thoughts back to where I needed them—and to what I needed from Jeanne.

"Can I get a ride later?" I asked.

She looked over her shoulder at me. "I thought you didn't want anyone to know you were here."

More like I didn't dare, but she didn't need to know that I couldn't afford to be noticed at all, lest word get back to Paul and through him to Kate Abraham.

"It can be after dark," I said, though I didn't relish the idea of traipsing around in the woods without benefit of daylight. The way my luck had been running, I'd break something. "Or if now is better, maybe I can just duck down in the back seat until—"

"I'm working." Jeanne went back to washing dishes, presenting me again with her plaid back. "I have to be at the hospital in half an hour."

The truth, I wondered, or her not-so-subtle way of pointing out how much more in her debt I should feel?

"Maybe tomor—" I began.

"A double shift." She didn't look over her shoulder. She didn't need to. Her tone of voice made it quite clear I should stop pressing.

If only I could.

"It's important," I said. An understatement if I'd ever uttered one, given what was at stake: the fate of the remaining four Crones and their protectors, the fate of humanity, perhaps the fate of the very planet itself. Because who knew what would happen if the god inhabiting Kate achieved his goal of opening multiple portals between Earth and its many splinters?

"I wouldn't ask if it wasn't," I added.

Jeanne's back went still. Then her shoulders lifted, and she expelled a long, slow breath. "I'll take Gilbert's car to work and leave my keys in the mailbox. He'll be asleep by ten."

"Won't he hear—"

"He takes a sleeping pill at nine. It knocks him out for at least seven hours. You'll be fine."

I nodded at her back. "Thank you. I appreciate—"

She whirled, her wet, soapy hands crossed across ample breasts. "Don't," she snapped. "I don't want your thanks. I'd rather not be involved with any of this, so let's just do what we have to and get it over with, all right?"

"I—" My mouth flapped a couple of times without further sound as I stared at her, taken aback by her reaction. She didn't want to be involved with any of what? How much did she know? How much *could* she know? Had Edie told her—

Questions piled up on the back of my tongue, but I held them back. Jeanne had the look of a cornered animal ready to bolt, and whatever she did or didn't know—or did or didn't *want* to know—I needed her. Needed her connection to my family, needed her ability to run interference with the world for me …

Needed her car tonight.

I nodded my head. "All right," I agreed. And then I caught the tip of my tongue between my front teeth and bit down—hard—to keep my thanks to myself.

CHAPTER 3

I PARKED JEANNE'S CAR AT THE SIDE OF MORGAN'S WAY—
that was how the road was marked on the maps of Confluence,
Ontario—and turned off the engine. The headlights remained
on for a few seconds before they, too, switched off, and darkness
swooped in from the surrounding woods to encase me. Encase,
not envelop, because for a moment, it felt so solid that I couldn't
breathe. As if I were back in the cell where Morok had left me.
As if I were on the most foolish of all fool's errands.

Because I was.

It had been hard enough to find the iron gate marking the
entrance to 13 The Morrigan's Way—that was what I knew to be
the real name of the road at the edge of town—even in full
daylight and with a magickal Crone's pendant around my neck
and a crow to point the way.

I had none of those things now. Only my decidedly non-
magickal staff and a nearly dead flashlight I'd dug out of one of
Edie's kitchen drawers. My fingers ached from their grip on the
rigid plastic barrel of the latter. The light it had emitted when I
tried it at the house had been watery at best, but I hadn't been
able to find fresh batteries for it and could only hope it would
hold out long enough to find the gate.

I pulled on the door handle and pushed stiffly out from
behind the steering wheel, regretting my impulsive and likely ill-
advised return to staff practice after Jeanne had left me pushing
my scrambled eggs around my plate. Given what I'd been
through and how I felt, I should probably have waited another
few days before taking up such hard physical work again, but I
wasn't sure how many days I had left to find the Crones before
Kate convinced them to raise their powers and split the world
again. Because even if they realized who she really was and kept

their powers from Morok, the very split itself could—would—spell disaster for the planet.

"But no pressure," I muttered to myself as I reached back into the car to retrieve my staff from the passenger side. The long wooden pole had become a nearly inseparable part of me since Lucan had given it to me. At first because he had insisted, and then because I'd become so used to its presence that it felt like an extension of me—even now, with or without whatever properties it might still possess that I couldn't access.

Plus, it was the only connection I had left to him and to the world I was trying to find again.

My fingers closed over the familiar, smooth wood, and it settled into my grasp. I backed out of the vehicle and closed the door with a thump muffled by the silence of the woods. The darkness tightened its grip on me. I switched on the flashlight and played the weak beam along the edge of the woods alongside the road. I'd parked close to where I thought the path would be, but now I wasn't sure. Even though most of the leaves had fallen, the underbrush remained a solid, impenetrable wall of interwoven branches, raspberry brambles, and wild rose bushes that gave no hint of having been parted by human footsteps. I knew from experience they wouldn't be kind to me, but at least this time, I'd come better prepared.

I held the end of the flashlight in my teeth and dug out Edie's old leather gardening gloves from my pocket. I would have preferred something warmer on this cold October night that smelled like snow, but they were all I could find, and they would protect my—

A twig snapped in the trees to the right, and my head whipped toward it. The flashlight dropped from the precarious grip between my teeth and rolled under the car.

"Shit," I muttered. I held still for a few seconds, barely breathing as I listened with my every fiber to the night around me. But the woods remained silent, and at last I dared ease myself to my knees beside the car so I could peer beneath it for the runaway flashlight. It hadn't rolled far on the gravel, thank the goddess, and I clutched it firmly as I pushed to my feet, determined not to let it escape again—especially once I was away from the road and into the trees.

My bravado quailed a little at the thought. One of the reasons I'd wanted Jeanne to drive me out here was so someone would know where "here" was. Where *I* was. *That* I was. Because goddess knew my son wouldn't come looking for me. He didn't even know I'd returned to Confluence—or that I'd left in the first place.

I swallowed against the little hitch of pain in my chest at the thought of how my son hadn't reported me missing, hadn't asked any of my neighbors if they'd seen me, hadn't done anything. Which was all good, in the grand scheme of things, but it still hurt like hell. I swallowed again. Then I squared my shoulders, held tight to flashlight and staff, and marched around the car to do battle with the unforgiving thicket of brambles and thorns.

It took a good ten minutes to force my way through, but at last I stood on the other side of the roadside growth and at the edge of the forest—puffing from exertion and bleeding from a nasty scratch on one cheek, but victorious all the same. For roughly half a second. Then, just as I pointed the flashlight into the trees, its beam dimmed, flickered, and died.

"Oh for goddess' sake," I muttered under my breath, shaking it with increasing force. "You've got to be kidding me."

But the flashlight was quite serious—and immune to my desperation. As was the goddess I appealed to but hadn't heard from since her cryptic *"Beware!"* had foreshadowed Morok's possession of Kate. If I were going to do this quest thing, I would be doing it alone and in the dark.

I stuffed the instrument into my pocket and peered into the woods. Stumbling around in the dark with no one knowing I was here was *so* not a good idea, but Morok had already had five days to bend Anne, Nia, and Maureen to his will. Five days to convince them to raise their power so that he could co-opt it and turn it to his own purposes.

I wouldn't—couldn't—allow him a single one more. Which left me little choice but to proceed with my plan—and a great deal of caution.

But not, as it turned out, much success.

My eyes adjusted to the lack of light enough to keep me from walking face first into the trees, but tripping over things was another story. And there were a lot of things to trip over in a forest. Fallen logs, rocks hidden beneath the autumn leaves, holes ... I found all of them, each one further undermining my attempts at stealth. Between thumps and thuds and faceplants onto the forest floor, I sounded like an entire herd of bison crashing through the woods.

Although I doubted bison would squeak the way I did. Or swear.

And it was all to no avail. I ventured as far as I dared, first in one direction and then the other, keeping to the trees parallel to the road and searching for signs of the gatepost atop which Keven had once sat. But I found nothing. No mound of stones, no brass plaque bearing the number 13, no iron gate—closed or otherwise—no break in the trees that so much as hinted at a path. Nothing.

I admitted defeat when my head connected with a low-hanging branch hard enough to make my ears ring. I was cold and wet—how had I not noticed that it had started to rain? I stood in the dark, chest heaving and breath fogging with my efforts, rubbing at the rising lump on my forehead, and trying hard not to give in to the threatening tears. Cheesy rice on a cracker, did *everything* have to be this hard?

I waited, but no Edie-voice broke into my thoughts to give me what-for about my lapse into improper use of language, which made things seem even worse. I sniffled and swiped at my nose with the back of the gloved hand clutching my staff. No Edie, no Keven, no Lucan, no fellow Crones ...

Hell, I would have been happy to see even Bedivere right now, and that—I shuddered at the thought of the surly, one-handed wolf-shifter that protected the Water Crone—that was saying a *lot*.

Frustration gathered in my core, building into a bellow that demanded release, but I didn't dare. Yelling might alert one of the protectors to my presence, but it might also alert Morok-Kate, and I couldn't risk that. If no protector—no Lucan or Bedivere or Yvain or Percival—had heard me crashing about in the woods by now, they weren't going to. Not tonight.

Or ever.

I hunched my shoulders against the unbidden thought—the possibility that no one had heard me because no one was here. That Morok had already achieved his goal.

The world still existed, I reminded myself, letting out a shaky breath. And as long as it did, I had to assume—to believe —that I had time to reach the others, warn them of the traitor in their midst, and stop them from inadvertently destroying the world.

But again, not tonight.

I cast a last, lingering look into the dark forest and turned toward the road. Pushing back through the bramble thicket seemed easier on the return, as if the woods were as glad to be rid of me as I was to leave them. I pondered the impression as I slogged my way through the puddles toward the shadowy hulk of Jeanne's car. Was it because I'd lost my magick? Was this the Morrigan's way—I snorted at the irony of the thought in relation to the road I trod, then snorted at the irony of *that* thought, too, then changed my mental wording before I lost it altogether.

Because if this was the goddess's way of telling me I had no part to play in this anymore, if it was her way of telling me that she had abandoned me, it was no laughing matter.

17

CHAPTER 4

I woke to the sound of the roller blind over the bedroom window rewinding itself, followed by a mighty clatter as it flew from its brackets and dropped to the floor. Heart pounding, I jolted upright in the bed—Edie's bed—one hand clutching the rumpled duvet over my legs, the other raised in the instinctive but useless gesture I'd once used to summon Fire.

I stared at my outstretched hand, then at the pale gray rectangle of light in the opposite wall that heralded daybreak, then at the blind rolling across the wide, pine planks. Freak accident? Or—

The bedroom door crashed against the wall, flung open by an unseen hand.

"Good morning to you, too," I grumbled, equal parts happy to have her back in my life and seriously annoyed at her way of announcing her presence. Not to mention waking me at the crack of—

My gaze went to the bedside clock, an old-fashioned, windup one with a hammer-between-two-bells alarm. My eyes widened. It was already ten? I looked back at the window and the barely-there light coming through it—and the huge, wet snowflakes slapping against the glass.

Shit, I thought. Snow was the last thing I needed right now. Finding a little-used path beneath fallen leaves on a forest floor was hard enough. Finding one under the snow would be impossible.

And then, *shit*, I thought again. Because if it stayed on the ground, that same snow was going to make me a prisoner in Edie's house. I'd planned to borrow Jeanne's car again tonight for a return to the woods, but short of levitating down the front walk to the street, my footprints would—

The bedroom door swung closed and banged open a second time. I turned my attention back to the invisible Edie. "I'm awake," I said. "What more do you—"

The faint sound of someone knocking at the front door reached my ears, and the rest of my words froze in my throat. Jeanne? No, she had a key and came in the back door. A neighbor? But I'd been so careful to keep my presence hidden, and they all knew that Edie was dead, so—

Oh, goddess.

Kate. Kate had found me…and with her, Morok.

Adrenaline jolted through my veins, and for a fraction of a second, blind panic rendered me incapable of movement. Reaction. Thought. I shrank back against the pillows, my lungs screaming for air I couldn't give them.

The knock at the front door became an insistent, loud pounding, and reason slowly returned. Not Morok-Kate. They wouldn't knock at the front door. They wouldn't have to. If they knew where I was, they would have used a ley line to get to me, and I would already be dead.

The bedroom door slammed shut and opened a third time, returning me to the here and now. Not knowing where exactly Edie stood—or floated, or whatever ghosts did—I scowled at the room in general.

"Stop that!" I hissed at her. "Do you want whoever it is to hear you?"

Indeed, the pounding at the front door had stopped, as if whoever stood on the porch *had* heard, and my gaze swiveled to the bared window. The ground-floor window that was accessible to whoever might walk around to the back of the—

Shit.

I scrambled from the bed and scanned the room, assessing the signs of my presence. Then I leapt into action, pulling the duvet into place and plumping the pillow, stuffing the fallen blind under the bed, grabbing my clothes from the floor and my staff from the corner by the dresser. Through the window—fuck,

I'd left it open!—came the distant crunch of footsteps on gravel as someone walked along the side of the house protected by the eaves from the snow.

I dived for the window and feverishly, fumblingly, cranked it shut. The footsteps rounded the corner and came closer. I'd run out of time. I dropped to the floor beneath the window and pressed my back against the wall, my belongings clutched tight against me. A faint shadow loomed on the opposite wall, and I caught my breath.

Long seconds ticked by. The shadow remained. My lungs began to burn, and spots floated across my vision.

Then, just as I thought my chest might explode, the shadow withdrew. I let out a soft whoosh of stale air and gasped for fresh, straining to hear the footsteps on gravel again—to be sure that my unwanted visitor was leaving. There. There they were, walking back the way they'd come, rounding the corner of the house, heading toward the front.

Leaving my bundle of clothing on the floor but keeping hold of my staff, I scrambled to my feet and tiptoed out of the room and down the hall toward the living room. The blind there mercifully remained in place for a change, and I edged it open at one side until I could peer around it at—*Gilbert?*

I blinked at the sight of Jeanne's husband retreating down the front walk toward the gate and the sidewalk and street beyond. What in the world was Gilbert—Jeanne. Of course. He was looking for—

"Is he gone?"

I whirled around at the voice, dropping the edge of the blind and slapping my hand over my mouth to muffle the shriek that erupted. Jeanne stood in the living room doorway, wiping her hands on a tea towel, her face closed and eyes weary behind her glasses.

"Gilbert," she said. "Is he gone?"

I lowered my hand and nodded. "He was looking for you?"

"Who else?" She turned and headed back toward the kitchen.

I peeked past the blind one last time to where Gilbert was climbing the stairs to the front porch of their own house across the street. I couldn't deny my relief at knowing that he didn't know I was here and hadn't come looking for me, but the fact that Jeanne was avoiding him couldn't be good, either. I let go of the blind again and followed my neighbor-friend to the kitchen.

The table was set for one when I entered—with a plate, fork, knife, glass, and mug on the single placemat—and Jeanne was removing something from the oven. She straightened as she turned, and the delicious aroma of eggs, mushrooms, cheese, and onions reached across the room to tickle my nostrils. My mouth watered. Frittata. I love frittata. And I actually felt hungry that morning, for the first time in I couldn't remember how long.

Without waiting to be told, I set my staff in its usual kitchen corner and took a seat at the table, knowing better than to offer my help. In silence, Jeanne brought the skillet to the table and set it on a trivet. She sliced into the egg dish, lifted a slab from the pan, and set it on my plate, then went to the counter to pour coffee from the waiting pot.

Two cups.

I raised a brow. Then braced myself. I was on day six here, and we hadn't yet shared a single companionable moment such as the kind that came with coffee. Jeanne had been all business —nursing business—as she'd tended to my injuries, seen to my well-being, fed me, checked on my progress. Given the terseness of our conversation yesterday, I had no reason to believe that would change, which didn't bode well for the upcoming shared beverage.

My new appetite nosedived.

Jeanne remained quiet as she returned to the table with the coffee, however. She set my mug beside my plate before taking a seat opposite and staring into her own, not seeming inclined toward conversation of any kind. I picked apart the frittata, taking a small bite here and there to be polite. Jeanne didn't seem to even notice. I set aside my fork and took my courage in both hands.

My neighbor spoke before I could open my mouth.

"She was right, you know." Jeanne's brown gaze lifted from the study of her coffee to meet mine, tired, sad, wistful ... a little bitter. "Edie. She was right about Gilbert. How he talks to me. You were right, too. You weren't as ... direct, but you were still right."

I knew exactly what Jeanne was talking about, but I wasn't quite sure how to frame my response.

Edie had been blunt in her criticism of how Gilbert Archambault treated his wife over the years we'd all been friends, and while I had shared her concerns, I'd been less vocal about them. I'd been less vocal about a lot of things. My own marriage and divorce, my son, pretty much my entire life in general. The last few weeks had shown me—in spades—how misguided my silence had been, but like any ingrained habit of a lifetime, it wasn't easy to change.

"You can say it," Jeanne said. "*I told you so.* You can say the words."

"But I can't," I said, "because it's not that simple. You saw my marriage to Jeff—and I'm sure you noticed Paul's treatment of Natalie before she was ... well, before."

Jeanne studied her coffee again, capable hands wrapped around the mug. I waited for her to volunteer more about the Gilbert situation, but instead, she changed the subject.

"He loves her, you know. Paul, I mean. He loves Natalie—and their son. I can see it in his eyes."

"I know," I said.

"Gilbert loves me, too. In his own way."

I was less sure of that, but I nodded anyway. Jeanne lifted her gaze and looked at somewhere faraway, over my shoulder.

"But that's not enough sometimes, is it?" she murmured.

I lifted one shoulder in a helpless shrug. "I can't answer that for you."

"I called him on it, you know, the way he speaks to me. For the first time ever. He made some kind of comment about breakfast this morning, and I told him that if he didn't like it, he could cook his own damned breakfast—swear word and all. Me, who never swears at anything. I'm not sure which one of us was more surprised, him or me."

Her brown eyes met mine, looking faintly astonished even now at her audacity. "And then I left. I told him I was going out, and he asked where, and Edie's voice in my head said it was none of his business, so I told him that, too." Jeanne snorted, shaking her head. "Even dead, that woman has opinions."

I heard the living room blind—a roller type, like the one in the bedroom—spontaneously roll itself up, as if in agreement with her words. Jeanne's head turned toward the sound as well, but neither of us commented on it. I cleared my throat.

"What are you going to do?" I asked, returning to the topic of Gilbert.

"I don't know. He came after me, so I should at least go home, I suppose?"

"Do you want to stay here tonight?" The question slipped out before I could reconsider—before I even knew it was forming, actually, and Jeanne looked as surprised by it as I was. I hoped I didn't look as horrified as she did, however.

"*Here?*" she echoed, her expression aghast. "In *this* house? With *her?*" She made a visible effort to recover herself and her manners, forcing a tight grimace that I took to be a smile. "Thank you, but no. No, I'm sure I'll be fine. Besides, I'm on shift tonight, so I won't even be home with … him."

Not knowing what else to say or do—and frankly relieved that she'd turned down my offer—I nodded, mumbled something unintelligible but vaguely sympathetic (I hoped), and followed her small change in subject.

"Speaking of the hospital, I'd like to see Natalie. Is there some way you can get me in without anyone seeing me?"

Jeanne's brown eyes softened even as she shook her head. "I wish I could, but even if there was a way, Paul's instructions were explicit. He is to be her only visitor, and if you—if anyone else asks—"

"Me," I interrupted, my voice cracking. "You mean me. I'm not allowed to see her."

My neighbor reached across the table and placed a warm hand over mine. "I'm sorry."

But still not sorry enough to ask what had happened, or to offer help. I pushed away the uncharitable thought—I was having a lot of those lately—and stood up from the table.

"I understand," I said, even though I didn't. I tugged my hand from hers and picked up my mostly uneaten frittata and cold coffee and carried them both to the sink.

"If there's something else I can do ..."

"Thank you, but no—wait." I turned to her. "Actually, there is. Can I use your car again tonight?"

"I'll leave the keys in the mailbox," she said.

CHAPTER 5

My SECOND NIGHT OF TRAMPLING AROUND THE WOODS IN the dark resulted in more bruises and scrapes and still no Earth house. I decided I needed a new approach. When Jeanne checked in on me the next morning—already my seventh day back, not that I was feverishly tracking time, or anything—I asked her for a lift to Morgan's Way.

It was a simple enough ask: drive me there in the morning while I hid in the back seat, drop me off, and come back for me in a few hours, with the hope that I would have more success (and fewer new injuries) in the daylight.

Things, however, didn't quite go according to plan.

First, once Jeanne agreed (reluctantly), she dawdled about and found so many reasons to delay our departure that the shadows were already long on the ground by the time we reached the woods. And then, once we were there, she insisted on accompanying me. I tried in vain to get her to at least remain in the car, but to no avail.

Having her climb over logs and push through the under-brush in my wake was more hindrance than help. No matter how many times I reminded her to be quiet, she repeatedly grumbled about our foray, pointed out that we'd already taken this path or that, suggested we try another direction—all while wanting to know what, exactly, I was looking for, waving me off with a "Never mind, forget I asked," and muttering under her breath about "The things I do for you," before starting the cycle anew.

We'd been crashing around for less than an hour, and I was already on the verge of leaving her out there—even if I had to walk home—when we heard it. A long, low, sustained growl, deep in the early evening shadows, too far from us to ascertain its source, near enough I had no doubt it knew exactly where—and what and who—we were.

I slapped a hand over Jeanne's mouth as she squealed, hissing at her to shut up. Eyes wide behind her red-framed glasses, she smacked away my hand.

"How dare you hush me!" she said shrilly. "I'm risking life and limb to help you out here!"

I managed not to roll my eyes at that, instead turning away to peer into the shadows in time to see a huge, four-legged one separate from the others and bolt away into the night. From Jeanne's renewed squeals, I knew she'd seen it, too.

"That's it," she announced. "I'm done. *We're* done. I'm taking you home, Claire Emerson. *Now.*"

I didn't argue. In fact, I couldn't propel her ahead of me back to the vehicle fast enough, my mind racing the entire way and the tiny hairs over my entire body standing on end in warning. If that had been one of the protectors, surely they would have recognized me and said something. Or, if they hadn't wanted to out themselves to Jeanne, at least they wouldn't have run like that, right?

I had a bad feeling about this. Such a bad feeling.

On the way home, I peered into the side mirror to see if we were being followed and cast anxious glances over my shoulder so often that Jeanne snapped at me to stop squirming before I caused an accident.

I did, in part because I was giving myself a crick in the neck, but also because even if the shadow had been one of Morok's minions, and he knew I was here, it wouldn't do me any good at all to see him coming. Goddess knew I couldn't do anything about it.

"Maybe you're looking for the wrong thing," Jeanne said, when we were back at Edie's house. "Or you're looking in the wrong place. Or both."

"You have no idea what I'm looking for," I growled back.

"You don't want to know—not about any of it. You've made that patently clear."

We faced off across the living room, she beside the front door and me in front of the fireplace, both tired and fed up and done with the day, and in my case, jumping at shadows, voices from the street, and passing cars, because any of them might be Morok.

"I'm only trying to help," Jeanne said huffily, pulling me back into the current argument. "I'm not the enemy here." She held up a hand against my reply, as if sensing my biting rejoinder along the lines of, *"Maybe not, but you sure as hell drew the enemy's attention, didn't you?"*

"All I'm saying," she continued, "is that sometimes a new perspective—"

"I appreciate the concern," I lied, "but I really don't—"

"Then what about a spell?"

"A—what?" I stared in astonishment at her utterance of what surely amounted to blasphemy, given her upbringing and ties to the church. I gave my head a tiny shake. I must have heard wrong. She couldn't possibly have said—

But no. She hadn't just said it, she now repeated it.

"A spell." She squared her shoulders against my gape. "It's more like a prayer, really, but Edie called it a spell, and—well, it might work for you."

"A spell," I repeated.

"It's for finding things you've lost."

I'd gathered that, but I was still stuck on the churchgoing-Jeanne-plus-spell idea, even if it was more like a prayer.

"You and Edie discussed spells," I said, "and she shared one with you."

"We discussed prayer. *She* called it a spell. Do you want to try it or not?"

I thought about the spell work Keven and the Water Crone, Anne, had tried so hard—and failed—to teach me. If I hadn't been able to work a spell then, when I still had my magick, what chance did I have now that I'd lost it in the ley lines? I started to shake my head, then paused.

It probably wouldn't work—no, it almost certainly wouldn't —but on the other hand, I was desperate, and what harm could it do to at least try?

"Fine." I sighed. "I'll try. What do I have to do?"

"The *prayer*," Jeanne emphasized the word, "goes like this: *St. Anthony, come around. Something's lost and must be found. Please help me find*—and then name what it is you're looking for."

"That's it?" I raised one rather skeptical eyebrow. "That's all I do? Just say the words? There are no herbs or hand movements or anything?"

My neighbor scowled and crossed her arms. "I told you. It's a prayer."

Whatever. I drew myself up and nodded. "All right. Here goes. St. Anthony, come around—"

"Not while I'm here!" Jeanne uncrossed her arms again and flapped them at me. "I don't want to know anything, remember?"

"But you came with me to look for—"

"I went with you because I'm your friend, and friends don't let friends wander around the woods in the middle of nowhere by themselves," she corrected tartly. "The second you'd found what you were looking for, I was out of there. Just like I'm out of here now." She reached for the doorknob. "And before you ask, I'm not going back out there with you, and I'm not letting you have my vehicle again to go by yourself. Not with whatever that —thing—was that we saw out there today."

"But—"

"No. I already have one of you haunting me." She jabbed a thumb over her shoulder at the house as she pulled open the door and stepped out onto the porch. "I have no intention of being responsible for two of you doing so. Whatever it is you're looking for, St. Anthony can darned well bring it here for you."

"You don't understand—"

"Nope. I don't. And I don't want to, remember? Do what you need to do, Claire Emerson, but do it *here*, where at least you won't get eaten."

The door slammed shut on Jeanne's last word, leaving me alone in the gloom of the unlit living room. I stood without moving for a moment, staring at the empty space she'd left behind, not quite sure what to do next. A part of me wanted to believe she hadn't meant it, that she was just being dramatic and of course she'd lend me her vehicle again; another part of me— the part that had known Jeanne for thirty-plus years—knew better.

Now that my neighbor knew what I'd been up to—that I'd been driving her car out to the woods at night and wandering around in the dark the way we'd done today—I wasn't getting near her vehicle again.

Which left me two options: walk two hours to The Morrigan's Way, stumble around the woods for a while, then walk home again—all in the dark—or hope St. Anthony could find a way to let me warn the others about Morok from here.

Assuming I still had time to do so.

With that thought in mind, I walked around Edie's favorite chair to the front door and framed my eyes with my hands as I peered through the partially frosted sidelight at the street. It was snowing again. Jeanne had reached her driveway on the other side, and I watched her march determinedly up it toward her house, leaving a trail of footprints in the skiff of white on the ground. I wondered how things were going with her and Gilbert. She'd said nothing today about their spat, and I'd been so focused on keeping her quiet that I hadn't thought to ask. I hoped she hadn't backed down from him, and I smiled a little at the thought of the man's bewilderment at his wife's sudden backbone. It would have come as a hell of a shock after thirty-three years of the obedience she'd promised him in their marriage vows.

Vows that had been peddled to her as desirable—no, neces-

sary—by her church, her father, the society she'd grown up in …
everything she'd ever known in her entire life. My smile faded as
the door across the street closed behind her.

I knew I'd been molded by my own upbringing, but Jeanne's
hadn't just shaped her, it had cut her off at the knees before she'd
ever learned to walk—mostly through the lies and deceit that
were fed to too many women by too many men.

All a part of the patriarchy that Morok had invented, and
that was *without* his full power.

I gritted my teeth and shifted my gaze to the darkening
street, first in one direction and then the other, looking for unfamiliar vehicles or lurking shadows. Would he send his Mages
after me to do his dirty work for him? One of his monsters,
perhaps? Or would he use Kate's body, her identity as a cop, to
come for me himself?

I pulled back from the sidelight and dropped my hands.
Whatever he might do, he hadn't done it yet, so I had to keep
trying. I returned to the center of the dark living room and
began reciting the words Jeanne had given me, my voice oddly
loud in the empty house.

"St. Anthony, come around. Something's lost and must be
found. Please help me find—" I stopped in sudden perplexity.
What was it, exactly, that I wanted brought to me? It couldn't be
the path or the Earth house, because I had no way of getting
back to the woods to search for either, nor could it be Keven,
who was tied to the house, or any of the shifters, who were
bound to their Crones—Lucan included.

I pushed away the latter thought and stood, hands on hips,
nibbling at the inside of my bottom lip. What the hell was I
supposed to ask for? I'd lost my magick, but that was hardly an
object that could be delivered to me—was it? I'd lost the
pendant, too, but not in the same way. I knew where it was, and
Morok wasn't likely to let it out of his grasp. Which left …

"Fuck if I know," I muttered. But I was uneasy at the idea of
leaving the spell—or prayer, or whatever Jeanne wanted to call it

—unfinished, and so I shrugged, hoped for the best, and landed on the ephemeral but desperately needed. "Magick," I said. "Please help me find my magick."

My words had no sooner died into silence when the blind over the front window rolled itself up beside me with a loud clatter. I jumped and gave an involuntary shriek, then leaped forward to close it again.

"Seriously?" I grumbled at Edie. I hadn't turned on any interior lights, so no one could see into the house, but I wasn't taking chances—and I didn't squander the opportunity to take another quick, furtive glance outside, either. Still nothing. I pulled the blind into place and turned to scowl at the room. "What is *with* you and this damned blind?"

The damned blind rolled itself up behind me again.

"Jesus Christ," I muttered. I pulled it halfway down again, then paused. Maybe Edie was trying to tell me something. I tugged the blind the rest of the way down and then stood to one side, lifting an edge away from the window to take a longer look outside. But I still saw no unfamiliar cars, no shadows—

The blind snapped up a third time, its bottom bar narrowly missing my nose as I jerked back.

"Oh, for goddess' sake!" I snarled at it. I gripped the bottom with both hands, wrestled with its unexpected resistance, and then stopped and stared across the street at Jeanne's house.

More specifically, at the blue-green glow seeping from around the edges of one of the windows overlooking her front porch.

CHAPTER 6

CLINGING TO THE BOTTOM OF THE RECALCITRANT BLIND, I blinked at the window I knew belonged to Jeanne's library, converted from their dining room shortly after Jeff and I had moved into the neighborhood. I'd tried to convince Jeff we should do the same thing, but he'd insisted we keep the formal space for entertaining clients.

To this day, I would have preferred the library.

The light seeping around Jeanne's blind pulsed and danced, waxing and waning. It didn't look or behave like a ley line but more like an aurora borealis.

My hands released the blind and drifted back down to wrap around my waist. I hugged myself as a dozen thoughts flitted through my mind. I'd never seen the glow before—had Jeanne installed some kind of fancy light in my absence? But the way it behaved, it didn't look man-made, so … magick? If that was the case, what was the source? And why was it at Jeanne's house? Was I supposed to go over there to find out, or was this some kind of a trap?

I might have stood debating it all night—and wishing I had some way of calling Jeanne to reassure myself about the possible trap—if it hadn't been for a solid shove between my shoulder blades that face planted me into the plate-glass window.

"Ow!" I rubbed the bridge of my nose as I glowered at the room through watery eyes. "Jesus, Edie, that hurt! What in hell was that for?"

The front door flew open, letting in a swirl of snowflakes and dried leaves. I hastened to close it, but it resisted my efforts, and another shove—this one to my shoulder—made me stagger sideways toward the opening.

"Fine," I said. "I'll go, but not yet. It's not dark enough, and someone might—"

A third shove knocked me backward onto the floor of the porch, and the door slammed shut. I gaped up at it from my sprawl, melting snow seeping through my jeans and underwear. For fuck's sake—seriously?

The porch roof above me took on a blue-green tinge, a reflection of the light coming from Jeanne's house, and I craned my neck to peek between the porch rail balusters. The aurora spilling from the library window was dazzlingly bright now, and my breath caught. Whatever it was, there was no doubting that both it and Edie wanted me to go to it. I just wished I wasn't going in both blind and empty handed.

I scowled at Edie's door. "Can I at least have my—"

The door opened, my staff landed with a clunk on the porch beside me, and it—the door, not the staff—closed again. With a sigh, I climbed to my feet, picked up my one and only weapon, and brushed the melting snow from my butt. Here went nothing.

I so would have preferred to wait until full darkness before venturing out, I thought as I ducked behind a parked car in front of Edie's house and scoped out the street. If one of the neighbors saw me, there would be questions. Visitors coming to Edie's house. Talk.

So much talk.

It was bound to get back to Paul at the very least, and from him to others, and from them to the police—because, small town—which included Kate, if she was still working at that job. I supposed she might have quit, given her new dual nature and hardly law-upholding new goals in life, but I couldn't know for sure, and I couldn't take the chance.

I ducked behind the car's fender as a bicycle headlamp approached. The bike's tires swished past on the wet pavement, and I released a shaky breath. Damn, but I would have liked to have had a ley line to travel right about now. I poked my nose up over the car hood. There was no one else on the street, and no one that I could see looking out their front windows.

"Now or never," I muttered to myself. Clutching my staff and running in an awkward half-duck, I skittered across the open to another vehicle on the other side, rounded it, and crouched on the sidewalk side by the driver's door.

Two houses down, a door opened and closed, footsteps sounded, and a vehicle started. The damned thing then took forever to back out of its drive and head down the street past my hiding place. By the time its taillights disappeared into the distance, I was cursing it roundly. It, and as I stiffly uncurled and stood upright, the knees that liked to remind me that, even with taking up my staff practice again, being Fifth Crone hadn't made me any younger.

The blue-green light beckoned.

After a final scan of the street, I scurried up Jeanne's driveway and climbed the stairs to her porch. Then, finger on the doorbell, I hesitated. If I rang, I had a fifty-fifty chance of Gilbert answering instead of Jeanne. There would be shock. Questions. Messiness I didn't need. I pondered the situation.

I hadn't checked the time in a while, but given how quiet the neighborhood was, it would be a fair guess that it was nearing the end of dinner hour. And given Gilbert's penchant for schedules, another fair guess would be that Jeanne would be serving their meal at the kitchen table on time—assuming they were speaking, and she'd cooked for him at all, and oh, *why* hadn't I thought to ask her how things were going between them?

I took a deep breath. There was only one way to find out, I supposed. I put my hand on the doorknob, twisted gently, gave silent thanks for safe neighborhoods where people didn't lock their doors, and stepped into the front entry.

The floor plan of Jeanne and Gilbert's house was similar to that of my old house, before it had burned to the ground. A two-story Cape Cod, it had a central hall leading to the kitchen at the back and a living room to the left when you came in—mercifully unoccupied at the moment. In my house, there had been a main floor den to the right, which Jeff had used as an office, and the dining room had been to the rear of the living room. Here, the dining room took the place of the den and had been converted to the library I sought. The library with a distinct blue-green glow seeping from beneath its door.

So. Definitely not my imagination, then.

I slipped off my shoes—not as a courtesy to Jeanne, but so I could move more quietly—paused to be sure the murmur of voices I heard was coming from the kitchen, and eased open the library door to step inside. The blue-green glow promptly disappeared, plunging the room into darkness. I closed the door quietly behind me, reached for the switch beside the door, and turned on the overhead light.

The room was Jeanne's pride and joy—a true oasis—and with good reason. I'd forgotten how beautiful it was. The doorway at the back that had once led to the kitchen had been closed off during the renovation, leaving the room private and entirely separate from the rest of the house. Floor-to-ceiling bookshelves lined all four walls, with a built-in reading nook beneath the window, a long, narrow wooden table before it stacked high with more books, and a rich, red-patterned wool carpet overlaying a dark hardwood floor.

I tamped down my ongoing library envy as my gaze fell on the single reading chair in the center of the room with its little table and reading lamp. Gilbert, Jeanne had told me apologetically when she'd first shown me the room, wasn't much of a reader. I hadn't known either of them well at that point, but I'd felt vaguely sorry for her that she'd felt the need to apologize for him.

That was before I'd learned that Gilbert wasn't much of anything, and my sympathy for his wife had become more personal. But that was neither here nor now, and—

On the opposite wall, a thick book tumbled from the shelf

to the left of the window seat and dropped to the carpet with a not-so-muffled thud.

Shit.

I pressed my ear to the door and, through it, heard the approach of footsteps down the ceramic-tiled hall from the kitchen. I switched off the light again and stood with my back pressed to the shelves beside it, my tap-dancing heart lodged in my throat. If I stayed still, if I didn't so much as breathe—

I remembered the shoes I'd left in the entry and closed my eyes.

Shit, shit, *shit*.

The library door opened beside me, and Jeanne stood silhouetted against the hall light. I saw her gaze go to the book on the floor, captured in the beam of light that passed her and crossed the room. She stared at it for a long moment without moving, then she came into the room, closed the door and locked it behind her, and crossed to the table beside the chair. She switched on the lamp that sat there and turned unerringly to face me.

"It took you long enough to come for it," she said.

I peeled myself away from the shelves. "I—what?"

"The book." She nodded at the fallen volume. "I wondered when you'd finally come for it. I'm guessing that's what you've been looking for. I should have told you about the St. Anthony prayer days ago."

"I—no. I mean, I don't think so?" I flexed stiff fingers that had been clutching my staff and shook my head to clear it, trying to make sense of her question. "What book, exactly?"

Her expression turned guarded. Worried. "You don't know?"

My gaze dropped to the fingers of her right hand, twitching at her side. Were those hex motions she was making? *Jeanne?* I shifted my staff across my body. I sneaked a quick glance at the book on the floor. It was obviously the one she meant, but even if I had been looking for a book—which I hadn't—why would she have it?

Jeanne's fingers danced a little faster, drawing my eyes back to them.

Yup. That was definitely a hex, all right.

"Hold on," I said, raising my own hand placatingly. "I'm sure we can——"

A flash of light arced toward me, the air sizzling in its wake. I yelped and ducked, instinctively blocking the attack with my staff. The wood sparked and smoldered under the hit, and I smacked at the charred embers with my free hand.

"Damn it, Jeanne, *wait*," I snapped. "Let me think this through!"

"You either know or you don't, Claire, and if you don't…" My neighbor shook her head, and her left hand joined her right in front of her. The finger dance began again.

I looked around for—and failed to find—shelter from her. Tried—frantically—to make sense of what was happening. St. Anthony. She'd mentioned St. Anthony, but I hadn't asked for help finding a book, I'd asked for help finding my magick. And then I'd seen the glow over here, and then Edie had pushed me out of the house, and——

A second hex blast slammed into the staff, knocking me back a step, but I barely noticed, my gaze riveted on the book on the floor. Its carved leather cover. Its obvious age. Its undeniable familiarity. My breath caught in my throat.

Impossible.

There had only been four books, one for each Crone. Earth, Fire, Air, Water. None of them had been accessible to me as the Fifth Crone, to be sure, but there had never been any mention of the existence of a fifth. No one had so much as hinted at the possibility, and——

And what if they didn't know?

"Edie?" I croaked, but more in desperation than true belief that my friend was able to speak to me again—or that I would be able to hear her if she did.

Jeanne's fingers hesitated in their dance. "Edie?" she

37

repeated, looking up into the corners of the room with more than a little apprehension. "Did she follow you here?"

"No—maybe—" I shrugged, overwhelmed by too many possibilities. "I honestly don't know. But Jeanne, the book—I asked for help finding—" I broke off and tried to reword my thoughts. Despite Jeanne's obvious skill at hexes, I still couldn't bring myself to tell her I'd been searching for my magick.

"The book," I blurted, pointing with my staff across the room, "is it the Book of the Fifth Crone?"

"Oh, thank God," Jeanne muttered. Her fingers stilled, and the sparkles forming around them fizzled out of existence. She took a deep breath, her broad, perpetually plaid-covered shoulders rising to the level of her ears before dropping again. She shook her head at me. "You had me worried for a minute there, Claire. I thought I'd made a terrible mistake. But never mind." She flapped a hand toward the book. "Go on. Pick it up. It's yours, now."

Mine. I stared at the volume on the floor, then at her. If it really was the Book of the Fifth Crone, then it was absolutely mine, but I had so many questions—

Jeanne marched over to me, gripped my arm above the elbow, and—fingers sunk into me like claws—towed me across the library. She thrust me toward the book. "Take it."

I shot a surprised look at her. Was her voice *wobbling*?

"Um," I replied. "Are you okay?"

My neighbor sagged into her reading chair and covered her face with both hands. "I thought you'd never come for it," she whispered. "And I had no daughter I could pass it to, and—"

I hesitated, torn between her and the book at my feet. Then I stooped, picked it up, and went to crouch at her side. "I don't understand. Why did you have it in the first place? And how do you know what it is?"

I glanced at the leather cover in my hands, carved with the same symbols as the other Crone books, but lacking a title or anything that might—as far as I could see—identify it as what she claimed it to be. I tugged gently at one of the hands covering her face, and with a deep, quavering sigh, she dropped both to her lap. In fists.

"I know," she said, "because my entire purpose has been to know. And to wait for you."

"Me? Specifically?"

"You, as in the Fifth Crone."

"But how … why … you …" I stumbled to a halt, trying to reconcile what I'd always known of Jeanne with what I was seeing now. I wasn't succeeding. It was my turn to sigh deeply. "How are you even involved in this?" I asked. "And for how long?"

She answered my second question first. "My whole life," she said simply, and then blew my mind with her answer to the first. "And I'm a Daughter of Hestia, handmaid to the Morrigan."

CHAPTER 7

I MIGHT HAVE GAPED AT JEANNE FOREVER IF GILBERT hadn't knocked at the library door.

"Jeanne?" The wood muffled his voice, but not enough to erase the usual petulance from it. Jeanne gave the door a pained, sour look.

"I'm with a friend," she replied.

"I just—"

"I *said* I'm with a friend," she snapped.

There was silence on the other side, and then the shuffle of retreating footsteps. I met Jeanne's gaze, not quite sure what to say—or if I should say anything. She took the guesswork away.

"I blame you and Edie for this," she muttered, resting an elbow on the arm of the chair and pinching the bridge of her nose above her red glasses frames as she glowered sideways at me. "I was quite happy being who I was until the two of you started needing me to be something else, you know. Quite happy. The sooner I'm done with both of you, the better."

She heaved herself out of the chair and began pacing the room. "You know about Morgana and the Morrigan," she said, "and how Morgana allowed the Morrigan to possess her body in order to fight Merlin and Morok, then divided her powers into the four pendants of the Crones."

I almost choked. Of course I knew about Morgana and the Morrigan—only it hadn't been four pendants, it had been five, and how in the name of the goddess herself did Jeanne know about all of that?

"Of course you do," Jeanne echoed my thought, waving an impatient hand at herself. "You wouldn't be here if you didn't know about them—or about the fifth pendant. You all know about those."

"I—"

"But you don't know about Hestia, because no one ever has except the Daughters."

Hestia. The name was familiar, but I was certain it didn't belong in Arthurian lore. I cast about in my memory. "Wasn't she a Greek goddess?"

And if that's who Jeanne meant, and "daughters" was literal, wouldn't that also mean the neighbor I'd lived across the street from for the last thirty years was—

"Yes. And as I said, handmaid to the Morrigan. But none of that matters." Jeanne's continued sour expression dared me to argue—or to ask how a Greek goddess had ended up as handmaid to a Celtic one. I did neither. "What matters," she said, "is that when the Morrigan created the fifth book, she entrusted its care to Hestia and her female line of descendants until such time as the Fifth Crone arrived to claim it. That's you."

I nodded. "So your mother...?"

"And her mother, and her mother before her, and all the others." Jeanne's face was grim, the lines around her mouth and eyes tight. "Yes."

"And you..."

"I'm the last of the line."

By choice, I remembered, my thoughts turning uneasy. Jeanne had made it clear throughout our friendship that she never considered herself mother material, and she had flatly refused to produce the expected progeny. It had been her one and only act of rebellion against the lifetime of control exerted over her by others—and, Edie and I had privately agreed, it had been a wise decision, given the idea of Gilbert as father material.

But all that aside, if her story were true—and I had no reason to doubt it—then ...

"What would have happened?" I asked. I hoped I was wrong. Hoped that the way she'd placed the entire world at risk hadn't been deliberate. "If I hadn't turned up, if you'd died with no one to pass the care of the book along to ..."

"It would have been lost." She lifted her chin. "I'm not proud of what I did, Claire, but by the time I realized my mistake, it was too late. I never believed my mother's stories growing up. Or perhaps I did, but I didn't want to subject a daughter of my own to the prison she imposed on me. From the time I was old enough to walk, I knew that my only purpose— the only reason I'd been brought into existence—was to protect that damned book." She jutted her chin at the leather-bound volume I clutched against my chest, and her eyes glittered with cold animosity.

"It went against everything my father taught me to believe. Everything my church taught me to believe. Everything I *wanted* to believe. Witchcraft? Magick? Blasphemy!" She spat out the word. "My mother swore me to secrecy, and I lived a dual life. The dutiful daughter and then wife, learning hexes on the side. It was hell." Her face turned sad. "And then monsters attacked— oh, yes, I saw them at your house—and Edie died, and you disappeared, and I knew my mother had been telling the truth. At least about magick. And if she'd been telling the truth about that, maybe the rest was true, too. Only I had no way to continue the line anymore."

"Jesus, Jeanne ..."

"Don't," she grated. "What's done is done. You have your book, and the work of the Daughters of Hestia is done. The line will die with me. It dies now, actually, because I'm done, too. With you, with Edie, with all of it."

"But—"

"No. Don't you get it? I never wanted *any* of this. I like safe, Claire. I don't like excitement, I don't like living in fear, and I sure as hell don't like what I've become because of both of those. I want to go back to being what I was—who I was. Me. Jeanne. Nurse, wife, upstanding citizen ... and a church-going woman who doesn't freaking swear, damn it. That's enough for me. It's always been enough, don't you understand?"

I didn't. I couldn't. But neither could I force change where it wasn't wanted. Not my circus, I thought, sadly recalling the proverb. And not my monkeys. I hugged the Book of the Fifth Crone to my chest and nodded my head.

"If you're sure," I whispered.

She raised her chin, defiance in the set of her jaw and flare of her nostrils. I thought I saw her lips tremble, but I couldn't be sure, and so I had no choice but to accept her cold silence as her response.

I reached for her then, to give her a hug and thank her for all she had done for me, for the book, for the world—but she side-stepped my embrace and skirted the long wooden table to go to the door.

"I'll distract Gilbert until you've gone," she said, and then she stepped out of the upheaval of my life, back into the safety of the one she said she wanted.

CHAPTER 8

BACK AT EDIE'S HOUSE, I LOCKED THE FRONT DOOR AND felt my way past the coat closet and down the dark hallway to the kitchen. There, by the faint light of the streetlamp outside—thank goodness the house sat on a corner lot—I stood my staff in its usual place near the fridge, closed the blinds over the window in the back door and the one above the sink, and then turned on the light in the hood fan above the stove, which was least likely to draw attention.

Then, and only then, I loosened my grip on the book I clutched against my chest.

I held it away from me and ran the fingertips of my right hand over its cover, barely grazing it. The shock and sadness that had followed Jeanne's story and her absolute and utter abandonment of me faded, and a sense of wonder bloomed in my chest. Anticipation. A tiny flicker of hope. This was it. There had been a book for me all along—a Fifth Crone's book—and I'd finally found it.

No, I corrected myself. My spell invoking St. Anthony had found it. I'd asked for help finding my magick, and St. Anthony had brought me to the book. A book that would be filled with everything I needed to—

My spark of hope gave a little hiccup, and my brows twitched together as I peered closer at the book. The other one I'd seen, *The Crone Wars* book that had come with the house and Keven and Lucan, had been different. It had been thicker. Worn. Aged. And its title had been carved into the leather. This one was thin and unblemished. It had no title, no marks of any kind. What if Jeanne had been wrong about it? It didn't even look like it had ever been opened, never mind—

I stopped, thought about it for a second, and then rolled my eyes at myself. "Duh," I muttered. "There's never *been* a Fifth Crone before, Claire, remember?"

The cupboard door beside me popped open in agreement. I reached out and pushed it shut again, then set the book on the stovetop beneath the light. Anticipation thrilled through me, a low buzz of energy that started in my belly and traveled to my fingertips. It was time. Time to learn the full story of who I was, what I was supposed to be, how to reconnect with my magick—hopefully without needing the pendant ...

And goddess willing, how to find and save the others, and reclaim said pendant.

I reached out and opened the book to the first page. A single word sat in the center of the page, written in a scrolling cursive in black ink.

Know

A little taken aback, I raised an eyebrow at it. An odd way to start a grimoire, but ... okay? I shrugged and turned the page. The same word appeared in the same position in the same writing.

Know

"What the hell," I murmured. "Know? Know what?"

I turned the page again. Same word. Same place.

A frisson of unease crept across my shoulders, and my belly turned cold. I flipped to another page, then another, then another, my movements jerky and increasingly frantic, threatening to tear the fragile paper. The same word appeared on every page. All of them, from beginning to end.

I sagged against the stove, book between the hands I rested there, disbelieving, uncomprehending. Shattered.

This was it? This was all I got? With everything I'd been through, everything I'd sacrificed, everything I *still* fought to do, this was the sum total of the help I could expect? I blinked back a sheen of tears and stared at the "book" that had been written for me, for this moment in history, more than fifteen centuries before.

Betrayal gutted me. I thought about Natalie, lying unconscious in the hospital. The grandson I might never see again. The best friend I had lost. The comfortable, safe life that had been ripped from me.

I thought about the god of darkness and deceit who had possessed Kate Abraham and left me to rot in the filth of a nowhere cell. The Crones who had no idea they were being manipulated by him, or that they would tear apart the world if they tried to split his remaining powers.

And I thought about Jeanne and her ancestors, who, for those same fifteen centuries, had guarded a book containing a single word. In retrospect, it was a damned good thing I *hadn't* opened it at Jeanne's house. She would not have taken this well at all.

Know.

What was I even supposed to do with that? Know what? Know what was coming? I already had a fair idea that whatever it was wouldn't be good. Know thyself? Much more introspection on my part, and I was going to go mad—or madder than I already felt.

Know.

Fury flared in me, and I swept the book off the stove and sent it flying across the kitchen. It landed face down on the floor beside my staff, bringing the latter down with a loud clatter to lie across it. I stood by the counter and stared at both, fighting to hold back the tears. The disappointment. The disillusionment.

The utter, bone-deep weariness.

No miracles. No magick. No help. Not even any more Jeanne, my last link to the world outside the house. I'd been alone before, but this was different. Now ... now, I was utterly bereft.

"What the *fuck* am I supposed to do, Edie?" I whispered to the empty room.

My staff lifted away from the book and returned to its corner, and the book lifted from the floor. It floated across the space and hovered in front of me, waist high. A short bark of laughter—hysterical, if I were honest—burst from my lips.

"Seriously?" I asked.

The book opened. *Know*, it said.

"Fuck you," I retorted.

The page flipped. *Know.*

I stared at it for a long, long moment, waiting for it to become more. It did not. Neither did I. Turning, I headed toward the hall and the oblivion of the bed beyond, not even bothering to take the staff with me.

I was done. With book, with staff, with trying. I had gone above and beyond every call made upon me, and I was done. Finished. Emptier than I had ever been in my life. I was out of ideas, out of hope, out of—

A thump sounded behind me, coming from the enclosed porch outside the back door.

I hesitated for a split second, then made myself keep walking. I didn't care. A summons from the Morrigan? It was too damned late. A Mage or monster sent by Morok? It could have me. I had nothing to fight it with, and no fight left in me.

Done, I reminded myself.

A scrabbling noise sounded from the porch as I turned down the hall toward the bedroom, and I heard the book's pages flipping wildly under the unseen hand that I'd left holding it. Both sounds called to me to turn back, as did the book itself and my friend's presence, and everything in me urged me to obey, dragging at my feet, slowing my steps.

I was having none of it.

"No," I told Edie harshly. I took another heavy, dogged step.

"You and the ancestors can damned well find someone else to be your pawn. I'm done. I'll leave in the morning."

I had no idea where I'd go, of course, but—

A faint, plaintive yowl cut across my thoughts, and I stopped dead in my tracks. I knew that yowl. Knew and—

I whirled and raced back into the kitchen, fumbling for the switch inside the doorway, neighbors be damned. The floating book dropped onto the table as I arrived, the back door flew open, and my gaze dropped to the porch floor and the filthy, barely recognizable ginger cat that sprawled there. *My* ginger cat.

My Merlin-Mergan-Gus.

With my pendant glinting beneath a bloodied paw.

"SHIT," I WHISPERED, DROPPING TO MY KNEES AND scooping the cat's wet, dirty body into my arms. Gus—the latest name for him—flopped against me with a pathetic mewl. I made to rise again, then hesitated. The pendant still lay there. My pendant. The one that Morok had taken from me, that I had missed like I would have missed an actual part of myself.

Now, I wasn't even sure I wanted it anymore.

Gus rumbled with a sad attempt at a purr, and my heart squeezed in on itself as I took in his half-closed eyes, mud-streaked fur, and long, red gash along one side.

"Shit, shit, *shit*," I muttered. I stared at the pendant for a second before I picked it up and dropped it inside the door for a later decision on what to do with it. Then I gently scooped Gus into my arms and cradled him against me as I carried him out of the kitchen and down the hall to the bathroom. I laid a towel on the counter beside the sink and set him on it. He didn't move.

The bathroom light blinked off and on, and I looked up to see the mirrored door of the medicine cabinet standing a little ajar in front of me. I swung it the rest of the way open and scanned the cabinet's contents, then pulled out a bottle of saline solution, suspecting that was what Edie had wanted me to see—still wishing she could confirm that.

We'd gotten okay at communicating without words—at least on her part—but goddess, I missed talking with her.

I hardened my heart, reminding myself as I turned on the tap and filled the sink with warm water that it didn't matter anymore, because I wasn't staying. I dropped a cloth and a bar of Edie's homemade soap into the water. I was going to clean Gus up and feed him, and as soon as he was strong enough, we were both leaving.

I poured a slow stream of saline solution into Gus's wound. With the blood washed away, it was smaller than I'd first thought, and it looked superficial. I didn't think it would need stitches. I went back to my escape plan as I capped the saline bottle and set it back in the cabinet. I still had no idea where we'd go, but we were absolutely leaving. There was no question, because, finished.

I met my own gaze in the mirror. The woman who stared back at me had aged shockingly since that fateful morning after my sixtieth birthday. Grief and fatigue had carved new lines in my face and deepened the ones that had already been there. I looked as old as I felt right now, and I felt bloody ancient. Ancient, and worn out, and fucking tired of having to be strong and—and, holy hell, had my language deteriorated since the start of all of this.

I pulled my attention away from the study that was just making my mood worse and soaped up a corner of the cloth. Cradling my cat's head in one hand, I began to wipe away the worst of the grime from his face. Gus, who detested wetness of any kind, closed his eyes and rumbled with contentment.

As for the pendant ...

I tried to dismiss it, but the thought that formed was less along the lines of *fuck the pendant* and more like *fuck ... the pendant*, because, questions. So many questions. How had Gus gotten hold of it? How had he gotten it here?

I tried not to think the questions, because I knew where they were leading, and sure enough, my hand stilled in the washing of Gus's face, and my gaze returned to the mirror. This time, my reflection was frowning.

Morok-Kate wouldn't have given it up voluntarily. Did that mean they'd been overpowered? But if that were the case, if the Crones had won, the question wasn't how Gus had managed to bring the pendant to me, but why he would have. And the answer was, he wouldn't, because he wouldn't have needed to, because the Crones would have already made the split and the world wouldn't even be here anymore.

Which then begged the question of what had happened to the others. And that answer? Nothing good.

"Fuck," I said, rinsing the soiled cloth and soaping it up again.

And then the doorbell rang, the injured and supposedly semi-conscious Gus leaped off the counter and bolted from the bathroom, and the entire house plunged into darkness.

"Fuckity, fuck fuck *fuck*," I told it.

CHAPTER 9

"I KNOW YOU'RE IN THERE, JEANNE," GILBERT'S VOICE CAME through the front door. "I saw the lights. Open the door and talk to me."

Great. I rested my forehead against the cool metal. That was all I needed right now—a marital spat. I willed Jeanne's husband to turn around and leave so I could go back to tending Gus—so I could *find* Gus. But his next words—Gilbert's, not Gus's—disabused me of the possibility.

"I'm not leaving until you open the door. I'll sit out here all night, if I have to. You know I will."

I didn't know—not for sure—but I highly suspected he spoke the truth. And if he continued beating on the door like that, I'd have half the neighborhood looking out their windows to see what the problem was.

"Oh, for—" I flicked on the light switch beside the door, unlocked the deadbolt, and pulled open the door.

The smug, satisfied expression dropped from Gilbert's face. He gaped at me. "You! What are you doing here? How long— are *you* the reason Jeanne has been spending so much time over here?"

"It's nice to see you, too," I said. I waved him in from the porch, still wanting to avoid unnecessary attention, even though the Morok-Kate ship had apparently already sailed and closed the door behind it … not to mix metaphors, or anything.

"And yes," I answered Gilbert's second question, "Jeanne has been … helping me."

His gaze narrowed. "With what?"

"With none of your business."

"Huh." He sniffed and puffed up his chest. "Well, whatever it is, I want it to stop."

I raised an eyebrow so high that my forehead felt stretched. "Excuse me?"

"She's not herself. She's—angry all the time. Combative. I don't like it."

"And that's my fault."

"It started when she began spending so much time here, so yes, I'd say it's your fault." He took a threatening step toward me. "And I want it to stop."

I held my ground, refusing to give way to him as I might have—had—done in past. I was done giving way to men like Gilbert Archambault. I tipped my chin up. "And Jeanne?" I asked. "Does *she* want it to stop?"

I already knew the answer to that, obviously, but he did not, and I enjoyed seeing him hesitate for a moment before his eyes narrowed again and his expression turned sly.

"What *are* you doing here, anyway?" he asked. "And why haven't you let anyone know? Are you hiding from someone? Is that why you were away for so long? Why, Claire Emerson, you dark horse, you."

I knew exactly where this was going. I could see the calculation behind the beady little gaze that told me he was already trying to figure out who he should tell and what might be in it for him. So, because I knew he'd think I was mocking him, and goddess knew I wanted to, I told the truth.

"You got me, Gilbert," I said, "I'm in hiding from an evil god, and I've been trying to regain my magick so that I can defeat him."

Sly turned to startled, then to scowling, then to disdainful outrage. I was delighted. Even more so when he huffed, wheeled on his heel, and stalked out the door again.

"Just stay away from her," he tossed over his shoulder in parting. "I'm warning you. You're nothing but trouble for her."

And because he wasn't wrong about that last bit, I let any retort I might have made die on my tongue as I closed the door and turned out the light. Wearily, I went in search of the injured

Gus, found him bathing himself on Edie's bed, and crawled in under the covers beside him.

As my body sagged into the mattress, I remembered the pendant and book I'd left in the kitchen, but I couldn't have gotten out of bed again to go in search of them if I'd tried. The weight of the day was simply too much.

I rolled over, put one hand out to Gus's warmth, and closed my eyes. The Fifth Crone would have to wait until tomorrow. Claire needed her sleep.

Huh, I thought as I drifted into sleep. *I guess that's my decision, then.*

And as unremarkable as it was, it was all it needed to be.

CHAPTER 10

I woke to Gus purring on my chest, his face close enough that his whiskers tickled my chin. Seeing that I was awake, he rumbled a little louder and gave a slow blink of contentment. I smiled. Despite his rough condition on arrival, he was going to be just fine.

"Good morning," I said, craning my neck to see the wound on his side without disturbing him. He'd obviously been busy with self-care overnight, because the wound had almost disappeared behind his sleek, clean coat. Still, I'd have a better look once I—

"It's about fucking time you woke up," a voice snapped.

I jolted upright, sending Gus tumbling to one side and nearly falling off the bed. "Jesus!" I yelped. Then I caught my breath. Was that—had that been—

"Edie?" I asked, my voice cautious. "Is that really you?"

"Unless you've been cheating on me with another ghost, of course it's me. Who else would it be? And I repeat, it's about fucking time you woke up. We have a lot to do. Get up."

"But—"

"A lot." An invisible hand tugged at the duvet covering me.

"Wait. How come I can hear you again? Is it because—" I stopped mid-question, suddenly aware of a weight hanging around my neck. My hand crept up to my chest. A fingertip brushed against something cool and inanimate—or as inanimate as magick could be. I drew back with a hiss.

"The pendant—but how—?"

"Don't look at me," said Edie, as if such a thing were even possible. *"That's one thing I cannot touch or move. None of us can."*

A reminder that she ran with the ancestors.

"Then how ... ?"

"You don't remember getting up in the middle of the night?"

Had I sleepwalked? But I'd never sleepwalked in my—I sighed. Never mind. I'd just add that to the list of firsts, too. I touched the pendant again, tracing its outline, feeling its weight against my skin. It felt both familiar and ... not. Could it sense my lack of magick? Did it no longer feel like it belonged with me? I shivered and turned my thoughts back to what *was* working in my favor. Because at least I could hear—

"Can you please get your ass in gear?" The duvet landed in a heap beside the bed. *"You have work to do."* Yup. I could hear her, all right. Loud and clear.

WHILE EDIE MADE COFFEE—SHE REALLY HAD MASTERED this whole ghost thing, hadn't she?—I placed the book on the table and rolled up my figurative sleeves. It would be different this time, I told myself. Just as the pendant had once revealed an otherwise invisible address in my newspaper that had led me to the Earth house, surely it would likewise reveal whatever secrets were hidden in the Book of the Fifth Crone.

I took a deep breath and put my left hand up to the crystal magnifying lens hanging from the chain. I had to believe—I did believe—that it could show me what I needed to get my magick back and find the others.

I looked over at Gus, loafing by the sink as he watched me through half-closed eyes.

"Ready?" I asked.

He yawned. I reached my right hand out to the book. *Please,* I thought. My fingertips hooked beneath the cover. *Please let it say more than "know."*

I opened the cover, braced myself, and stared at the word in the middle of the page.

Accept

I blinked. Blinked again. Blinked yet again. The word didn't change. *Accept*, it said. A single word in the middle of the page where *know* had once been. My fingers flipped through the book, one sheet of paper at a time, slowly at first and then faster. On every page. I looked at them through the pendant's magnifying lens, first holding the book under better light, then against the light so it shone through the pages rather than on them. I squinted and even tried using Edie's old prescription bifocals that she'd left on the kitchen windowsill. But nothing changed. No other words or shadows of other words, or even the faintest hints of shadows of other words appeared. There was only the one. The same one.

On
every
damned
page.

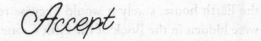

What the hell, I thought.

"What the fuck," I said.

"What?" Edie asked. A chipped stoneware mug floated through the air from the counter toward the table.

"*That.*" I pointed at the book. "A single word on every freaking page. That's all I get?"

"*Huh,*" said Edie. The mug settled beside the book.

"Not helpful," I growled. I slammed the cover shut and crossed my arms, then threw them wide, then raked my fingers through my hair. "Jesus goddess, Edie, what am I even supposed to do with that?"

"Jesus goddess?" she repeated. *"That's a new combination. I'm not sure either one would approve."*

"Will you be serious?" I paced the kitchen floor from stove to sink to fridge and back again, following the workspace triangle that had been the hallmark of kitchen design when the neighborhood was built, flapping my hand at the book. "What the hell am I supposed to do now? Morok may already be opening a portal, and even if he's not, I can't stop the Crones from splitting the world again if I can't find them, and I don't have a hope of doing that when I don't have my magick, and—"

"Don't you?"

My feet tangled and I almost face planted into the fridge. "What?"

"When is the last time you tried to use it?"

"My magick? I—" I stared at the empty kitchen, nonplussed. When *had* I last tried? Certainly not since ... I had no idea.

"Not since you got here," Edie finished for me.

I rested my hands on my hips and did another, slower circuit of the kitchen as my brain sorted through the past few days: arriving here, healing, starting my staff work again, tramping through the woods ...

Surely at some point in there I had at least tried to find Fire in me. It had been my first connection to magick and had remained the easiest one for me to access, likely because it felt pretty much identical to a menopausal hot flash, making it hard to miss.

But no. Edie was right. I hadn't just not tried, I hadn't even considered the possibility—which was staggering, because dear goddess, maybe I'd had my magick back all along, and I could have already found the Crones (*and Lucan*, my mind whispered), and—

I stopped beside the table and looked down at the book. And maybe, if I could connect to the elements again, it would unlock the secrets the book was hiding from me. Because I refused to believe that all I would get to defeat Morok was a couple of words. There *had* to be more.

And there was only one way to find out. I settled my feet more firmly against the worn vinyl floor and took a deep breath. Closing my eyes, I focused inward, reached deep, and—

Something nudged my shoulder.

"Stop that," I muttered at my friend. "I'm trying to concentrate."

"Stop what?" asked Edie.

Another nudge.

"That," I said.

"Um," she replied.

My entire being went still. "You're not pushing me?" I whispered, elemental connections forgotten.

"Nope."

An ice-water sensation trickled down my spine. "And there's nothing behind me?" I opened my eyes but didn't dare turn so much as my head.

"Nope again," said Edie, and her voice echoed my own caution. *"Nothing."*

The book on the table flopped open, and I jumped, only just holding back an accompanying shriek. Whatever had nudged before shoved now, right between my shoulder blades, and I staggered forward, putting a hand out to steady myself. And then I exhaled a long, slow breath as I looked down at the open page and saw that the word there had changed. Again.

Trust

"ARE WE SURE ABOUT THIS?" EDIE'S VOICE FOLLOWED ME down the hallway to her—my—bedroom. *"We don't know what*

you're going to find out there, and you still haven't reconnected with your magick, and—I mean, I'm sure you will, but don't you think you're being a bit hasty?"

Trust.

For some reason, that word resonated with me in a way the others hadn't, and I had known in an instant and without a doubt that I needed to get back to the Earth house. Now.

"I have the pendant," I replied to Edie. "It will have to be enough."

"The pendant can't wield its own magick, it needs you to do that. What if—"

"If you have another suggestion, make it," I said. I opened the closet door and dug through the mess of shoes and boots in the bottom. "But if you're just going to point out problems, save it. I already know about them."

"Then why—?"

Trust.

I scowled over my shoulder. "Do you have any other ideas?"

Edie sighed. "Fine. Then how are you going to get there? Have you even thought about that?"

"I'll walk." I would have said *take a taxi*—as Lucan and I had once done—but I had no cash, no credit cards, and no bank access, and while Edie had left me the house, her accounts had been frozen when she died, and she hadn't kept so much as a spare change jar in the house when she'd been alive. I'd already asked.

"It's two hours. You'll be exhausted before you even get there, and then you still need to find the house and face who knows what. Assuming you don't freeze to death first."

A possibility, yes. But it didn't change my mind. And where in the goddess's name was the canvas crossbody bag Edie had used for her forest forays? I was sure she'd kept it in here. I stuck my head further into the closet, muffling my response.

"Again, if you have no suggestions—"

"Ask Gilbert."

I pulled back so quickly that I whacked my head on the side of the door frame. "Say what?" I rubbed at the lump already rising above my ear.

"Gilbert. He wants you out of Jeanne's life, let him drive you."

Huh. That suggestion had actual merit. And it raised a whole other possibility for me, too. An idea I'd been wrestling with for days. I gave up my search, withdrew from the closet, and turned to find the bag I'd been searching for sitting on the bed with Gus on top of it.

"You can be a real pain in the ass sometimes, you know," I told my ghost friend, who was cackling in delight inside my head.

"Yes," she agreed, *"but you love me, and you're glad I'm back."*

She had no idea.

CHAPTER 11

GILBERT LOOKED DOWN HIS NOSE AT ME, AN INTERESTING trick given we were roughly the same height. We were standing on his front porch, in full view of any neighbors who might be watching, but I didn't care, now that I was leaving.

The stiff October breeze carrying the scent of snow stirred the comb-over on Gilbert's head. I watched it flap a couple of times and then settle again, trying not to wrinkle my nose. Even if he wanted me out of Jeanne's life as Edie had said, it wouldn't take much for him to turn me down flat.

"Drive you somewhere," he echoed. His air quotes around the words were implied rather than actually sketched, but he still managed to sound condescending, and I still had to bite back the urge to tell him to never mind. I hated that I needed this favor from him. And I was antsy as hell to get on the road after watching and waiting all day for him to return home from his junk shop, and he *would* pick today to be late.

"Antiques, darling, not junk," Edie drawled. *"Remember?"*

I ignored her and focused on willing the man in front of me to cooperate. Hating that I needed him to, but Edie was right. I'd probably have frozen to death if I'd walked out to The Morrigan's Way. I tucked my fingers between my ribs and arms to warm them.

"And why, pray tell," he said, "would I drive you *any*where?"

"Because I'm leaving," I said. "And if I leave, Jeanne won't be able to come see me anymore." Jeanne's own desire not to see me again didn't seem pertinent here, so I conveniently left it out. "Well? Will you do it?"

The comb-over lifted again, and beneath it, Gilbert's bald spot gleamed in the porch light. He pursed his lips. "When you say leave ... "

"I mean leave. As in go and not come back." I thought. Or hoped. Or something. Because I honestly didn't know what to expect or how I would handle it. So much of everything was up in the air right now—including Gilbert's hair—that I didn't dare dwell on nebulous ideas like *hope*.

Trust, the memory of the book reminded me. An equally nebulous idea, but somehow a more reassuring one. And as it was all I had right now, I'd take it.

"Huh." Gilbert folded his arms and narrowed his gaze speculatively as he considered my request. No doubt trying to figure out what was in it for him.

How in the world had Jeanne tolerated the man for so many years? And why—

I cut the thought off. Not my circus, I reminded myself. And thank goddess Gilbert wasn't my monkey. I gritted my teeth and grimaced a semblance of a smile.

"It's a simple yes or no, Gilbert," I said, and then sudden inspiration struck, and I made to brush past him into the house. "I suppose I could just ask Jeanne instea—"

He slapped his comb-over down and held it in place. "No. I told you, I don't want her to see—" He glowered at me, knowing he was beaten. "Fine. After dinner."

"I'd prefer—"

"*After*," he repeated, his enunciation exaggerated, "dinner."

"*You sure you can't access any magick?*" Edie growled. "*Just enough to turn him into a toad?*"

I turned the snort that would have likely made Gilbert change his mind into a cough and nodded my head. "Thank you," I said, forcing the words past the gagging sensation in my throat. Then, as he turned to go, I added, "But I'll need to make a stop on the way, and there's one more thing I need."

Because without it, the idea that had just occurred to me wouldn't stand a chance.

CHAPTER 12

It was almost nine o'clock when Gilbert pulled up in front of the hospital to let me out for the first of my stops.

"Ten minutes," Gilbert snapped as I unclipped my seatbelt and reached for the door handle. "If you're not back in ten minutes, I'm gone."

I paused, door half open, and looked over my shoulder at him. I tried to imagine living with someone like him, wondering how in the goddess's name Jeanne could tolerate it, never mind actively want to stay with him. Remembered that I'd lived with a similar situation myself—albeit a somewhat politer-on-the-surface version—for almost forty years. I would almost certainly still be living with it if Jeff hadn't left me for Julia.

When this was over, I decided, if I somehow got through it, I would come back to Confluence. I would return to the neighborhood and to Edie's house ... and to Jeanne. And I would support that woman with every fiber of my being, because goddess knew she needed it, especially if maybe—just maybe—she found the courage to walk toward her strength after all.

"Tick-tock," said Gilbert.

Or maybe, if I found my magick again, I'd follow up on Edie's idea of turning him into something. But not a toad. I liked toads.

"Fair point," Edie's voice said. *"I vote cockroach."*

"I'll be back when I get back," I said, ignoring my friend and injecting a thread of steel into my quiet voice as I responded to Gilbert, "and you will be waiting for me. *With* my cat."

I added the latter bit because I didn't put it past Gilbert to "accidentally" release Gus from his carrier in the back seat—and from the car. It had been hard enough in the first place to wrangle the cat into the carrier Edie had directed me to in her basement. I didn't think I'd get a second chance after his last experience in one. Specifically, being used as a battering ram through a gauntlet of gnomes.

Gilbert hadn't answered me, so I shrugged. "Unless, of course, you'd prefer to have me back in Edie's house."

His jaw worked back and forth as he ground his teeth together, but his gaze slid away from mine. "Just be quick," he muttered, as he turned to stare out the driver's side window.

Letting him have the last word, I lifted the crossbody bag from the floor—because no way did I trust him not to go through it—and got out of the vehicle. I closed the door behind me and instantly felt cleaner. Goddess, but that man was an odious presence. I hated leaving Gus with him, but this was going to be dicey enough without trying to take a cat in with me.

I glanced around at the thirty or so cars in the staff parking lot. A full complement, given the Confluence hospital's small size. With luck, that same small size would mean my presence would go unnoticed—and more importantly, unchallenged—because at least there wouldn't be security guards wandering around the way I'd seen in city hospitals.

At the front entrance, yes. Which is why I started toward the side door, clutching the security pass in my pocket that would unlock it. Jeanne's, "borrowed" under duress by Gilbert at my insistence. He really did want me out of his wife's life, didn't he?

I made it into the building without incident and, after wandering the sterile, empty corridors following Gilbert's less-than-helpful instructions, finally stumbled upon the long-term care ward. There, I stopped at the blessedly unoccupied nurse's station, discovered the patient list posted on the wall, and found the room I needed without anyone even knowing I was there.

I hoped.

I paused outside the room, wiping sweaty palms against my jeans and praying to every deity in existence that the room would be a private, unshared one, and that it was late enough that Paul would be at home with Braden. That he wouldn't be inside.

"You good?" Edie asked quietly.

"Not even slightly," I whispered.

"I'll keep watch out here," she said.

Her way of telling me she would give me my privacy with Natalie. I nodded, pushed open the door, and stepped into my daughter-in-law's room. An invisible weight lifted from my shoulders. My son wasn't there.

But my relief was brief. The weight settled again, heavier than before, and I locked my knees to keep it from pressing me to the floor. Because Natalie *was* there. Pale and unmoving in the bed, wires sprouting from her, monitors blinking and beeping around her. She looked ... fragile.

The memory of the last time I'd seen her seized me by the throat and filled my brain with horrifying, technicolor detail. The battle of monsters raging outside the Earth house, water flooding the clearing, Natalie on the ground, cradled in my son's arms, their child's *"Mamamamamama,"* an unbroken howl that I had never stopped hearing. *Would* never stop hearing.

I inhaled on a half-sob, fingertips pressed to my lips and back to the door, wanting to flee from what I had wrought. From my failure to keep my family safe. Out in the corridor, the intercom called for a doctor to report to the ER. The tinny voice jolted me back to the present, reminding me that my time here was limited. I was already well past the ten minutes Gilbert had allotted me. If I was going to do this, it had to be now.

I gritted my teeth and squared my shoulders. Then I crossed to the bedside.

Carefully, and with the utmost gentleness, I lifted my daughter-in-law's hand from beside her and held it between my own for a moment. It felt warm, limp, empty of—I brought my thoughts harshly to heel. She *was* still alive, I told myself fiercely. The steady beep of the machines by her bedside proved it. She was alive, and she would come back. She had to come back.

I swallowed the sharp pain in my throat that heralded unwanted tears and reached out to brush her hair back from her forehead. Goddess, but I had misjudged her. Misjudged and underestimated her, for so many years, only to find that she was the only one who embraced my new role as witch and Crone. The only one—Crones, protectors, gargoyle, and me included—who'd believed in me so wholeheartedly and without reservation.

I almost smiled at the thought, but then I remembered how little her faith in me had meant, because I'd still failed her. And through failing her, I'd failed her son, too.

Hell, let's be honest. I'd failed them all. Natalie, Braden, the Crones, the protectors, Lucan … even my obstinate, arrogant son.

But Natalie—beautiful, vital, innocent Natalie—she was the failure that hurt the most, and everything in me rebelled at the idea of leaving her like this. I would not, *could* not, simply walk away.

Know, the Book of the Fifth Crone whispered to me. *Accept.*

No, I thought, in a flash of anger. *I will not accept this. None of it. It can't end this way. I won't let it.*

Trust, said the book.

"Fuck you," I told it. I leaned closer to my daughter-in-law. "I'm not done, Natalie," I whispered to her. "If there is any way to fix this, darling heart—any way at all—I promise I will find it. I will find it, and then I will come back and fix you. You have my word as Crone."

Outside the room, the intercom paged housekeeping, and a murmur of voices passed by the door. It was time to leave.

Mindful of the wires and Natalie's fragility, I pressed my lips to her temple in a brief kiss. "Stay strong," I said. "Stay strong for your son, darling girl. And for me."

CHAPTER 13

"YOU SERIOUSLY WANT TO BE LEFT HERE."

Gilbert had pulled up at the intersection of Barrymore Street and The Morrigan's—Morgan's—Way, and I was unloading the cat carrier (complete with cat—I'd checked when I got back to the car at the hospital) and crossbody bag from the back seat.

"In the middle of nowhere," he continued, "in the dark. Where will you stay?"

"What's the matter, Gilbert?" I asked. "Have you suddenly grown a conscience?"

My newfound "attitude," as my ex would have called it, still had the power to surprise me, and I had to bite back the automatic apology that wanted to follow. I was done apologizing to the jerks—no, the assholes—of the world, I reminded myself. Particularly the entitled male ones who had helped Morok retain his control over the world for all these centuries.

Beneath the dome light, Gilbert leveled a malevolent glare at me. I ignored it and heaved Gus's carrier out of the car and set it roadside, then I tucked Jeanne's hospital pass under the mat on the floor, hoping Gilbert might have heart failure when he realized he'd forgotten to get it back from me and had to explain its absence to his wife.

Or at least a serious moment of discomfort, especially if Jeanne retained a little of her own new attitude.

I slammed the door shut and slung the bag's strap across my chest. I was traveling as lightly as I could, but its weight still pulled at my shoulder, and I adjusted the strap twice to make it tolerable.

I blamed the tins of cat food I'd made Gilbert buy for me—and the useless Book of the Fifth Crone that I'd felt compelled to bring.

"It's your funeral," Gilbert retorted, leaning toward the open passenger window to deliver his words. He had no idea how accurate they might be.

"Give my love to Jeanne," I replied sweetly, closing my hand around the staff I'd leaned against the vehicle, "and thanks for the ride."

He pulled away in a spray of gravel that bit into my legs and pinged off the carrier, making Gus hiss. Such an asshole. I watched his taillights disappear down Barrymore Street toward Confluence, and then, as my eyes adjusted to the night, I looked down at Gus's carrier.

"Well, dude, I guess it's just you and me, now. You ready for this?"

The cat meowed in response, but I couldn't tell if it was agreement or objection. Either way, it was too late to turn back. Far, far too late. I reached down and opened the carrier door, and Gus emerged to wind around my ankles, his purr a comforting rumble. Leaving the carrier where it sat, I started up the snow-dusted gravel of The Morrigan's Way. The earlier snow had stopped, and the skies had cleared, and I was grateful for the light of the three-quarter moon rising above us.

Gus trotted ahead, a pale ghost of a cat in the moonlight, his tail high and curved at the tip. He stopped to wait for me at an unmistakable break in the roadside brambles. It was the one I'd searched for in vain for days, now as plain as day itself—even in the dark—and impossible to miss. I stared at it and then at the stone gatepost beyond—also as plain as day. All those hours I'd spent tramping around out here, and I'd never stood a chance of finding them without the pendant, had I?

I put a hand up to the chain at my neck beneath my pullover. I might be its wielder, as Edie said, but I was nothing without it. I wouldn't let it out of my hands again. Not ever.

Speaking of Edie … I frowned, then sighed. I should be used to her appearing and disappearing, and I supposed I was on some level, but I still wished she'd give me some kind of warning. Or a farewell. A farewell would be nice, too.

"Right," I said to my cat. "Are you leading or following?"

Gus picked his way through the break in the brambles, and I fell in behind him. But where he walked past the gatepost without pause, I stopped beside it, staring at the wrought iron gate that hung open. It sagged from one hinge, rust marring its formerly pristine surface. A frisson of unease edged down my spine, and the hair at the nape of my neck stirred.

My gaze dropped to the brass plaque embedded in one of the stones. The one that once held the address, 13 The Morrigan's Way, and in smaller print, instructions for waking Keven, the gargoyle that had once sat atop the post: *Knock three times on the gatepost if you want me. Twice on the gate if the answer is no.*

Once held. Because now, the address was barely visible under layers of grime, and the small print beneath it had obliterated by scratches.

I glanced up at the empty top of the gatepost and brushed the fingertips of my free hand over its stones. I'd never paid particular attention before to the magick in the gate before, but I certainly felt the lack now. The cold. The nothingness. Unease flared into alarm, and my grip on my staff tightened. I scanned the silent, dark woods surrounding me. Too silent, even for the edge of winter. Not so much as a dried leaf on a branch stirred, let alone the presence of anything living.

The hand I held against the stones dropped back to my side. *Goddess help me*, I thought. *They're gone.*

I'd taken too long to get here, and they were gone. All of them. I could feel it.

A few feet ahead, Gus meowed, his voice muffled by the absoluteness of the quiet. I stared at him, my little ginger cat sitting in a patch of moonlight on the snow-dusted path, wondering what he would tell me if he could. What he had seen. What he had escaped—and endured—in his quest to return the pendant to me. Had it really been all for nothing?

My fingers rested against the rough canvas bag, tracing the outline of the book within. *Know*, it had told me. *Accept.* My lips twisted bitterly. Know what? That I was too late? Accept that I'd failed?

But ... no. No, those words didn't fit. Didn't feel right.

Gus meowed again. *Trust*, the book urged. I hesitated for a second more, then squared my shoulders and stepped through the gate and onto the path. I wasn't at all sure about the trust idea, but I did know that whatever the book wanted me to know and accept, it wasn't failure. It couldn't be, because according to Edie, I hadn't tried yet.

It was time I did.

CHAPTER 14

FIVE MINUTES LATER, MY NEWFOUND RESOLVE HUNG IN tatters as I stared at what remained of the Earth Crone's house. Unobstructed by trees, the three-quarter moon shed an almost brilliant light over the clearing—and the rubble strewn across it.

Slate shingles from the roof.

Stones from the walls.

The thick front door, its oak shattered into chunks and splinters.

Bits and pieces of furniture, some still draped in scraps of fabric.

Keven's woodstove from the kitchen, battered and dented.

Keven.

Oh dear goddess. Keven.

I dropped my staff and sagged to my knees on the grass, hugging my arms around myself to keep from falling apart, oblivious to the snow melting through my jeans. Through a shimmer of tears, I gazed at the unmoving stone gargoyle in the midst of the wreckage. At the familiar face, twisted into a grimace of fury made macabre by the shattered side of her mouth. At one arm upraised with claws outstretched—and the other lying on the ground at her feet. At the snow blanketing her shoulders and muzzle and dusting the tops of her wings.

At the blank, staring stone eyes.

Nausea rose from my belly and tangled in my throat with sheer anguish, emerging in a retch that tore at my very core but produced nothing more than a raw, guttural moan of denial. Of agony. Of empty, hollow, impotent rage.

I squeezed my eyes closed against the destruction. Against the remains of the battle that had been fought—and lost. Gus nudged his way onto my lap and into my arms, and I clutched him close, desperate for his warmth, for his reminder that life still existed, that not all I loved had been lost. My heart ached at the thought of Lucan and the other protectors. Had they died, too, trying to save their Crones? Had Morok—

A twig snapped behind me and I froze, holding fast to Gus, barely daring to breathe, terrified that my thought of Morok had conjured the god himself. But the throat that cleared, the deep, husky voice that spoke—neither of those could have ever belonged to darkness.

"Milady," the voice said. "Bedivere was right. You survived."

For a moment, I didn't move. Shock sucked every atom of air from my lungs. A surge of elation followed—and then crashed, battling with disbelief. Distrust. What if I was hearing things? What if my desperation had conjured hallucinations, and I turned around and no one was there? Or perhaps the voice *was* Morok's doing after all. His deceit. My heart shredded at the possibility, and I put a hand to my chest.

But I had to know, and so I pushed Gus gently from my lap and climbed to my feet, staff in hand out of sheer habit—and just in case.

I turned.

My breath caught again, but this time in sheer joy. It was him. It was really him. His face was cast in shadow, but I knew him instantly. The tilt of his head, the broad chest and shoulders, the dangerous edge to the energy rolling off him, the—

The slow topple to the ground?

I abandoned my staff and leaped forward to catch the shifter, grunting under his weight as he crumpled, then I grunted under his weight.

He was too heavy to hold upright, of course, but I managed to break his fall and get him to the ground without further injury—because, dear goddess, he already had enough of those. Panting with the unexpected effort, I stared at the moonlit body stretched before me. He was naked and bleeding from a dozen wounds, each seeming worse that the last.

"Shit," I muttered, taking in the blood-matted hair and beard, and the oozing wound in his belly. I glanced around the ruins and the clearing that surrounded us, and my gaze settled on Keven's snow-dusted hulk. Goddess, but I could have really, really used her healing magick right now. Or at least some of her herbs. Or shelter of some kind, or ...

"*Fuck*," I snarled.

I stripped off my gloves, then lifted the strap of the cross-body bag from my shoulder and tugged it over my head. Its contents spilled onto the ground. The book, a change of clothes that would never in a million years fit Lucan, the tins of cat food I'd made Gilbert buy for me, and—

I pounced on the cloak I'd packed and shook it out to place it over Lucan's inert form, pausing to stare at the soft, clean, intact fabric. Huh. So its magick worked again, too, did it? I hoped that meant it would warm Lucan against the encroaching night cold and I prayed that his immortality would let him heal himself while he slept, because I ... I had nothing else to give him.

I arranged the cape to cover as much of the naked shifter as I could. He didn't so much as twitch beneath it. Beside him, Gus nudged through the cat food tins and gave a plaintive mew. I picked one up. Whether by chance or design, Gilbert had bought the kind of tins with the tab and peel-back top—most likely by chance, I decided. If he'd thought about it at all, he would have purposefully bought the kind I needed a can opener for, and I hadn't thought to pack one of those.

I opened the tin for Gus and set it on the ground a few feet away. While he ate, I ignored the rumble of my own stomach and packed the rest of my things back into the bag, arranged them to be as flat as possible, and tucked it under my butt as a seat to keep any more of me from soaking up melted snow. Then I wrapped my arms around my legs, rested my chin on top of my wet knees, and took stock of the situation.

It wasn't pretty.

A cat. An injured shifter. The Earth house in ruins. Keven returned to lifeless—and broken—stone. No sign of the Crones or other protectors. The world's most unhelpful book. No shelter or food (unless you were the cat).

And me.

A breeze stirred, swirling snow across the clearing and laying it over the cape-covered Lucan. Lucan, who was not my protector but, by his own words, would have been my friend had circumstances been different. I blinked back tears of self-pity. Goddess, I'd missed him. The kind of missing that went well beyond the initial jolt of hormones that had surprised me when we first met. I missed his presence, his ability to sense when my mood had gone even slightly off track, his—well, everything about him.

And now he was unconscious and injured—fatally, for all I knew—and what the hell was I supposed to do?

"Edie?" I whispered into the dark. But I hadn't heard from her since the hospital, and no answer came now.

The night breeze crept down the collar of my coat—adequate for an autumn walk but not for spending a night outdoors in the encroaching winter. I shivered and tucked my half-frozen fingers into my armpits to warm them and looked down at Lucan's still form. Then, with a sigh, I lifted the edge of the cape, stretched out alongside him, and arranged the cape to cover us both—more or less. As an afterthought, I pulled the canvas bag over and tucked it under my head as an uncomfortable but oddly comforting pillow.

Gus finished his meal and joined us, curling up at my back, and—with the waxing moon shining down and Keven's lifeless hulk watching over us—I wrapped one arm around Lucan's naked torso, willed what little warmth I possessed into him, and closed my eyes.

Know, the book beneath my head whispered to me as I drifted into an exhausted sleep. *Accept. Trust.*

CHAPTER 15

Know.

My eyes flew open, and I stared at the shadow my nose was pressed against, trying to get my bearings. It was dark and cold, except for something warm lying against my back—and the shadow against my nose. That was warm, too. And pliable. And—

I remembered. I pulled back to lever myself up on one elbow and peered down at the shadow. Lucan. Still sleeping—or unconscious? Either way, he hadn't moved, and he was still breathing, despite the fact I'd pulled most of the cape off him to wrap around myself in my sleep. I sat up and rearranged it over him, steeling myself against the loss of its warmth. Gus meowed a protest behind me, and I reached around to give him an apologetic scratch around the ears.

The moon had moved from overhead to just above the branches of the trees surrounding the clearing, and in the absence of its earlier bright glow, the shadows of the ruins loomed larger, darker. Deader, if that was a word. My gaze sought and found Keven's shape amid the tumble of stones from the house. Definitely deader.

Know. The word floated through my thoughts again. *Know. Accept. Trust.* Had that been what woke me? Dreams of the book? My subconscious trying to decipher its obscure words?

A tiny light sparked beside Keven's head. I blinked. Another light sparked a few inches above the first. I squeezed my eyes shut, hard, blinked twice more, and opened them again. A light sparked above Lucan's still form.

Fireflies? I dismissed the idea. Wrong season, too cold, too small, and—understanding dawned. *Wards.* They were wards. And they were everywhere.

Awe crept through me as the clearing filled with hundreds and then thousands of the tiny lights, blinking on and off, then rising to form a net-like dome above the ruins. Above Lucan. Above me. The blinking synchronized and settled into a steady on-off pattern. The wards. The wards had come back at last.

I blinked back tears of gratitude. Remorse. Guilt.

"I'm sorry," I murmured to them, cringing from the memory of the devastation I had caused in my battle with the Mages and their goliath. The thousands of wards that had perished while trying to protect my own family. "I am so, *so* sorry."

The lights gave a quick double-blink before settling back into their pattern. An acknowledgment? Forgiveness? Goddess, I hoped so. I hoped they'd understood, because I wanted them to know—

I sat up straighter as a sudden thought crystallized: *The wards were back.* A half-dozen more thoughts followed on its heels. The wards were back, I had the pendant again, the cape's magick had returned, I'd been able to find the Earth house (at least what was left of it), Lucan had found me, and—

I inhaled a long, slow breath and exhaled it again. Then, tentatively, I turned my focus inward—and found it. The heat that had been missing from my core since my last solo trip through the ley—the one I'd made in my search for the Air and Fire Crones ... and Lucan—had returned. It was weaker than it had once been, to be sure, but it was there. I pressed both hands to myself, one resting on my chest, the other just below it on my diaphragm, as if to protect the small warmth there. I had no idea what had precipitated the return, or why it hadn't come back when Gus brought my pendant to me, but—

Know, the book coaxed, reaching out to me from the bag I'd used as a pillow. I closed my eyes and wrestled with the word, beginning to understand that it held more meaning than I'd realized. But whatever that meaning was, it remained elusive, ethereal, hovering just out of my grasp.

Accept, the book whispered.

I focused on that word, instead. Perhaps its meaning would be less obscure. More befitting the circumstances. Because I didn't know how or why my magick was returning the way it was, but … it was. I could accept that, right? Accept it, and maybe—just maybe—

Trust.

Ignoring the cold seeping into my bones from the ground I sat on, I stared across at Keven's stone bulk and remembered how she was connected to the house she served. Had drawn her very life from it. Remembered, too, how the house had once healed itself from the devastation I'd wrought in my battle against the Mages—and from the many accidents I'd caused after that as I'd sought, and failed, to connect with the elements and control my magick.

I frowned. It had healed itself then, but it hadn't now. Why? What was different? What had—

The answer struck like the proverbial light bulb going off in my head. Crones. There were no Crones. The house needed Crones to survive. All of them did—Earth, Air, Water, Fire. They were entwined with them, with each house coming into being when a pendant chose its next Crone. And now Elysabeth —the Earth Crone—was gone.

Sick horror filled my heart and made it lurch down to my toes, and the hands I held against myself turned to fists. All the Crones were gone. And if the Earth house hadn't been able to heal itself, it meant—

But wait.

A glimmer of an idea prodded at the edge of my mind. I slogged my way through my panic and reached for it—and then the proverbial penny dropped. Of course! Elysabeth had already been imprisoned in a cell when the house had healed before. She'd been nowhere near Confluence. Which meant the house had come here for me, not her. I had been the one to find it, and to wake Keven and summon Lucan, because …

My brow cleared and a small, "*Oh,*" left my lips. Because I was Crone, too. I mean, I knew that, but I was the *Fifth* Crone, and until now, I'd forgotten what that meant. I wasn't just supposed to find and warn the others about Morok's plan or their possible destruction of the planet if they raised their powers; I was supposed to bring them together to defeat the dark god once and for all. To be the center of their wheel.

The house wasn't mine per se, but it had accepted me, housed me, sheltered me, and ...

Accept, the book coaxed, and my thoughts shifted, slid sideways, and emerged from a fog I hadn't even realized overlay them.

And the house had repaired itself after the battle with the Mages for me, not for Elysabeth. It had repaired itself *because* of me.

Which meant Elysabeth wasn't necessarily dead. She might still be alive. All of them might be alive ... and I might have a chance to find them ... and they—*we*—might yet be able to save the world.

But to do that, I would need Lucan—who showed no sign of waking on his own—and to heal Lucan, I would need Keven, and to bring Keven back ...

The fog crept back, swirling through my brain and obscuring the path I knew I needed to take. But this time ... this time, I recognized it. Knew it for the doubt that it was—doubt of myself, my ability, my very worth. Doubt born of a paralyzing mixture of both fear of failure and fear of success.

Fear of my power.

The book nudged my mind again.

CHAPTER 16

KNOW, THE BOOK HAD SAID, AND I DID.

I knew the Morrigan had chosen me as Fifth Crone for a reason. I knew I *could* connect to the elements—and now it was time to figure out what stood in my way.

Accept, my mind whispered to me, and I exhaled a shaky breath. That was going to be a little tougher, because knowing was one thing, but acceptance ... acceptance was akin to admission, and that was something entirely different. It was more. It was owning what I knew. What I'd failed at, what I'd failed to try, what I'd done wrong ... and what I'd done right.

It was accepting *me*.

Me. Claire Emerson. Ex-wife, mother, friend, grandmother, reluctant Crone, deeply flawed. I was stubborn, inclined to think I was funnier than I was, filled with self-doubt, far too willing to set aside my own wants and needs in favor of others, lonelier than I wanted to admit, terrible at making decisions and taking action, and terrified of growing old on my own. My flaws were multiple, and easy to name.

Their counterparts, not so much.

The self-study was uncomfortable, like a prickly sweater, and I wanted to turn away from it but knew I needed to see it through. Because there was more to me than my flaws, and the truth was that I was as determined as I was hesitant, and I was fiercely loyal and caring and compassionate, and somehow, I had managed to muddle through life despite its—and my own —obstacles.

Which meant that perhaps I was more capable than my ex had spent thirty years telling me. More competent.

Stronger.

Strong enough that I'd defeated the goliath once. And the

fire pixies. And the three Mages. Strong enough to have traveled the ley lines on my own, an impossible feat according to the Water Crone's protector, Yvain. Strong enough to have confronted Morok himself, even without my magick.

Stronger than I'd ever allowed myself to notice—in part because heaven forbid I should let my own capacity go to my head, but in greater part because ...

My gaze dropped to Lucan's dark, cloak-draped form beside me. Deprived of my warmth to cuddle against, Gus had overcome his dislike of the shifter—or maybe that had happened in my absence from the house—and was now curled up on Lucan's chest. I watched for a long moment as the cat-shaped shadow rose and fell with each breath the protector took, then shifted my attention to the remains of the hulking stone gargoyle, the claws of her remaining hand outstretched toward the battle I had missed.

The doubt I'd brushed away hung in shreds at my edges, ready for the chance to creep back. It would have been easy to let it. So easy. Just as it was easy for Jeanne to remain with Gilbert —to step away from her strength back into the safety of the familiar. I understood that, now, because stepping into strength was hard, and it was terrifying, and it was filled with the unknown, and oh goddess, how I wished I could be like Jeanne and turn away.

But I wasn't, and I couldn't.

Know.

I wasn't Jeanne, and I'd come too far to be just Claire anymore. Like it or not, I was more. I was strong. I was powerful. And I was Crone.

Accept.

"I am the Fifth Crone," I said softly, reaching for my staff. "And I am chosen by the Morrigan."

I struggled to my feet, wincing at knees and hips stiffened by the cold, giving them a moment to adjust to the demands of standing before I drew fully erect. Overhead, the net of wards pulsed with light, magick, promise. I surveyed the ruins. Earth magick, I decided. Not out of any particular sense of certainty, but because it seemed to make sense, given that I wanted to move stones.

Plus, I had to start somewhere.

Trust.

I closed my eyes, reached into my core, and began my search. It wasn't easy. Any connection to magick that I'd had in past had been born of emotion: fear, anger, desperation. This time, I felt none of those things—or rather, I felt all of them (and more), but without the wild intensity of the past. This time, I sought my connection from a place of control. Intention. And a weird, unfurling confidence in my ability to find it.

To be honest, that latter one was damned distracting. But I held tight to the staff and my intentions, stilled my mind, and delved deeper.

I found the warmth of Fire first and let myself bask for a moment in my connection to it, then I moved on. Air tugged at me, ruffling my hair and caressing my face, and Water next, rippling through every cell of my body, but they weren't what I wanted, either. I ignored all of them and continued further. Deeper. Seeking … there. The roots. *My* roots. The ones that came up from the ground beneath my feet to wrap around my ankles and my body—until they became part of me, and the strength of the very earth itself flowed through me. Until I could feel every rock, every tree, every blade of grass …

The house.

I could feel the house. The stones and the trees that had been broken and bent to become a part of it, the life that still vibrated within them. The life that was still within Keven.

My eyes snapped open, and joy leaped in me. My concentration wavered for a second. I steadied it. There would be time to celebrate *after* the work was done, I told myself. First—I hesitated, because I had no idea what came first, or where to even begin. My gaze settled on the staff I gripped in my right hand. A staff carved from a tree grown from a wand that had been a twig of another tree. It had been a physical weapon of late, but before that, it had been a wielder of magick. Could it be that again?

As if in response to my unspoken question, the staff quivered and began to grow. Where it rested against the ground, it sent out roots to anchor itself. Where it reached toward the sky, it reached further. Its circumference became too great to hold, and my fingers gave up their grip, able only to rest against the rough bark that enshrouded the wood that Lucan had polished for me. To continue to feed my magick into it.

Branches sprouted along its length, stretching up and out until they blotted out the net of wards above us. The tree groaned beneath their weight, but still it grew. And then it stopped. Before I could do more than notice the pause, the trunk beneath my hand shifted—almost as if the tree took a deep breath of its own—and then the real work began. Branches swept low and plucked stones from the ground, sorting through them, sifting out the debris, slowly and painstakingly setting them one on top of another.

A wall took shape. Then another, then another, then a fourth. The three-quarter moon disappeared behind the trees, and my legs ached from standing. The sky to the east turned pale. A chimney rose from the rubble. Splinters of wood became a crooked door that was fitted into an even more crooked opening. My hand against the tree trembled with fatigue as the battered wood stove was lifted from the snow-dusted grass and set inside. Then, as the first rays of the morning sun poked through my tree's branches, the roof went on—a mosaic of shattered slate shingles that fell far short of covering the whole house.

It was …

I stared at the hodgepodge structure, and then at the lifeless Keven, one arm outstretched and the other still on the ground by her feet. It was nothing like the Earth house. Not even a little. Disappointment welled up in my chest. Beneath my hand, the tree trunk quivered. I leaned against it and laid my cheek against its rough bark in reassurance. Gratitude. Because goddess knew, it had tried.

"It's not you," I whispered. "It's me. I'm not ..." I trailed off. I wasn't what? Strong enough? Skilled enough? Practiced enough?

Enough?

Know, said the book.

The disappointment in my chest rose into my throat and turned dry and bitter on my tongue. What was I supposed to know this time? My limitations? I was pretty sure I'd just proved those. In spades.

I pulled away from the tree, swaying in exhaustion as I broke my connection with it. The branches rustled above me and then began to retract. The trunk shrank. Its roots pulled away from the ground. In a fraction of the time it had taken to grow, it was just a staff again, standing for an instant on its own and then toppling to the snow-dusted grass. I stared at where it lay but didn't move to retrieve it.

Then, shuffling forward on half-frozen feet, I crossed the dozen or so feet between me and the gargoyle and stood looking up at the carved visage. A stony gaze stared past me into the distance. If Keven were still in there, there was no sign. I bowed my head and rested my forehead against the granite chest, letting the tears flow at last, feeling the cold trickle in their wake.

"I am so, so sorry, my friend," I whispered. Because in spite of her denial of our friendship on that last day my magick had gotten away on me, that's what she had been. Would always be. Because I was loyal to that friendship, fiercely so, whether she liked it or not.

Which reminded me that I still had Lucan to care for, too, though without so much as a roof to put over his head, I hadn't the slightest idea of how I was going to do that.

With an indelicate sniffle, I stood away from the gargoyle and wiped my jacket sleeve across my eyes, then aimed a glower at the ramshackle pile of stones behind her that vaguely—so vaguely—resembled a house. And that so clearly illustrated my magickal shortcomings.

"Fuck," I muttered, because I'd almost believed I could do it. "Fuck, fuck, *fuck*."

I turned my back on both house and gargoyle, ignored the staff on the ground, and started back to where I'd left Lucan and Gus.

A heavy hand landed on my shoulder and almost knocked me from my feet.

CHAPTER 17

INSTINCTIVELY, I WRENCHED AWAY FROM THE HAND AND dived for the staff I'd let drop to the ground. My fingers closed around it, and I rolled onto my back, swinging it up in an arc toward my attacker. The staff slammed into something, and the impact jarred through my arms and shoulders, numbing my hands so that the weapon dropped from them back to the ground. A dozen thoughts crashed together in my mind.

Who—?

How—?

The ley lines—monster!

Stop using the staff just as a weapon—call your magick!

And then sheer astonishment silenced my brain, and I stared at the stone gargoyle I was sure I'd failed to resurrect.

"*Keven?*" I croaked.

The gargoyle towered over me, still missing one arm. The grimace of fury she'd worn frozen in place had been replaced by sadness, despair, bottomless grief. Not for the first time, a distant part of me marveled at the capacity of stone to be able to show such emotion. A greater part of me wanted—*needed*—to ease the pain etched there. I surged to my feet, leaving my staff where it lay, and threw my arms around the cold granite.

"You're alive again," I whispered against her rough, thick torso. "I did it. I made you alive a—"

My *again* was cut off by a guttural groan that vibrated through the stone beneath my cheek. Keven's claws closed over my shoulder, and she shoved me away with enough force to make me stagger and fall to the ground. She looked down at herself—at the shoulder of the severed arm—and then her gaze swiveled back to me. She groaned again, and her massive, disfigured head shook slowly from side to side. The despair etched in stone became agony.

What have you done? she seemed to be asking, and suddenly, I had no answer. Or I did, but I didn't like it.

The blood in my veins turned cold, washing through me like ice water as slow understanding—and horror—dawned. *I* had done this to her. I had caused the agony beneath that groan and within whatever was at the gargoyle's core. Me. I had overstepped my capacity, my knowledge, and made this ... whatever this was. Because it wasn't Keven. Not like this, and we both knew it.

And that—my gaze went to the tumble of stones that barely resembled a structure, let alone a building—that wasn't even a faint shadow of the Earth house.

My breath snagged like shards of broken glass in my throat as I faced my arrogance. My conceit. How could I have thought for so much as a fraction of an instant that I could rebuild something so marvelous? That I could feel life in stone, or worse, try to create it? Me, who could barely—

Something soft and warm settled around my shoulders, interrupting my mental tirade against myself. I stared down at it. My cloak? I blinked up at the tall, naked form silhouetted against the bright, cloudless morning sky. In silence, Lucan surveyed the gargoyle before him and the house—the attempted house—beyond. He lowered himself to the ground at my side. Amber eyes turned to me, the brow above them furrowed.

"Did you do this?" he asked.

Shame washed through me. My gaze slid from his, and I gritted my teeth against the tears I felt building. I would not cry, damn it. I pulled the cape around me and wrapped my hands in its fabric. It brought scant comfort.

"It's ..." Lucan trailed off.

"A mess?" I supplied, my voice tight. "A disaster? Yes. I know. I thought—I tried—"

"It's magnificent," he said.

My gaze snapped back to meet his. To meet the awe there. The pride. I gaped. "It's ... what?"

"Magnificent," he repeated. "You did it, milady. You learned to control your magick."

I narrowed my eyes at him. "Do you have a fever? Because I think you're hallucinating. Look at it, Lucan." I pulled an arm out from under the cloak and waved it at the house. "It's barely standing, and Kev—Keven—" My throat closed, and I turned away, unable to finish. I didn't know how to finish. How to even begin to describe what I'd done to poor Keven.

Magnificent, my ass.

But Lucan's hand cupped my chin and gently, insistently tugged it around so that I faced him again. "It's enough," he countered. "You've seen the house repair itself before, milady. It will do so again. It *can*, because you've given it the chance."

I wanted to believe him, but I couldn't find belief in me. Not for Lucan, not for the house, and sure as hell not for myself. One of the tears I'd tried so hard to hold back spilled from my eye and trickled down my cheek, leaving an icy path in its wake. Another followed.

"You're exhausted." My not-protector and not-friend-because-circumstances wrapped an arm around me and pulled me close, cradling my head against his chest.

I resisted for an instant because said chest was naked—and not-friend or otherwise, I doubted I would ever not notice when that happened. But he was right. I was exhausted, weary to the bone and beyond, and I didn't have it in me to object.

"Sleep," his chest rumbled beneath my ear, "and let your magick do its work. It and the gargoyle will both be back. You'll see."

I drifted off to the sound of Keven's mournful groan.

CHAPTER 18

I WOKE ALONE, UNLESS YOU COUNTED GUS, WHO SAT ON my chest in loaf position, staring at me with the half-closed eyes that came with a cat's contentment. He gave a slow blink, likely approval at me regaining consciousness, and a purr rumbled through him.

My lips twitched upward. "Good morning to you, too," I told him.

But it wasn't morning. Not with the sun hovering just above the treetops in the west.

West.

How did I know——? Why was I——?

The events of the last hours rushed back, like a river released from a dam. Natalie. Gilbert. Lucan and the house and Keven. Connecting with the Earth element and raising its magic in an attempt to heal, to rebuild, to …

Failure.

I pulled a hand out from under the cape covering me like a blanket—Lucan's doing—and rubbed it over my eyes, remembering the crooked, ramshackle house that my magick had cobbled together. The remnants of the gargoyle I'd tried to bring back to life.

Her anguished groan echoed in my head, and I cringed from it. Oh goddess, what had I done? And what in hell was I supposed to do now? Lucan——

Lucan.

I jolted upright, summarily dumping Gus to the ground. Lucan—had he succumbed to his injuries? Crawled off somewhere to take his wolf shape and die when I'd only just found——

My jaw dropped and I stared at the tableau before me. At the house—not the Earth house as I remembered it, but a proper house nonetheless, with a solid door that stood ajar, mullioned windows across its front—two to the left and one to the right, a flagstone porch, walls as straight as stone could be … and a slate roof that covered it all.

"You've seen the house repair itself before, milady. It will do so again," Lucan's voice had whispered to me. *"Let your magick do its work."*

I released a long, slow breath. Awe filled me. Had he been right? Was it possible? Had *I* done this? Or at least begun it? I looked up at the curl of smoke rising from the chimney. Gus, his tail held high and twitching in annoyance at my perceived treatment of him, stalked away from me, across the flagstone porch, and into the house. No sooner had he disappeared into the interior than a huge shadow filled the opening. Stone ground against wood as Keven stepped through, sending the house an irritated look over her shoulder.

"For the fifth time," she growled, "could you *please* take care of the doorways before I do it myself?"

The house trembled—in annoyance, I suspected—and a fine cloud of dust slid from the eave onto the one-armed gargoyle standing beneath. But the doorway Keven had scraped through creaked and groaned, visibly growing taller and wider.

The gargoyle gave a brusque nod. "Better," she grumbled, "but it took you long enough." Then she turned her stony— both literally and figuratively speaking—gaze on me.

For long, silent seconds, she said nothing, and I could think of nothing *to* say. Not after how things had been left between us.

"Friends?" The memory of her voice, her denial, had never stopped echoing in my heart. *"Milady, we were never meant to be friends. We served you as our Crone when we thought that was who you were. And now you are not."*

And now? What was I now? To her, to Lucan … where did I fit into their lives? Did I fit at all?

On the porch, Keven turned and stomped back into the house, and my heart plummeted at the unspoken answer to my question. Not her Crone, it seemed, and still not her friend. I took a moment to absorb the heaviness of the knowledge, to let it fill me, to decide what it meant.

Nothing, really. It meant nothing, because the task ahead of me remained unchanged. I was here to find the others, then to find Morok and stop him. I folded the cloak across my lap, first in half, then half again. It didn't matter whether Keven and Lucan were my friends; it mattered only that they helped—

"In or out," bellowed a gravelly voice from within the cottage. "I'm not keeping dinner for you forever."

I gave a start. Those words. I recognized those words. They were imprinted on me forever. The exact words Keven had bellowed at me on the night I found the original cottage. It had been dark, and I was hungry, and my stomach had growled, and I had chosen "in," and I had gone into the house and found—

Lucan.

I still didn't know where he was now—or how he was doing. Had Keven been able to heal him? I stuffed the cape into Edie's canvas bag, slung the latter over my shoulder, climbed stiffly to my feet, and hobbled toward the house, past the stone arm still lying on the grass. My cold joints loosened up enough that I wasn't limping by the time I reached the flag-stone porch, but goddess, my sixty-year-old body was cranky about sleeping on the half-frozen ground at the end of October.

My steps slowed and stopped at the door. The house and I had been on uneasy terms after my previous attempts to do magick within its walls—especially after I'd set fire to its kitchen door when I'd tried (accidentally, I swear) to kill Bedivere. Would it still be wary of me?

The heavy oak door, already ajar, opened a little more, as if nudged by the wind—or an invisible hand. I put my own hand out to the wood frame, touching the scrape made by Keven's shoulder as she'd passed through.

"I'm sorry," I whispered to the house. "I know I was—unpredictable. But I'm better at it now, I think. And the wards are back, if that counts for anything."

A soft rustle sounded, and I looked down at a welcome mat taking shape on the floor inside the doorway. I smiled at the gesture and patted the frame under my hand.

"Thank you," I said, and then I stepped over the threshold.

INSIDE WAS NOTHING LIKE I REMEMBERED. GONE WAS THE huge, vaulted entry with the stone stairs ascending to a second floor. Once, Lucan had taught me to use the staff in this space, with ample room for our practice. Now, there was barely enough room to get past the door and close it, and scratches along the walls at eye-level were silent evidence of Keven's difficulty in navigating the space.

Once, a set of double doors to the left had opened onto a spacious, wood-paneled sitting room with a fire blazing in a huge stone fireplace flanked by matching sofas. Now, a cramped room held a single stool drawn up before feeble embers in what was little more than a hole in the wall.

Tears welled in my eyes. So very much had been lost. How would all of it ever be recovered? Was it even possible? And if rebuilding a house was this difficult, how would my magick ever be able to manage more?

As if responding to my thoughts, the timbers above my head groaned and creaked, and the ceiling lifted a few inches higher. *A work in progress,* the house seemed to say. *Be patient.*

"Dinner!" Keven bellowed again, her voice coming from the end of the narrow passage before me.

I closed the door and started down the hall toward the kitchen at the back of the house. This part of the layout, at least, felt right—at least until I spotted the gaping hole in the back wall and the inky, impenetrable darkness within it. There had been two doors here once, side by side. One had led to a second set of stairs to the upper floor, and the other to ...

A familiar, damp scent emanated from the opening. The cellar. I would recognize its smell anywhere—as I should, given the number of hours I'd spent down there, trying to learn magick. First with Keven, then under Anne's tutelage.

Never with much success.

I edged closer to the hole. I had Fire, now. I could—

In the kitchen to my right, a pot banged down on the stove. I would have recognized that sound anywhere, too. I stepped back again and pushed open the door leading to Keven. Dinner first. Then ... then, we'd see.

CHAPTER 19

LIKE THE REST OF THE HOUSE, THE KITCHEN WAS A fraction of the size it had once been, and Keven's bulk—with the addition of Gus draped around her neck—seemed to fill most of it as she turned from the battered woodstove, a steaming bowl in her only hand. She waved it at a bench sitting along one wall.

"No table yet," she grunted. "You'll have to hold it."

I made no move to follow her directions. My attention had been seized by a curled-up form on the floor beside the wood-stove, and my heart skipped a beat. Then another. Lucan. But an unmoving Lucan, who hadn't so much as lifted his head from the floor at my entry.

"He'll heal," Keven said, her voice gruff, "but it will take time. My herbs were destroyed in the ... well. They were destroyed. I'll plant the garden again tomorrow, but that will take time, too."

"How much time?" I asked.

"For things to grow? We'll have vegetables in a day or two. The herbs will need more time—a week, maybe more—to acquire their power. It will take longer than it would if the house were whole. Most of its energy is focused on rebuilding right now."

The house shuddered around us as if in agreement, and Keven gave a nod of satisfaction as the walls of the kitchen expanded outward by a foot in each direction. I ducked instinctively, then straightened when nothing collapsed on me.

"I didn't mean the garden," I said. "I meant Lucan. How long will it take him to heal?"

She shrugged her intact shoulder. Gus shifted with the movement, then settled again as she indicated the bench a second time. I moved over to it, set the bag down, and leaned my staff against the wall beside it. Then I eased myself down to sit. Tomorrow, I thought, I would take up my staff practice again for real, before my inactivity and the general abuse of my body caused it to seize up altogether. For now, though …

I took the bowl Keven held out to me. Its sparse, watery contents were a far cry from the thick, meaty stews she had once produced, but the fact she'd been able to make anything with one hand and virtually no ingredients was downright astounding in my book. I murmured my thanks. She nodded acceptance. My eyes followed her return to the stove.

I recalled Lucan's words to me two scant weeks ago—though it felt like a lifetime. Another lifetime, because goddess, every week that passed seemed to feel like a lifetime right now. But I digressed, and I went back to Lucan's words. *"You do know that you are the Crone, right? And the gargoyle is your servant?"*

Strictly speaking, that wasn't exactly true, now that we knew I wasn't their Crone, but it was enough for me to gather my courage and clear my throat. The oblique stone gaze met mine.

"Tell me," I said.

Silence stretched between us for so long that I thought she might refuse, but at last she turned to face me and settled back on her haunches to talk.

"We thought you were dead," she said. "When Kate returned with the pendant, she—*Morok*—" Her top lip, a chunk of it still missing, lifted in a snarl at the thought of what I knew had returned to the house in Kate's body. "We had no reason not to accept the story he told, that you had known you were dying and had passed the pendant on to him—to Kate—as the new Crone. He gave up Kate's job and moved in here with the rest of us and helped to heal Lady Elysabeth. We suspected nothing. His magick was strong, he connected with all the elements …"

Her gaze slid away from mine, and I knew we both thought the same thing. They suspected nothing because Morok-Kate had been everything the Fifth Crone was supposed to be. Everything I had not been.

"Go on," I said.

"There were many discussions about what to do, whether to create another split or try to destroy Morok outright as the Crone Wars books said would happen. Lucan knows more than I do about that. I was ... excused from participation."

I frowned. "Excused ...?"

Keven's shoulders hunched more than usual. "My purpose is to serve," she said, her tone flat, "not to take part in conversations or offer suggestions. I had forgotten that, but Morok reminded me, and the others did not object."

My hands tightened around the cooling bowl of soup I held. "Not even Lucan?"

"He tried, but the mutt is as constrained as I am by the bonds of the magick that made us." Her lip curled again, this time in a sneer that spoke of centuries of resentment—and internalized pain. The same pain I had seen in Lucan.

"What did magick do to you?" I had asked him once.

"Choice," he had responded. *"It took away our choice."*

The Morrigan's magick, it appeared, was far from perfect. I wasn't sure if that made me feel better about my own or even more unsettled.

Keven shifted her weight, a grinding of stone against flagstone. She sighed. "Then one night, Percival returned from a hunt to say that he had seen you in the woods, but he hadn't been able to talk to you because you were with another woman."

Jeanne. I knew we'd made too much noise that night. Or perhaps I'd just made too little on the occasions I'd come alone. Goddess, but how different things might be if I'd been alone that night and could have warned Percival. But then ... my hand strayed to the bag at my side and the book within it. A book I might still not have found if Jeanne had *not* been with me that night.

Though its actual value had yet to be ascertained, in my mind.

"Lucan wanted to go after you to confirm it was actually

you," Keven continued. "Elysabeth was in favor of the idea, but Morok convinced the others that it would be a mistake. He said"—she gave a short, humorless laugh—"he said if there was anyone out there who looked like you, it was a deception—a ruse perpetrated by Morok himself, trying to flush them out."

Morok had blamed Morok. Because, of course.

"Then this ...?" I moved one hand away from the bowl to encompass the house in a wave. "How did this happen?"

"Morok tried to accelerate the timeline. He wanted to create the splinter immediately, because of the imminent danger he claimed we were all in if you weren't you, and the god of deception had found us. But Lady Elysabeth was still far from ready, and the others refused." The gargoyle shook her ponderous head. "He lost patience. A dozen Mages attacked, with twice that number of shades and the goliath. We were overwhelmed. While the protectors fought the monsters, the dark god and his Mages seized the Crones. I saw them bound and pulled into a ley line, and then the house fell beneath the goliath, and ..."

She trailed off, staring into the distance for a moment before looking back to me. "And then I woke to find you and this"—she waved her clawed hand at the kitchen—"and him." She nodded at the wolf curled up by the stove. "I have no idea what happened to the other protectors."

A long silence followed her story, and I sipped my cooling soup while I processed her words and let them sink into me. On one hand, I ached to know that I hadn't been here to help. On the other, I knew that if I *had* been here, I could have done nothing anyway. But what really hurt was knowing that I had been the cause of all of this by letting Morok take my pendant in the first place.

I looked across the room at the wolf curled up by the stove, then at the one-armed gargoyle hunched nearby. I'd made a mess of things, yes. The question now was, how did I go about cleaning it up?

CHAPTER 20

I SLEPT—OR AT LEAST DOZED—ON THE KITCHEN BENCH that night. In part because there were no bedrooms or beds as yet, but mostly because that's where Lucan was, and I had no intention of leaving him. Keven lumbered from room to developing room in the rest of the house. In between my fitful bouts of sleep, I listened to her heavy tread against the flagstone floors that had been re-laid, and to Gus's contented rumble from her shoulders when they returned every so often to the kitchen so Keven could check on Lucan and put more wood into the stove.

I listened, too, to the creaks and groans of the ever-expanding house. I wondered how long it would take to heal, and what it would look like when it was done. Given that it had been my magick that set it on the road to recovery, would it shape itself to my memory of it? I had loved what it had been before. Loved that it had felt so welcoming. So much like home … at least until the discovery that I wasn't its proper Crone and my feeling of belonging had evaporated.

I fell into my deepest slumber just as the morning light crept through the window over the sink. By the time I woke, sunlight streamed in, and Keven stood over the stove again, stirring a pot.

I eased myself upright on the bench, wincing at the twinges in my back and neck that accompanied the previous stiffness in my hips. My sixty-year-old body didn't appreciate sleeping on hard benches any more than it did the hard ground, apparently, and oh goddess, but I missed the luxury of a mattress.

And a hairbrush. I ran fingers through my tangled curls in an attempt to unravel them slightly, then stopped. Lucan's wolf was gone. I lurched to my feet and teetered for a second before finding my balance. Keven looked around at me, one brow raised.

"Lucan?" I croaked.

"Resting upstairs." She went back to stirring the pot.

I tipped my head back to look at the ceiling. "We have a second floor again?"

"We do. And a table." She pointed with the spoon she held.

She was right. We had a table. The same long wooden table with the knife-scarred top that I'd shared with her and Lucan so many times before. A tiny joy bubbled up in me, so intensely sweet that it brought tears to my eyes, and I reached out and ran my fingertips over the familiar surface, feeling as if I'd just found another friend.

In my peripheral vision, I saw Keven roll her eyes, and I pulled my hand back. Great. Now I was getting downright maudlin.

I firmed up my spine and, when I asked, Keven directed me to a flimsy wooden shack at the end of what had been the garden that housed what she referred to as "the personal facility." It was a far cry from the polished tile and chrome bathroom that had once abutted my bedchamber upstairs, but using it was better than looking for a suitable clump of trees for my call of nature. It even had an old-fashioned water pump beside it for washing my hands when I was done.

I returned to the kitchen and took stock of the changes while Keven ladled soup into a bowl for me. The battle scars on the woodstove had been smoothed away, and it looked like its old, well-used self again. The dish-laden shelves over the counter were back, as were the shelves that held Keven's herbs—although the jars there were empty, as were the drying racks above the table. A variety of seeds sat in carefully separated piles at the opposite end of the table from me.

"Is the rest of it ...?" I waved my hand toward the door to the hallway and the rest of the house.

"It's not finished, but it's getting there." The gargoyle ladled some of the pot's contents into a bowl and carried it to the table. "Eat."

98
98

I hesitated. "Lucan ..."

"Will still be there after you eat. He needs sleep if he's to heal."

I frowned. "What do you mean, *if*? You can't do anything to help?"

She cast a speaking glance at the empty jars. "I've done all I can," she said. "His life is in the hands of the Morrigan, as it has always been. Now eat. I have work to do." And with that less-than-satisfactory response, she lumbered out of the kitchen.

I heard her descend the stairs to the cellar and debated going after her—or, better yet, going to check on Lucan myself—but the gargoyle didn't seem overly worried about him, and my stomach chose that moment to growl, so I sighed and pulled my bench up to the table. It wasn't likely that Keven would be forthcoming in this mood, anyway. Keven in any mood wasn't particularly forthcoming, but this mood was worse, so I might as well eat now and try again later.

The bowl contained the same watery and unappealing soup as the night before, the strongest flavor of which came from the juniper berries floating in it, underpinned by what I was pretty sure was pine, along with something else that was darker, earthier. But it was hot, and I needed food, so I sipped at it in silence, letting my mind turn over the events of the last day.

It had been ... a lot.

Come to think of it, the last *few* days had been a lot. As had the last few weeks. But my brain skipped sideways at the thought of going over it all, and so I focused on the most recent events—the most pressing, and the most intertwined.

The house rebuilding around me. The magick that I had undeniably called on to start that rebuilding. Lucan's sudden reappearance. The battle that had destroyed the house in the first place—and that had injured Lucan and cost Keven her arm. The whereabouts of the others. The book that remained frustratingly obscure.

Lucan.

When my thoughts circled around to the shifter yet again, I set the bowl, still half-full, on the table and pushed myself up from the bench. I'd get nowhere until I saw for myself that he was still alive and healing.

CHAPTER 21

THE SECOND FLOOR HAD, AS KEVEN SAID, REAPPEARED—albeit in an as-yet unfinished form. The staircase was a rough, rickety affair that I climbed with not a little trepidation as it creaked and groaned under my weight. I wondered how it hadn't collapsed beneath Keven—especially with the addition of Lucan, whom she'd most likely had to carry, and who wasn't a small man. Or wolf, if he was still in that form.

But he wasn't. I found him in the room to the right at the top of the stairs, where he lay in very human form in the middle of a sturdy, plain, four-poster bed, covered by a coarse wool blanket. A single oil lamp on the nightstand beside the bed gave just enough light for me to see that his eyes were closed. Judging by the rise and fall of his chest, he was indeed still alive. I hesitated in the doorway, not wanting to wake him. But as I turned away, a violent shiver shook his frame.

Alive, yes. Healing? Maybe not so much. Leaving the plank door open, I tiptoed to the bedside and caught my breath at the sheen of sweat covering his face and the shoulders not covered by the blanket.

"If he heals," Keven's words whispered to me. *"His life is the hands of the Morrigan now."*

A frisson of fear snaked through my belly.

The Morrigan.

Serve her, I might, but I was under no illusions about the goddess. So far, she had proved herself to be mercurial at best and unfeeling at worst. She was there when she wanted to be—or, more specifically, when she needed something—but nowhere to be found when one needed her most. She might, deep down, perhaps, have the world's best interests at heart in her struggle against Morok, but I was beginning to understand that we individuals—even the supposedly immortal ones who had served her since the beginning of this damned war—were nothing but pawns to her.

Easily sacrificed.

Disposable.

In the bed, Lucan shivered again, and his head thrashed from side to side. I curled my hands into fists and waited in the hope that I was wrong, that I had misjudged the goddess, that she had heard my thoughts … but no rush of crows came together to form her dress, and no raspy voice told me what to do. Lucan really was on his own for this.

My mouth tightened. *We* were on our own, I corrected myself. Because the goddess may have deserted my not-protector, but that didn't mean I had. I looked around the room and found a pitcher and bowl sitting on a washstand beside the fireplace, with a small towel hanging from an iron hook on the stand's side.

I carried all three across the room, pausing as I passed the window overlooking the garden. Keven moved slowly and methodically through the prepared beds there, stooping every few inches to stretch out her hand and gently press down the soil. The seeds from the kitchen table, I remembered. She was replanting.

I cast back in my memory for the garden's previous layout. The heal-all had been there before, I thought, and I hoped that was what she planted again now. First. Before anything else. Because I would happily eat juniper-pine soup for the rest of my days, if it meant she could heal Lucan.

I watched her for a few seconds more, then continued to the bed and set the bowl on the bedside table. I poured water into it from the pitcher, dipped the end of the towel into it, and squeezed out the excess. Then I sat on the edge of the bed.

Scorching heat radiated from Lucan. His long hair was splayed on the pillow around his head, and both it and his beard were soaked with sweat. Using one end of the damp towel, I wiped his face, his neck, his shoulders. He didn't move.

I folded the towel into a rectangle and laid it across his forehead, then looked down at him. I thought of Natalie, similarly unconscious in a hospital bed. My son, who no longer spoke to me. My grandson, who was likely traumatized for life by the battle he had witnessed—and the potentially permanent loss of his mother. I thought of Edie, who died in my stead in the fire that had consumed my house. Of Jeanne, who had been torn between two conflicting worlds her entire life, guarding the Book of the Fifth Crone. Of the gargoyles that had died, nameless, in the battles that had destroyed three of the Crone houses. Of the Crones who had been taken by Morok, and the protectors whose fate I didn't know.

Of the thousands of wards that had died trying to protect the Earth house and my family.

So many deaths. So much destruction. And so much of it because of me. My indecision. My choices. My failures. My—

Through the window came the faint caw of a crow. I didn't think it was one of my crows—they tended toward silence—but it was enough to break my train of thought. Enough to make me blink and step back from the abyss I was creating for myself out of blame and failed responsibility, the way I always did when life went awry, when the truth was …

The last fifty or so years of my life flashed before me with startling speed and clarity. I *had* always done this, hadn't I? I'd made it my duty—my calling—to fix everyone else's lives and clean up their messes, and when I couldn't, I'd accepted the blame, because I should have been more understanding, more helpful, more thoughtful, more available—

More. Always more.

But the truth? The truth was, my marriage had ended not because I hadn't tried hard enough or worn the right clothes or had the right demeanor when meeting my husband's clients, but because Jeff had been a prick. *Was* a prick. And I may not have always been the perfect parent to Paul, but perfect didn't exist and I'd done the best I could, and he was a grown-ass adult who had chosen to follow in his father's footsteps. And Jeanne's weird upbringing? I hadn't even known her then.

"Well, fuck," I said aloud, with no small astonishment. Because what else did one say when she suddenly realized that she wasn't responsible for the entire world?

I wet the cloth from the bowl and wiped Lucan down again, sifting slowly through the many, many layers of my self-revelation. The fire that killed Edie? Morok, not me. Natalie's injuries? My insides did a little sideways skitter at the idea I might be trying to evade my role in that, but the final answer remained the same: Morok. The missing Crones? Morok.

It was all Morok.

Hell, even the patriarchy could—at least to some extent—be blamed on the god of deceit, who'd been feeding lies to the world for centuries.

A weight I hadn't known I carried lifted from my shoulders, and I took a deeper breath than I'd been able to since … I couldn't even remember when. Everything in me—every atom of my being—knew that I was right. I felt the truth. Accepted the truth. Was downright giddy with the truth.

Oh, I had without doubt played a role in the recent death and destruction, yes, but the start of it? That was on Morok, not me. And it was only part of the story. Only part of me. The rest of the story, however …

That part, I wanted a say in how it went.

I brushed my fingers over Lucan's hot, damp cheek. "Heal," I whispered to him. "Heal, my friend, because we're not done yet, and I need you."

CHAPTER 22

I SAT IN THE KITCHEN WITH THE BOOK OPEN ON THE TABLE before me, determined to find the elusive understanding I knew I needed in order to move forward. I'd hoped it would be more forthcoming this time around, but it contained the same three words as it had before, now on alternating pages as I flipped through them. *Know* on one, *Accept* on the next. *Trust* after that.

Repeat.

But I felt none of my former disappointment or betrayal or animosity. Because this time, I came to it with an open mind and a guarded but willing heart. This was the Book of the Fifth Crone, and I had to—*did*, I told myself—trust it to give me what I needed. If that was only three words, then I obviously needed those words.

Know.

I stared at the word and sipped at the soup I'd strained into a cup, having decided it was better as tea than it was as food. I thought about all the things I knew about myself. That I was Claire Emerson, that I was divorced and now estranged from my son, that I had been called to serve the Morrigan and had lost my best friend, that over the course of my life, I had been called on to be many things to many people—wife, mother, grandmother, friend, upstanding citizen, hostess ...

That I'd lost myself among all my many other identities.

I thought back to what I had been before those identities, when I had been a child, free from the constraints and expectations placed on me by family and society, from the masks I'd donned in order to meet those expectations. And yet ...

I turned the page. *Accept.*

And yet, those masks had all been me, too. I'd worn them

not just out of need, but out of choice. I'd chosen to marry Jeff
—and to remain with him even when I felt myself being smothered beneath his demands. I'd chosen to have Paul—and to
refrain from speaking up when I saw him begin to follow in his
father's footsteps. I'd dabbled in witchcraft and then turned my
back on it, choosing to fear it. And ultimately ...

Ultimately, I'd chosen to be here, too, on this path of Crone.
Here in this kitchen. Here in the service of the Morrigan. Here
to find the others—and myself. I flipped the page again.

Trust.

The third word was as oblique on the surface as the other
two had been. But I met it with curiosity rather than frustration
this time, because this wasn't about what the book could give
me, but what I could take from it—and find in myself.

Trust.

Trust who? Keven and Lucan? The Morrigan? The process?

Know. Accept. Trust.

Gus jumped up on the table beside my tea and walked over
to head-butt me under my chin. I gave him an absentminded
scratch around the ears and listened to the familiar, comforting
rumble of his purr as I frowned.

Know. Accept. Trust.

The words held more than a message for me. They held—
power. Or at least a key to power. I was sure of it. But I still
couldn't quite grasp—

The door from the garden opened, and Keven lumbered into
the kitchen. She set the basket she carried on the counter by the
sink and closed the door, then turned to me. Her gaze went to
the open book before me, and she frowned.

"Lady Elysabeth's book? But I thought you couldn't read it."

I closed the book and held it up for her to see the cover.
"Not Elysabeth's," I said. "Mine. Or at least, the Fifth Crone's."

She looked even more surprised. "There was a book for you?
But where—?"

"In the safekeeping of ..." I trailed off. I'd been going to say *a friend*, but I wasn't sure that's what Jeanne was, anymore—or if she ever had been. "An ally," I finished. "One of the Daughters of Hestia."

"Never heard of them."

"Hestia was another goddess," I said. "Greek. She was apparently handmaid to the Morrigan. I don't know how that came about, but she gave Hestia the book to guard, and Hestia's descendants have kept it safe ever since."

She narrowed her eyes at the book, then at me. "Is that the reason you were able to …" She waved her hand at the kitchen, then herself.

I set the book on the table again. "I don't know," I said honestly. "Maybe? My magick started coming back at around the same time as I found it, but Gus brought the pendant to me then, too, so—"

"What do you mean, your magick came back?"

Right. Lucan, the Crones, and the other protectors had known about my loss of magick, but Keven hadn't been there when I'd told them. I paused and stepped back in my story-telling.

"I lost it when I traveled the ley lines," I said. "At least, that's what I think happened. Every time I used one on my own, I emerged with less magick. By the time we went to rescue Elysabeth—" I frowned. "Actually, by the time I found Lucan and the others, I had nothing left."

The gargoyle stared at me for so long that it sparked a concern in me that she'd turned to stone again—the lifeless, unmoving kind. I was beginning to consider waving a hand in front of her when she grunted, making me jump.

"You knew you couldn't come back," she said, "and that the mutt wouldn't be able to go back for you. You knew you'd be trapped in that cell—which means you knew about Morok."

"About Morok, yes. About not being able to get out, no. Not for sure, anyway. I thought—hoped—I could make one more trip back to warn the others."

That had actually been the slimmest of my hopes. The other, more likely outcome had been that if I did make it into the ley myself, I would die in it—or, worst-case scenario, that I would get only the pendant into the ley and, as Keven had said, be trapped in the cell until I died.

Any of the three possibilities would have kept the pendant out of Morok's hands and kept him from infiltrating the Crones as Kate, pretending I had chosen her as my successor. If they had worked out. Which they hadn't.

I looked down at the hand I'd clenched into a fist in my lap, remembering the feel of Morok-Kate's fingers working at it, trying to pry the pendant from my grasp. I heard again the whisper of the voices of a thousand ancestors: "*Let go, let go, let go...*"

"And now?" Keven asked, pulling me back into the kitchen and our conversation.

"Now ..." I flexed my fingers and returned my hand to the tabletop and the book there. I sighed. "Now, I'm not sure."

She grunted. "Well. You obviously have at least some of your magick back. And more control of it than you once did. What does the book tell you? Does it give you the spells you need?"

"It's ... complicated." I almost choked on the resurrection of my go-to phrase. Not too long ago, it had been my answer to almost every question asked of me and, frankly, I could have done without ever uttering it again.

"Isn't it always with you?" Keven muttered, not quite under her breath.

I changed the subject. "How bad is Lucan? I looked in on him a while ago. His fever ..."

Keven turned away. "As I said, it is in the goddess's hands."

I decided I must be imagining the extra gruffness in her voice. "You can't do anything?"

"I have made him comfortable. I can do nothing more without my herbs." She gestured with her hand, and my gaze followed to the empty jars lining the shelves that had been her dispensary.

Like a lightning bolt, the image of similar shelves flashed into my mind. Edie's shelves. Of course! Why had it taken me so long to think of it? I surged to my feet, almost knocking over the bench—and my tea—in my excitement. Startled out of his nap, Gus jumped to his feet, gave me a baleful glare of disapproval, and leaped down from the table, his tail three times its normal size as he stalked away.

Keven looked askance at me, her one hand resting on its corresponding haunch and her brow furrowed.

"I know where to get herbs," I said, swinging the cloak I'd been sitting on around my shoulders and fastening it at my neck. I shoved the book into my canvas bag and slung the strap over my head and across my shoulder. "What exactly do you need?"

I couldn't very well transport all of Edie's jars back here, but fortunately, my friend—unlike Keven—had thoughtfully labeled all of hers.

Keven frowned. "Where—?"

"A friend," I interrupted, desperate to leave now that the idea had occurred to me. Even more desperate to return, so her healing of the shifter could begin. I might find some answers in the book, but I still needed Lucan's help.

I still needed Lucan.

I clutched the bag to my side and swallowed, then continued, "She's gone, now, but she was a midwitch—and skilled with herbs. I'm sure she'll have what you need."

But the gargoyle's ponderous head shook in the negative. "You cannot leave, milady. Morok—"

"Trust me," I said, my voice grim. "Given the condition I was in when he left me in that cell, he won't consider me a threat."

"Given that he knows you escaped the cell," Keven countered, "you can't be sure of that."

I hesitated, because she had a point. And then I shook my head, because all the points in the world aside, we needed those herbs. "I have to take the chance. If I'm going to go after the others, I need Lucan."

Keven's scowl deepened, and I braced for another objection. Then she inclined her head. "As you wish, milady."

She studied the empty jars, muttering to herself as if mentally cataloging what they had once contained, nodding to herself in agreement, shaking her head in dismissal, and at last turning back to me.

"Heal-all is best," she said. "But if you can't find that, then calendula and marshmallow will do for wound healing and infection. Slippery elm, too, if it's there. Yarrow, to be safe, in case the bleeding starts again. Angelica to restore his energy; rhodiola, his endurance. And violet and linden flowers for his grief."

My breath caught at the last. His grief? I swallowed, remembering how Lucan had told me about his brother Bedivere's enduring pain at the loss of Lady Isabelle, the only Crone to have ever died under the protection of a wolf-shifter. Of course. If Lucan's own Crone had been taken from him, if she had already died and his bond to her was severed the way Bedivere's had been, his grief would be just as bottomless.

And it would be just as eternal, if we did manage to save his life.

For an instant, I faltered at the thought of consigning him to the same anguish I'd seen in his brother. *Know*, the book in my bag whispered to me. *Accept. Trust.*

Know that there were risks. Accept that not everything would be easy.

Know that Lucan would accept those risks.

Accept that it was not up to me to refuse him the chance or, no matter how much it made my heart hurt, to try to protect him from it.

Trust that he would survive the grief.

"Heal-all if possible. Failing that, calendula, marshmallow, slippery elm, and yarrow, plus angelica, rhodiola, violet, and linden," I recited the list back to Keven, then took up my staff from its resting place against the wall. "I'll be back as soon as I can."

CHAPTER 23

I WAS NINETY-EIGHT PERCENT CERTAIN THAT MY assurances to Keven were accurate regarding Morok's attention being elsewhere. The other two percent, however, followed me like a dark cloud through the woods and along the increasingly populated streets as I made my way back to Edie's house. The two-hour walk felt like it took an eon., and I'd been right—I could never have made it while toting Gus in the cat carrier.

Despite the sun being high in the sky and no shortage of people out and about, I jumped at every noise I heard—the snap of a twig, the rustle of a dried leaf, the sound of a car starting, the rattle of a garbage can being dragged to the curb. I spent as much time looking over my shoulder as I did looking where I was going. And when I let myself into Edie's kitchen via the back porch, the relief that washed through me made my knees sag and the air whoosh from my lungs.

But the relief didn't last.

I stared at the wreckage before me. Stunned disbelief didn't even begin to cover the reaction that welled in me. Shock, horror, a rising panic at the thought that I had misjudged the dark god—those were closer. But as my gaze panned the shattered dishes and torn-off cupboard doors, the unending flow of water from the sink where the tap still ran, the toppled fridge with its ruined contents strewn across the flooded floor, panic gave way to a slow fury—and a slow heat building in my core.

This wasn't Morok. It was more personal than that. Pettier. And closer to home. Much closer.

"Gilbert," Edie's grim voice said the name I'd been thinking.

Her sudden reappearance—figuratively speaking—didn't even startle me. I was too focused on the idea of what I'd do to Gilbert if I could get my hands around his throat to worry about where my friend's ghost had been for the last two days. And I was far too pissed at him to be more than passingly annoyed with her.

"Yes." I set my staff against the door I'd closed, gathered my cloak in my hand, and waded through the ankle-deep water to turn off the tap and pull the plug from the sink. "Gilbert."

The water drained away, and I willed the heat inside me to do the same. Now was not the time to lose control and accidentally finish what Gilbert had started. I turned back to the devastation, wondering if it extended beyond the kitchen, dismissing the idea of going to check. Whatever damage Gilbert had done, it had to remain secondary to my purpose in coming here. The herbs Keven needed for ...

My gaze found the empty shelves that had held Edie's dispensary, then dropped to the jars lying in the water, some broken, some just open but with contents soaked—a scant few intact and still dry inside. My heart catapulted to my toes.

Lucan, I thought.

"Fuck," said Edie.

"Fuck," I agreed, my voice hoarse with rage, worry, despair. Without the herbs, there might be no Lucan, and without Lucan—

"Maybe it's time to revisit the cockroach idea," my friend said, her voice tight.

"Don't tempt me," I growled. I made myself concentrate on flexing my fingers as my internal fire surged again. It was a damned good thing Gilbert was no longer at the scene of his crime. I scanned the jumble of broken glass and sodden herbs, my hatred of Jeanne's husband filling my mouth with a bitter taste. If Lucan died because of him—

"Let's not panic yet," Edie said. *"Some of them are still good. See what's there."*

I slipped off the crossbody bag and my cloak and set both on the stove top—the only dry spot in the kitchen—and then made my way to the jars. Carefully, I picked through them, mindful of broken glass as I searched for the intact, unspoiled ones. Of the fifty or so jars that had once lined the shelves—

"Seventy-two," Edie corrected with a sigh. *"There were seventy-two."*

Of seventy-two, eighteen remained usable—or might have done, if their labels hadn't come off in the water and I'd had a clue what they contained. I stared at the collection I'd amassed on the counter, each filled with dried leaves of one kind or another, all looking pretty much the same to the untrained eye.

"Fuck," I said again. "Now what?"

"Open the jars and sniff. I'll help you identify them."

It was slow and painstaking work—and taking too many deep breaths made my head spin—but with Edie's help, I found three of the herbs on my mental list. Calendula for healing, I remembered, yarrow for the bleeding if it started again, and angelica for energy. No heal-all had survived, and without either violet or linden, Lucan would have to face his grief for Elysabeth unaided.

Altogether, it was a far cry from what I'd hoped to find—and not nearly what Keven said she needed—but it would have to do.

As for the house—I turned from packing the jars into the bag with tea towels wrapped around each and surveyed the wreckage that had been Edie's home. The water level on the floor had dropped below my ankles, which meant it was draining into the crawlspace beneath, and I could only imagine the damage that had been done to the structure.

"Leave it," said Edie. *"It's just a house. It doesn't matter."*

But her tone said otherwise, and I hesitated another moment, tempted to take a stab at turning Gilbert into a cockroach after all. Then, as my gaze came to rest on the telephone on the wall by the back door, I had a better idea. Like me, Edie had been a holdout where keeping a landline was concerned—although she had admittedly been better about embracing cellphone use than I had. If the line was still connected …

I donned my cape, slung the bag around me, and picked up the receiver. A welcome dial tone sounded. Bingo. I dialed 911 and, smiling grimly, waited for the voice at the other end.

"911. What's your emergency?"

"I'd like to report a break-in and vandalism," I said. "The back door is open, and I can hear water running inside. The house is unoccupied, and the last person I saw hanging around there was the neighbor from across the street." I gave Edie's address, and then, before the dispatcher could ask for more—such as my name—I hung up, put the plug back in the sink, and turned on the water again.

"Take that, Gilbert Archambault," I muttered, leaving the door open as I walked out. I doubted he would be charged with anything—especially once the police realized the call had come from Edie's house itself—but at the very least, they would have questions for him. Uncomfortable ones, I hoped.

Edie grunted in my head. *"Not bad,"* she said. *"But still— cockroach one day?"*

"I'll do my level best," I promised from between gritted teeth. I stepped onto the sidewalk and settled into my two-hour walk back toward The Morrigan's Way—this time in the near dark. Oh, joy.

"And now," I said to Edie as I turned left at the intersection, "how about you explain where the heck you keep disappearing to all the time?"

KEVEN SCOWLED DOWN AT THE THREE JARS I'D UNPACKED. "That's all you could find?"

"Long story," I replied, easing myself onto the bench and wishing I'd thought to look through Edie's kitchen for foodstuffs that had survived Gilbert's kitchen rampage. I'd give my right arm for a—

The sight of Keven's shoulder, still missing its arm, brought my thought up short. I would give a *lot*, I mentally amended, for a meal that consisted of more than juniper and pine-flavored broth. To take my mind off my pinched, incessantly growling stomach, I leaned an elbow on the table, cradled my chin in my hand, and focused on the gargoyle, who was still frowning at my meager offerings.

"Can you do anything with them?"

She huffed her displeasure. "I expected more."

And I'd gotten more than I'd bargained for, with Gilbert's incursion. Not to mention Edie's revelation that I was the one who kept shutting her out, not vice versa.

"I've been yelling at you since the hospital," she grumbled, *"but you shut down tight in Natalie's room and nothing I did got your attention. What happened in there?"*

Of course, nothing had "happened," but I'd had a good idea of what had been keeping Edie from communicating with me. When I'd sighed and told her about my epiphany regarding not being responsible for the entire world's ills, she'd given a soft *"huh"* in response that had sounded remarkably like agreement. Or praise. Or both.

It was testament to our friendship that she hadn't commented further on how effective my self-inflicted guilt had been at shutting me down—or on how long it had probably been doing so.

I brought my attention back to Keven.

"But?" I prodded, pointing at the three jars. "Can you still use them?"

"They're better than nothing," she allowed. "If I get the proportions and the magick right, the angelica's energy might boost the power of the calendula enough to start the healing."

Something in me relaxed. Keven might doubt herself, but I'd seen her healing magick at work, and I had every confidence in her ability. Plus, I conceded to myself, I *wanted* to believe in it. I needed to believe Lucan would get better, because without him—

My stomach gave an extra-loud grumble, and Keven looked sideways at me. "There is more soup on the stove," she said. "I know it's not much, but it will keep you nourished. We'll have vegetables to put in it the day after tomorrow."

And no meat until Lucan recovered enough to hunt. *If* he did.

"I'll be fine," I said. "Let's just focus on Lucan."

CHAPTER 24

THE GARGOYLE HAD DONE HER BEST, BUT THE POULTICE she'd made glowed a weak, insipid shade of yellow as it rested against Lucan's skin. It was nothing like the neon green of the heal-all that she'd used on his wounds that first night, a lifetime ago. It might have been in part because she'd used calendula this time, but I suspected it had a great deal more to do with the house's available magick ... or lack thereof.

It was tired. The house, not the magick. Or perhaps the latter was tired, too. I didn't know for sure, and I didn't want to ask. Keven—still wounded herself, for all intents and purposes —had enough on her mind without having to answer my inane questions. The strain of her efforts to infuse magick into the concoction showed in the lines of concentration between her brows and in the set of her shoulders—rigid even for her—as she ministered to the shifter.

I thought about offering to help, but how? Healing magick was a delicate art if I'd ever seen one. My magick was big. Powerful. And prone to getting away on me without warning. The most deliberate, focused things I'd managed were resurrecting the house and cracking the stone in Elysabeth's cell enough to allow a trickle of water through to keep her alive. And, let's face it, moving and breaking stones required considerable force. If I were to turn that kind of power on Lucan's body—

I shuddered at the potential outcomes, none of them pretty. No, any healing was best left to Keven, while I ... what? Watched helplessly? Wandered aimlessly up and down the corridor outside Lucan's room? Chafed with growing frustration at the wait imposed on me while imagining the worst for the other Crones and their protectors?

I stared out Lucan's window at the garden below, arms

crossed and shoulder resting against the frame as Keven worked at the bedside. I might not have mastered my magick, I thought dourly, but worry? That, I had aced.

Keven cleared her throat behind me, and I looked over my shoulder. She stood, bowl in hand, halfway between bed and door.

"I've done all I can," she said. "It should help."

"Should?"

"He is strong. With luck, the poultice will draw out the infection and give him the edge he needs to begin healing."

With luck didn't sound much more positive than *should*, but I let it go, knowing the gargoyle would make no false promises, no matter how much I wanted to hear them.

"And the angelica tea?" I asked. "Did he drink any?"

She hesitated, then shook her head. "No, milady. He did not."

She didn't have to tell me that was bad. I stared at the shivering form in the bed. At the long hair still splayed on the pillow, still soaked with sweat.

"I'll stay with him," I said, "and keep trying."

"As you wish. I will bring you soup later."

Keven left the room, and the thud of her footsteps receded down the corridor toward the front stairs, because the back ones to the kitchen hadn't been rebuilt yet. As the sound of her steps faded, I crossed to Lucan's bedside and perched on the edge of it. The towel I'd used for him earlier sat on the bedside table, barely damp anymore, and I had an idea.

I picked up the towel, dipped a corner of it into the mug of angelica tea, and held it over Lucan's mouth, pulling his bottom lip down so I could squeeze a little of the liquid into him. Hygienic it was likely not, but—my heart skipped a beat as he swallowed reflexively, and I almost let out a cheer. I'd done it! I'd gotten Keven's tea into him. Only a tiny bit, but it was a start, and now—together with the calendula—it might give him that edge Keven had mentioned.

But it didn't.

Keven changed the poultice covering Lucan's belly wound twice over the course of the night, and I managed to get more of the tea into him, but there was no change in his condition. No improvement. No sign that any of it was working. And then, in those hours that always seemed darkest before the dawn, his fever spiked, his body turned rigid beneath the blanket, his back arched against the bed, and I knew we were losing him.

I was alone with him when it happened, and for an instant, I froze. Terror and horror battled for supremacy in my brain, tangled, became one. I didn't know what to do. I forgot how to breathe. Lucan's back arched higher.

Keven. I needed Keven. I sucked air into my lungs, preparing to scream for her, but another's harsh voice arrested my own and demanded my attention—and it wasn't in my head.

"Hold him!" it rasped. "Let your magick touch his before it's too late!"

My head snapped around toward the door, and I saw her again. The Morrigan. Her straight black hair fell from a severe center part to frame a narrow face with sharp features and a beak-like nose. Skin so pale that it seemed translucent gave way beneath her chin to black feathers that encircled her throat, and the feathers in turn became a long gown that moved and fluttered with a life of its own—or many lives, given the number of crows that made it. Her sharp, piercing black eyes, like those of the birds clinging to her, seemed to burrow into me, into the core that held my fire, which flared high and hot and barely controllable in response.

The Morrigan pointed her staff across the room at the bed. "Do it!"

I jumped, then started to climb onto the bed beside Lucan, but the bird-woman behind me hissed, and I looked back again. Her dress was beginning to come apart, with crows flapping in circles around her—or what remained of her, because there was no body beneath the gown.

Shit, I was losing her as well as—

"Skin to skin," she commanded, her voice more crow than human. "Save him!"

The rest of her dissolved into the flapping of wings that had rushed at me the last time she'd visited, and a cloud of crows swirled around the room.

The last shreds of my hesitation evaporated. The Morrigan had spoken. *Save him.*

Swiftly, I shed the cloak I still wore for warmth in the chilly house, then my shoes, my socks, my jeans, my shirt ... and after a split-second's pause, my underwear and bra. I lifted the blanket covering Lucan and crawled into the bed beside him. It had been a long, long time since my body had been naked with a man—and never at this age—but there was no time for vanity right now. No time to worry about the wrinkles and sags and softness accrued over a lifetime. This was about more than the physical. This was about—

Lucan's skin seared my own as our bodies touched. The fire in my core rose to meet it, touch it, envelop it. His fought to free itself, to separate from mine. To escape. Mine was stronger. *I* was stronger.

I held fast to the shifter thrashing in my arms. He morphed into wolf, then man, then wolf again. He snarled and tried again to pull away, his muscles bunched beneath the fur pressed against my breasts, my belly, my thighs. Ferocious amber eyes locked onto mine and fangs gleamed, scant inches from my face. His temperature soared until I was sure one of us would burst into flames.

Distantly, somewhere behind me, I heard a door crash open and Keven's voice shouting, but I couldn't hear what she said. Couldn't separate her words from the roaring in my head as the fire—my fire—threatened to consume both me and wolf. Every instinct I had once possessed as the old Claire urged me to let go —to give up—to run.

"*Save him!*" the Morrigan's voice echoed in my head.

Know, said the book. *Accept.*

Lucan threw back his wolf's head and shrieked in agony, and for the breadth of a heartbeat, I hesitated, terrified that I had been right about loosing my magick on his body. What if the Morrigan was wrong? What if I destroyed him instead of saving him, as I had destroyed so many before?

Trust, the book whispered.

"Fuck," I muttered into the fur of the wolf-shoulder pressed into my face. "Fuckity, fuck, fuck, *fuck.*"

I locked one hand around the other wrist and held on tighter. Held on for dear life. Held on for Lucan's life. Our fires meshed. Became one. Burned ever hotter until the bones in my body felt like they would melt, and I could no longer tell where I ended and the wolf in my arms began. And then, abruptly, my flames danced alone again. The smooth warmth of a man's skin replaced the coarse fur against my lips. Not hot. Warm. Normally warm. And not fighting me anymore.

My internal heat banked, ebbed, and died down to a soft glow. Lucan's breathing evened out and turned slow and rhythmic. He was sleeping. Or was he unconscious again? With difficulty—goddess, but I felt like I'd run a marathon—I pulled back to study him. His eyes were closed and his features relaxed. He looked exhausted, but peaceful. That was good, right?

My gaze strayed past him to the charred bed post and the smoldering wood paneling on the wall behind it. That, on the other hand, couldn't be good. Someone should probably do something about it. But not me. My own fatigue pulled at me like quicksand, and my neck ached with the effort of just holding up my head. I doubted I could have raised so much as a finger if Morok himself had put in an appearance.

So, no. Definitely not me. But someone.

As if summoned by my thoughts, a great stone hand reached across me and patted out the glowing embers of the wall, and Keven's voice behind me said, "He sleeps, milady. You should do the same."

I stiffened, every fiber of my being rejecting the suggestion I leave Lucan. But the gargoyle's hand pulled the blanket up to cover both me and the shifter, and I let my head sag onto the pillow beside Lucan's, grateful for Keven's understanding.

The quicksand tried to drag me under, and I struggled to keep my head above it. "He'll be okay?" I asked, wanting—needing—reassurance before I could let go.

"He will live," Keven replied, "because of you. You did well, Lady Claire. Now sleep."

And on that rare note of gargoyle approval, I did.

CHAPTER 25

I WOKE IN MY OWN BED, WITH THE SUN STREAMING between the curtains covering the window. *Curtains*, I thought. *The house has curtains again.* And then—

Lucan.

I bolted upright into a sitting position. Lucan—the fever—the Morrigan—

My magick.

Had it been enough? Had Keven been right? Had Lucan lived, or—

A knock sounded at the door. Reflexively, I reached for the blanket to cover myself, but it was a duvet again, not a blanket, and I was no longer naked. That sparked a whole flood of other questions, and—

"Dear goddess, woman, breathe. You're giving me a headache with all that noise."

Edie.

"Yes. Edie," she replied tartly. *"Unless you've acquired another ghost I don't know about."*

Heaven forbid. One was more than enough.

"Again, you do know I can hear you, right?"

Another knock at the door. I pulled myself together, summarily dismissed the ghost in my head, and called out, "Come in."

I was expecting Keven. I got Lucan. In spite of the fact I wore one of the nightgowns the house liked to provide for me —the kind that covered me from beneath my chin all the way down to my toes—I hitched the duvet higher. A dozen reactions seared through me, each vying for top place in my attention. Relief that he was okay. Shock that he was *so* okay so fast. The memory of our life fires—our magick—melding. The remembered sensation of our bodies pressed against one anoth—

I frantically swatted that last one away, because *friends*—or *not-friends*, to be more accurate—but I was too late. A blush had already started at my toes and was creeping inexorably upward, and the fire at my core flared in response. Shit.

"You, my friend," Edie said dryly, *"need to work on that little issue."*

So much for ghosts being summarily dismissible.

Lucan, for his part, appeared unperturbed by any of what had happened between us as he leaned a shoulder against the door frame and crossed his arms. "I've been sent to fetch you for dinner," he said. "Keven said to tell you there's meat."

More reactions. First, my mouth watered at the idea of actual food instead of tea-soup. Then, irritation flared at Lucan's seeming intention to not even mention last night. I mean, I wasn't expecting undying gratitude or anything, but maybe an acknowledgment of some kind that I had mastered my magick enough to do what I had? Abruptly, my brain circled back to the meat idea. Wait. Did that mean—?

"You're well enough to hunt?"

A smile quirked his lips between mustache and beard. "Well enough to go to the grocery store," he said. Then he flashed me a wider grin. "I got you some broccoli while I was there, too."

Warmth curled through me at his thoughtfulness, and at the fact that he remembered our first shared broccoli and chicken casserole (courtesy of Jeanne)—and especially at the idea that, friend or not-friend, we could still have a little inside joke. It almost made up for his lack of comment on the previous night. Almost.

"Thank you," I said.

He nodded and straightened up from the door frame, then turned to go, wincing as he did. So. Not quite fully healed.

"Lucan."

He looked back, and I steeled myself. I didn't want to cause him any more pain than he might already be feeling, but I had to know.

"Elysabeth … can you still feel her?"

A shutter came down over his expression, and for a moment, I wasn't sure he was going to answer. But I saw no indication of grief at my question, and so I waited. And waited. And—

Lucan closed the door and came into the room. He turned the wingback chair set by the fireplace around so that it faced me, then settled into it. "That's … complicated," he said.

"Great. You're contagious," Edie muttered.

I ignored her, even though she had a point. "Complicated?" I asked.

"I could feel Lady Elysabeth before you got here, but since your arrival, my sense of her is … clouded."

"Whoa," said my friend.

"Grk," said me.

Lucan scowled and raked long fingers through longer hair. He hadn't put it up in its usual man-bun. I wished he had. He leaned forward, resting elbows on knees and clasping his hands between them, his amber gaze unflinching.

"Things went foggy as soon as I saw you," he said. "I thought it was my injuries, but I've been trying all day, and at most, I have a vague sense that *maybe* I can feel her. I can't be sure if it's real, or if it's just wishful thinking. Your presence interferes with my bond to her."

Well, fuck, I thought, as I felt my mouth drop open in an "o" of shock.

Edie snorted in my head. *"Maybe that's what you and he should—"*

"Don't you dare," I snarled, remembering at the last second to use my "inside" voice, because I had yet to tell Lucan about my ghost and now really wasn't the time—especially if I had to explain her dirty mind as well. With an effort, I looked away from Lucan and down at the duvet twisted in my clenched fist, trying to gather my fragmented thoughts.

"As I said," Lucan murmured, his voice a disconcerting rumble. "Complicated."

No shit. I flapped a hand at him to silence further comment. What I needed was for him to go away so I could pull myself together, but complicated aside, we still had—theoretically—four Crones and three protectors to find, never mind a dark god to stop, and—

Did my presence really cloud Lucan's—

Stop it, I admonished myself. *You're old enough to know better, Claire. Now, focus.*

Preferably on something other than the breadth of Lucan's shoulders and the memory of their shelter.

"Well," I said as the silence in the room continued to stretch out. And then, because I really had nothing more to offer, I said it again. "Well."

What else was there *to* say? No problem? Piece of cake? No worries, I've got this? If that's what Lucan had been hoping to hear, he would be sorely disappointed, because missing Crones and protectors plus dark god plus monsters plus me being responsible for getting in Lucan's way of finding any of them? That was definitely a problem, and I so did not have "this." I didn't have anything.

Trust, the book in my bag, slung from a hook beside the wardrobe—oh look, I had a wardrobe again, too—whispered to me.

"Oh, fuck off, why don't you," I snapped at it—the book, not the wardrobe.

Lucan frowned, then raised an eyebrow as he followed the direction of my scowl. "Milady?"

I opened my mouth to brush off the outburst, then snapped my teeth shut with a clunk that echoed in my skull, then sighed. This was Lucan. My not-protector and friend-if-circumstances-were-different, who'd just admitted I interfered with his bond to his Crone, and with whom I'd just spent the night. Naked. In all my sixty-year-old, saggy glory.

I was pretty sure that meant we had no more secrets between us.

I pointed to the canvas bag. "Pass that to me?"

Lucan uncoiled his lean, muscular length—permanently imprinted on my body's memory—from the chair and stepped over to take the bag from the hook. He returned and held it out to me. I let its weight drop onto the duvet covering my legs, then unbuckled the two leather straps holding it closed and withdrew the book.

Know, accept, trust, it murmured.

I held it out to Lucan. He took it from me, his fingers brushing mine. I pulled away and tucked my hand under the duvet with the rest of me.

"I don't understand," he said, flipping through the pages. "This looks like one of the Crone books, but ... it's not."

"It's my book," I said. "The Book of the Fifth Crone." Briefly, I told him about Jeanne and the Daughters of Hestia, half-hoping he might have knowledge about them that he could share with me. Insight into Jeanne, and how she could be a powerful protector of the book and yet unable to stand up for herself.

But like Keven, Lucan had never heard of the Daughters, and in the end, I suspected the blame for Jeanne's internal struggle lay with simply being human—as did my own, seemingly unending battles with myself. Like the one raging in me right now as I fought not to reach for the fingers turning the book's pages.

"It looks like the same three words repeating throughout," he said. "What do they say?"

I'd forgotten that only I could read the book. I glanced down at the page he had open. "That one says *trust,*" I replied. "The others say *know* and *accept.*"

"Pithy."

I snorted. "Just a little."

He flipped through the pages again, then closed the book and set it down between us. "And you hear it whisper to you?"

I nodded, then shook my head, then shrugged. "I'm not sure. It could just be the words repeating themselves in my head, I suppose, because it's not the same as when Edie or the others talk to—"

"You have other voices in your head?" One of his eyebrows shot up.

Whoops. Oh, well. Maybe now was a good time to 'fess up, after all.

"My best friend, Edie. The one who—" I swallowed and drew my knees up to my chest under the duvet. My hips protested the movement. My heart needed the protection. "The one who died in the fire," I said.

"You have a ghost talking to you?"

Full disclosure, Claire.

"Yes and no—and more than one, actually."

Lucan frowned. "How many?"

"Exactly?" I hedged.

"Exactly," he agreed.

"Thousands," I admitted. "Sometimes I hear them all jumbled together, like a crowd, sometimes they speak as one. Edie says they're the ancestors."

"Voices," Keven said, staring at me. "Of the ancestors."

It would, I decided, be easier if I just made sure Lucan and Keven were together whenever I shared a story, so that I wouldn't have to keep repeating myself. I nodded. "That's what Edie told me, yes."

Keven looked sideways at Lucan in a way that I tried to pretend didn't question my sanity. I wasn't convinced. Her gaze came back to where I sat on the kitchen bench like a child sent to the principal's office. "Whose ancestors?"

"The ones you told me about, I think." Actually, it was hard to think at all, with that delicious scent wafting from the pot on the wood stove. I was so hungry that it felt like my belly button had stitched itself to my backbone, and Keven had yet to ladle anything into a bowl. I clutched the bench seat on either side of myself. The sooner we finished this, I assured myself, the sooner I could eat. I inhaled a breath, regretted it when it made me salivate all over again, and forced my attention back to the conversation.

"That day in the garden," I reminded the gargoyle, "when you told me I was a witch, and about all the women who had practiced witchcraft before me. It's their voices I hear."

"In your head."

I shook said head. "Not the way you mean, no. I think they just … are. Like magick just is."

"Can you summon them?"

I thought of all the times—like now—that Edie had disappeared on me. So to speak. I shook my head again. "I wish, but no."

The gargoyle grunted. "So it *is* like your magick, then."

Har de har har. I looked from her to Lucan, who stood beside her, arms folded, face grim. "There," I said to him. "I told her. No more secrets."

Now can I eat?

"You haven't told her about the book."

"She already knows I have it."

"She doesn't know what it says."

Keven harrumphed from the stove, where she'd moved to stir that delicious-smelling ambrosia she'd made. "*She* is still in the room."

Lucan raised an eyebrow at me in silence, waiting, but I continued to hesitate. Despite my having set the house on its path to rebuilding itself—bringing Keven back to life in the process—I was pretty sure the gargoyle continued to think of me as having failed at being Crone. Telling her that the book contained only three words for me would only confirm that opinion, and as ridiculous as it might be to care about a gargoyle's opinion, a part of me—a great part—did just that.

Even if we weren't technically friends.

Lucan cleared his throat, and I rolled my eyes. He wasn't going to let this go, and if I didn't eat soon, I was going to pass out.

"Fine," I snapped, and before I could talk myself out of it again, I told Keven everything about the three words the book had given me: how they'd appeared to me one at a time, how they repeated on every page, how they whispered to me like another voice.

For long seconds that felt like an eon, Keven didn't respond. She stood by the sink, staring out the window and tapping a sprig of rosemary against the counter's wooden surface, presumably intending to add it to the simmering stew—which was fine, as long as it didn't delay dinner any longer.

Tap, tap, tap—pause. The gargoyle looked over her broken shoulder at me, her expression thoughtful rather than accusatory. My own shoulders relaxed a fraction.

"The books have always held what their Crones need," she said. "It stands to reason, then"—she crushed the sprig in her fist to bruise it and then dropped it into the pot—"that you need to know, accept, and trust. But it will—"

"But I don't know what that means," I interrupted, "or what I'm supposed to do."

"*But*," she repeated, taking up a spoon to stir the herbs in as if I hadn't spoken, "it will be up to you to decide how to apply its words. Now, are you hungry or not?"

CHAPTER 26

"How do you know so much?" I asked Keven as she carried a second bowl of stew from the stove toward me. Lucan had devoured two bowlfuls already and then excused himself to go for a run in the woods—presumably in wolf form, as it was already dark—to work out some of the stiffness of his healing injuries.

Keven stopped on the other side of the table. "About what?" she asked. "Herbs? My knowledge is intrinsic in the magick that powers me."

I shook my head. "About people. Crones. Me."

She set the bowl before me. "I know little about any of those—"

"Stop," I said, because I'd been mother to a teenage boy, once, and I knew when I was being stonewalled. I'd been puzzling over her words since she'd spoken them, so much so that I'd hardly tasted the stew I'd been anticipating.

"*The books have always held what their Crones need,*" she'd said, "*it will be up to you to decide how to apply its words to you.*"

Not *how its words apply*, but *how to apply its words*. A small but critical distinction that somehow put me in control of the book rather than letting it control me. A distinction it seemed odd—no, impossible—that a magickal construct such as a gargoyle would be able to make. I looked up to meet the gaze of the stone creature towering over the table.

"You know more than you let on," I told her, "but you don't want anyone to guess that. Why? And how?"

Keven didn't answer for so long that I thought she might not. Then she pulled out the bench on the other side of the table and settled onto it. The wood snapped and groaned under the weight of her granite form, but it held. She rested her forearm on the table and regarded me with a narrow intensity that made the back of my neck prickle.

"No one can know what I'm going to tell you," she began.

"Lucan—"

"No. Not even him."

I stared at her, wrestling with the *full-disclosure-no-more-promises* vow I'd made to myself scant hours before. On the other hand, whatever Keven was going to tell me was her secret, not mine—technically—so maybe it didn't count? I sighed and nodded agreement.

"You know I'm not like the other gargoyles are—were." A brief flash of sorrow crossed her face at the reminder that she was the only one left, the only one not destroyed by Morok. Though he'd given it a damned good try.

"I know you have a name," I said, pulling my gaze from the scarred granite that marked where her arm had once been. "And you have feelings."

But not friends.

I kept the latter thought to myself, but Keven's mouth drew tight, as if she shared the memory of her denial—her rejection—of the friendship I had once believed was between us. If she did, however, she skirted it without comment.

"Because I wasn't always a gargoyle. At least, not only a gargoyle."

My face must have shown my confusion, because she scowled and exhaled a gust of wind, then muttered, "It's not easy to explain. The Morrigan—Morgana—there wasn't room for both of us."

"Room…?"

"In Morgana's body."

Right. The Morrigan had possessed—for want of a better word—Morgana in order to do battle with Morok, who had likewise possessed Merlin, and … wait. Had Keven just said there hadn't been room for *us*? What did she mean, *us*? The proverbial penny dropped, and I gaped at the gargoyle. She couldn't mean—she couldn't have—she couldn't be—

Oh hell, no.

But the ponderous stone head dipped in confirmation of the impossible-to-believe, and Keven's gaze remained steady. My jaw dropped.

"You're—" I began.

"Hush!" Keven hissed, and I dodged the massive hand headed toward my mouth, almost falling off the bench instead. I made a monumental effort to regain my equilibrium, both physical and mental, but the mental part was impossible, because—

"*Morgana*?" I hissed back. I darted a glance toward the doorway between kitchen and corridor, but neither wolf nor broad-shouldered form appeared, and I turned my shocked gaze back to the gargoyle. "You're *Morgana*?"

"Was," Keven corrected quietly. "I *was* Morgana. A very, very long time ago."

"But…" I trailed off, too many questions jostling for my attention to even know where to begin. Morgana. Keven was—had been—Morgana, the most powerful witch to ever live. The witch that had joined forces with the Morrigan herself to splinter the world that first time in Camlann and—

I stared down into the bowl of stew going cold before me—I really wasn't going to get to enjoy this meal, was I?—and tried to assemble my thoughts. To reconcile them. Morgana and Keven.

"How?" I asked.

Keven rested her hand on the table, tracing the knife scars there with one stone fingertip. "When the Morrigan joined with me, her powers overwhelmed mine and began to—devour them, I suppose. And to devour me. We realized that I would disappear if I remained—we thought that was what happened with Morok and Merlin, too—and so she placed me in the nearest living creature she could."

She lifted her hand from the table to gesture at herself. Her gargoyle. "It was supposed to be temporary."

"But…?"

"When I moved into this body"—another wave of a granite hand at herself—"I had to share it with the gargoyle it already was. It wasn't a creature that could be trusted with the powers I possessed, so the Morrigan placed my magick elsewhere for safe-keeping. It didn't survive the split, and without it, I couldn't reclaim Morgana's body."

Absently, I moved my spoon through the stew as I let the gargoyle's revelation settle into me. Two separate tracks of thought emerged, each vying for equal attention. First, the Morgana track, as I tried to imagine what it must have been like to go from living, breathing, powerful witch to being locked for eternity in what was essentially a block of stone. Second …

Come to think of it, that second track was the one that needed the attention.

"Wait," I said. "I thought Morgana's powers were divided among the pendants. When you and Lucan told me about Morok, that's what he—"

"It's what he thinks," Keven said. "What we let them all think."

"But if they weren't your powers …" My world gave a sudden wobble, and I dropped the spoon in favor of gripping the more solid table edge as I gaped at the gargoyle. "The *Morrigan*? The pendants' powers were *hers*?"

"Half divided among the four elemental pendants," Kevin agreed, "and half in the pendant of the Fifth Crone."

The Morrigan had put half her powers—half of a goddess's powers—into the pendant that had come to me and marked me as the Fifth Crone. The pendant I had handed over to Morok in the cell. The pendant which, if Gus hadn't brought it back to me, would have meant that the dark god might have controlled a goddess's full powers.

As it was, he still had half of them—if not yet, then soon—plus his own remaining powers, and I had—

135

The fire in my core surged through my body and danced along my fingers.

I had to leave before I exploded something.

I bolted from the kitchen.

"ARE YOU ALL RIGHT?" EDIE ASKED CAUTIOUSLY.

I gave a bark of laughter, bitter and unamused, as I let the curtain fall across the window I'd been staring out. I turned to face the sitting room, empty but for me and my friend's ghost. A fire crackled merrily in the fireplace, throwing cheerful light and dancing shadows across paneled walls and flagstone floor, but its warmth didn't reach me. I was pretty sure I could have been standing *in* its flames, and its warmth wouldn't have reached me.

"Define *all right*," I told my friend, folding my arms over my belly in a hug. Or an attempt to hold myself together. Or both. "I'm not curled up under a table in the fetal position, if that counts."

"It does," she said, her voice gentle. *"Very much so. That was ... a lot."*

Another bark of laughter. "You think?"

"For what it's worth, I had no idea. None of us did."

Wasn't that the whole point of a secret? I caught back the snarky thought before it reached my lips, forgetting that Edie existed in my mind and would hear it anyway.

"I'm not the enemy here," my friend reminded me. *"None of us is. Not even Kev—Morgana."*

"I know," I said. I leaned back to rest against the wall, shifting until the panels didn't dig into my shoulder blades. "And she wants to be called Keven."

Keven, because that had been the name of Lucan's son. The child she had killed on her way to attack Merlin—driven by the part of her that had been gargoyle, remembered always by the part of her that had been Morgana. Because she was both. For fifteen centuries, she had been both.

And I ... I was the Crone who had been given half the power of a goddess.

My stomach rolled at the thought, and the pendant around my neck—the one I'd been so glad to have returned to me—felt like it weighed a thousand pounds. A millstone around my neck, now that I knew what it contained.

A cold sweat bathed my entire body, and my teeth chattered. It was no wonder I couldn't feel the warmth of the flames in the fireplace. But as icy as I felt on my exterior, my insides were the exact opposite. The fire in my core had stirred as Keven told me her story, seething stronger and higher with every word, until I'd had to leave before I lost control. I didn't know if Keven knew how close I'd come, if the Morgana part of her had felt the surge of barely leashed magick. I didn't know, and I didn't care.

Never had I wanted to run away more than I had as I'd walked away from her and down the corridor, my hands in rigid fists at my sides. Not when I'd first learned about my calling as Crone, not when I'd killed the three Mages, not even when I had felt myself losing my magick, little by little, as I'd traveled the ley lines.

And never had I been less able to do so, because just when I'd realized I wasn't responsible for the whole world, I'd learned that actually, yes, I *was* responsible for it. Which was how I'd ended up here in the sitting room, unable to feel any fire but my own, desperately trying not to lash out at the gargoyle, the house, the entire goddess-forsaken situation.

Because the Morrigan *had* forsaken us—me and the others alike—by keeping this from us. We should have known whose powers we wielded. Should have been told the truth from the start.

"To what purpose?" Edie's voice asked. I tried to ignore her, but she persisted. *"Would it really have helped to know that you controlled half of a goddess's power?"*

My Claire-voice, rarely heard from these days but apparently still in residence, snorted. *"Hardly. You would never have agreed to any of this if you'd known."*

Edie grunted. *"For once we can agree on something. The Morrigan had her reasons, Claire. Accept that and—"*

I scowled and snapped, "What did you say?"

"I said—"

But I wasn't listening, because another voice had intruded, or more precisely, a memory. *Accept,* my book whispered to me. *Know. Accept. Trust.*

"Fuck," I said, thinking of the four pendants that held the Morrigan's remaining powers and the Crones who unknowingly wore them. Unknowingly, because their origin had been Morgana's—Keven's—secret. And now the secret was mine. I hated that. Hated the secret, hated keeping it, hated understanding why I must.

And really hated that I would do the book's bidding.

Accept. Accept the secret. Accept the power. Accept that the Morrigan didn't have—had *never* had, in all the time I'd known about her—the power to help me the way I'd been waiting for.

Whatever was going to happen next, it was all up to me.

"Fuck," I said again. And then I snarled, "Fuckity, fuck fuck *fuck.*"

My internal fire flared high, and the stool sitting in front of the fireplace burst into flames.

CHAPTER 27

"THAT'S IT. THAT'S THE PLAN." IT WAS A STATEMENT OF incredulity rather than a question, and it matched Lucan's expression as he regarded me across the table, fork poised halfway to his mouth. He looked better today, except for the expression, of course.

He moved without wincing, and he'd been out hunting already, as evidenced by the roasted grouse we were having for breakfast. A testament to the continued healing of the house's magick, or to Keven's secret identity and the knowledge that went with it? I decided I didn't much care and buried my nose in my teacup, waiting for him to continue, because I didn't think he was done.

I didn't wait long.

"We go after them and rescue them, just like that," he said. "The two of us. By ourselves."

Well, when he put it that way ...

I sighed. "Do you have a better idea?"

"Yes. We remain here until we have an *actual* plan instead of a half-baked one."

"No." I shook my head and set my tea back on the table, picking up my fork instead. "We can't. For all we know, Morok might already have one of the pendants—or all of them. The Crones can't hold out against him forever." An image of the emaciated Elysabeth popped into my head, and bile rose into my throat at the thought of her suffering that way again. Of all of them suffering that way.

I put my fork on my untouched plate and pushed both away, appetite gone, and continued with my argument to convince Lucan. "And, goddess forbid, if they're already gone, he could be on the verge of opening the portal to Camlann as we speak."

Over by the stove, Keven cleared her throat. Lucan and I both ignored her in favor of glaring at one another. Lucan jabbed his loaded fork at me.

"And if we go storming in without knowing what we're up against, he'll have your pendant, too. *Again.*"

"*Ouch,*" murmured Edie. "*But he does have a point. Maybe we should take a step back and—*"

"It's what the book wants," I said, my reply directed at both opponents of my … plan. "I have it, I have the pendant"—I touched the chain at my neck but avoided the crystal itself because, half of the Morrigan—"and I have you. It's not going to get any better than that."

"Two of us against who knows how many monsters he's called." Lucan's expression was becoming darker by the second.

"We have to take the chance," I insisted.

In the background, Keven *ahemmed* again, but my focus remained on Lucan, whose entire fist had curled around his fork in a rather alarming way.

"Milady," he gritted through his teeth, "might I remind you that I am bound by magick to keep you safe? If we go willy-nilly into Morok's lair without a proper plan—"

"But you aren't," I said, and my quiet words silenced him mid-objection. Angry denial began to form in his gaze. He knew where this was going, but I said it anyway, voice and gaze both steady. "Your duty isn't to me, Lucan, it's to the Earth Crone. To Elysabeth."

What I said was true, no matter what had passed between us as I held him in healing the other night. No matter how much my presence clouded his connection to her. Any bond he felt to me was one that he could not, should not, feel. And it was one that he absolutely could not give in to because of what magick had done to him. What it had taken away.

"For what it's worth, milady," his voice whispered in my memory, *"if I did have the power of choice, we would indeed be friends."*

I lifted my chin and met his scowl. I hated that I had to use those words against him now, but with the very world hanging in the balance, I had no other option.

"You are not my protector, Lucan," I reiterated, "and you are not my friend. You have no—"

"It's gone," Lucan said flatly, and the word *choice* died on my lips. "Whatever sense I had of Lady Elysabeth yesterday, it's gone."

My jaw dropped into a gape. I snapped it shut again. "Because of me? Because I—" I stopped short of finishing with *cloud your connection* and sent a quick look Keven's way. Would she understand the implications of my question?

"No," Lucan said. "Because *she's* gone."

Keven let out a gravelly hiss, and then utter silence dropped over the kitchen. With great care, Lucan set the fork, a chunk of grouse still speared on it, across his bowl. He rested an elbow on the table, fist against his mouth as he waited for my reaction.

I waited for it, too, but felt … nothing. No shock. No sadness. None of the despair I might have expected at knowing that Elysabeth was likely dead, and if so, the others probably were, too. Which meant that all of our efforts—and losses—had been for nothing, because Morok now possessed their pendants and would indeed be working to open the portal back to Camlann and the half of his powers trapped there.

"Overload," Edie whispered in the back of my mind. *"That's why you don't feel anything. This, on top of what Keven told you earlier … you need time to process everything."*

Perhaps, I thought, and perhaps I just didn't believe it. Or refused to. Or whatever. Either way, my plan stood. I slid from the end of the bench and stood up.

"Then we'd better get moving," I said.

Lucan slammed a fist onto the table, making the bowls jump and their contents spatter. "Have you heard *nothing* I've said?" he growled. "I cannot—*will* not—let you place yourself in such danger. If Elysabeth is gone, the others are almost certainly dead, too, and you're all—"

Keven cleared her throat loudly for a third time, cutting across his words. For a third time, we ignored her.

"*Let* me place myself in danger?" I snapped at Lucan. "I'm sorry, but who put you in charge? Just because Elysabeth *might* be gone"—my emphasis was deliberate—"doesn't mean you get to push me around. I know how this works, remember?" I deepened my scowl at him and crossed my arms for good measure. "You weren't my protector before, Lucan, you're not my protector now, and if the others *are* dead, then we're the last chance of stopping Morok. We're going."

Lucan pushed to his feet and leaned across the table toward me, resting his fists on the wooden surface. "And at the risk of repeating myself, if we go after him with just the two of us, we don't have a hope in hell. We're staying."

Over by the stove, Keven cleared her throat yet again, and Lucan and I both rounded on her, demanding as one, "*What?*"

"First," the gargoyle said, addressing Lucan, "Lady Claire is right. You're not her protector. Second, she's also right about needing to try. And third, there are three of us, not two."

My initial surge of vindication at her words disappeared in a blink of confusion. "Three," I said. "You mean, you want to come with us? But I thought you were tied to the house."

"She *is* tied to the house," Lucan said, looking as if he might like to bury Keven *beneath* the house for having interfered. "So, no, she can't."

"Unless ..." Keven's voice trailed off, and her gaze turned to me. Cold pooled in my belly. I didn't like the way she was looking at me. Not even a little. Like she was weighing possibilities. Assessing potential. Deciding ... what, exactly?

I started shaking my head, because whatever she had in

mind, I was pretty sure—no, I was *absolutely* sure—it was a bad idea. I opened my mouth to tell her so, but before I could, Lucan asked the fatal question, and my doom was sealed.

"Unless what?"

"Unless she can move the house, too."

CHAPTER 28

"MOVE THE HOUSE." STANDING IN THE CORNER OF THE kitchen as far from Keven as I could get, I echoed her words. Then I echoed them again. "*Move* the *house*?"

It made no difference whether I said it as a statement or a question. I still couldn't wrap my head around the idea. And I still felt like a cornered animal as I faced it and the gargoyle who'd suggested it.

"How in the goddess's name do you expect me to move all of this"—I waved at the ceiling and walls and floor and everything beyond—"when I can't even reattach your arm?" I changed the direction of my hand flap to encompass Keven.

"I didn't know you'd tried to reattach it."

"Because I wasn't able to budge it from the front lawn, never mind get it inside and onto you. And now you want me to try moving a whole *house*?" I flapped again.

"Not any house. This one. It's already sitting at a ley intersection. All you need to do is—"

I didn't let her finish. "Tell her!" I exclaimed, rounding on Lucan as I suddenly realized that he hadn't spoken since Keven had made her outrageous—no, her *ludicrous*—suggestion. I planted my hands on my hips and scowled at him, because he damned well needed to speak now. Needed to ...

My thought died away as I registered the same thoughtfulness in the shifter's expression that had been in Keven's as she'd studied me only moments before. My heart plummeted to my toes, and the air wheezed from me. Oh, no. I started shaking my head. No, no, no. He couldn't *agree* with her, could he? I shook faster. More emphatically.

More desperately.

But it did no good, because yes, he could agree with her. And, apparently, he did.

"It would give us an element of surprise," he said.

Surprise? For an instant, I pictured the house dropping— à la Dorothy's house in *The Wizard of Oz*—onto the heads of whatever Crones might have so far survived Morok, with my voice chirping, "Surprise!" as it did. I snort-laughed at the image, recognized the mounting hysteria behind the sound, and slapped a hand over my mouth.

Then I gritted my teeth, took a firm(ish) hold on my runaway imagination, and said unequivocally, "Absolutely not. Are you out of your minds? There's no way I can do something as big as that!"

Not with any semblance of control, anyway, and goddess knew where I might drop the house if I—

"If you can't," Keven's voice dashed across my panic like ice water, "what chance do you have against Morok?"

I opened my mouth. Flapped it a couple of times. Tried my utmost to find a response. And then began a slow deflate when I realized there was no answer, because—

"You're right," I whispered, as the fire that had danced again in my core since I brought the house back to life suddenly snuffed out. "There's no chance at all."

I bolted for the door leading to the garden.

LUCAN CAUGHT UP WITH ME AT THE EDGE OF THE GARDEN where it met the forest, as he had once before—after I'd tried to kill his brother. I would have liked to think of it as "accidentally tried," but I'd never been certain it had been a complete accident. More of a Freudian slip, because Bedivere had been such an ass.

Is such an ass, I corrected myself. *We don't know for certain that he's—*

"Milady." Lucan's deep voice sounded behind me as I stared into the trees, contemplating …

Hell, I had no fucking idea what I was contemplating. No idea what *to* contemplate. I closed my eyes and dug the fingers of my crossed arms into my ribs. I didn't turn. I didn't answer him.

"Milady," he said again, and then, "Claire."

The quiet utterance of my name, with no formality attached, was my undoing. The floodgates I'd put in place against my tears gave way, and everything poured forth. Grief for the losses I'd suffered, guilt for the losses I'd caused, terror at what I faced …

Rage at being the one at the center of it all.

Strong hands settled on my shoulders and turned me. Gentle arms folded me close. A warm, bare chest cradled me. Somewhere between leaving the kitchen and finding me here, Lucan had shifted to wolf, shed his clothing, and shifted back to human form. I didn't care. Didn't feel the usual surge of hormones. Didn't feel so much as a frisson of awareness.

I simply stood in the circle of his arms, neither fighting nor clinging, and set myself adrift in the dark morass of thoughts that tumbled through my mind. Natalie, Paul, Braden … Anne, Maureen, Elysabeth, Nia … their protectors … the wards I'd destroyed … Keven's lost arm … Morgana's lost powers … Lucan's near-death …

So much had already been lost in this war between god and goddess. So much nearly so. And so much more still rested in the balance. Rested on me. Me. Fucking hell, *why?*

A new wave of anger washed over me. I was a sixty-year-old grandmother, for goddess's sake. I was supposed to be taking life easier at this age: puttering in my garden, enjoying my grandson, laughing with Edie over a glass of wine on the porch, working on my cross-stitch (and knowing where my reading glasses were when I wanted them), and a myriad of other pleasant pastimes.

I was *not* supposed to be going up against the fucking god of deceit and darkness in a fight for the world itself.

"And yet," said Edie quietly, *"here you are."*

I wanted to tell her to fuck off—I wanted to tell *everyone* to fuck off—but to what purpose? It would change nothing. Natalie would still be in a coma. Paul would still refuse to let me see either her or Bradyn. Edie would still be dead. The Crones and their protectors would still be missing and Morok would still be on the verge of destroying the planet ...

And, as Edie said, I would still be here. At the crossroads I'd been avoiding all my life, because I knew now that I'd always had magick—I'd just never accepted that I had power, too.

Know, said the book, *accept, trust.*

And then it whispered a new word to me, one that I sensed being written across its pages even as it crossed my mind.

Be.

My thoughts stumbled for a moment, and I squeezed my eyes shut tighter, gritted my teeth, and clenched my fists until my fingers hurt, fighting the word and all that it contained: the magick, the power, the responsibility.

My chest ached with holding back the bellow of fury and denial that clawed for release. I didn't want this, damn it. I sucked for air, pushed the bellow deeper. I'd never wanted any of it, never *asked* for any of it. I wished with every fiber of my being that I could deny it.

But I couldn't.

Like it or not, all of it was mine, and—like it or not—it would remain mine, regardless of the choice I made now, regardless of which path I set my foot upon. And damn her hide to eternal hell, the Morrigan knew exactly which path that would be. She'd known since she'd offered me the Cup of Power and I had turned it down and she had announced, *"You'll do."*

Fucking, fucking hell.

I lifted my hands and shoved them against Lucan's chest. He

147

staggered under the unexpected assault, recovered, reached for me again.

"Claire—"

"No." I held up one hand to ward him off, even as I wanted to throw myself back into his arms, to bury myself in his protection. It was time to stop hiding behind him—and behind the Claire I had been. It was time to stand on my own. Time to choose my path.

This time, irrevocably.

As Lucan watched, I paced from the edge of the forest to the end of the garden, then back again, each step marking an event in the weeks since my birthday—since all of this had started. Learning about the pendant, the address in the newspaper, the gate and Keven, the house, Lucan, the shades. Surviving the gnome attack. Killing the Mages and defeating their goliath, finding Elysabeth in the cell, losing my magick to the ley lines, discovering Morok's possession of Kate—the list seemed endless. And yet, here I was, because I had lived through them. Risen to the challenge. Survived.

I hadn't wanted any of it, but it had been mine, and I had survived. I hadn't wanted much of what had happened in my life before sixty, either, when I thought about it—not the divorce, not Jeff's subjugation of me, not the too-early death of my mother that had left me floundering with my own motherhood when Paul had been at his most difficult—but all of that had been mine, too, and I realized now that I'd stepped up to those challenges. That the tears I'd shed over them hadn't made me weak. That I had dug deep, found the reserves I'd needed ... and survived.

Me. I'd done that. Sometimes with help, sometimes on my own. Sometimes with grace, more often with a sheer, determined refusal to quit, but always with strength. Always with ...

Power.

A thrill tingled over the skin of my arms and traveled down my spine, and I caught my breath again, but this time in awe and understanding. I'd refused the Morrigan's Cup of Power because I hadn't needed it, because I already had my own power. I just needed to—

Know, the book said, its whisper exultant. *Know, accept, trust,* be.

Know that you are powerful in your own right. Accept that you may wield her power, too. Trust yourself to do so. Be the Crone.

I whirled on my heel to face the concerned—and still naked, a part of me noted—Lucan. "I'm her," I announced. "I'm Lady Claire, the Fifth Crone."

The shifter's concern deepened rather than dissipated. "You thought otherwise?" he asked, his brow creasing as he folded his arms across his very bare chest.

My hormones tried to come back online and, impatiently, I shoved them back down.

"Long story," I answered. One that I hoped I would be able to tell him one day, when all this was behind us, and we had time. Time, perhaps, to explore the bond that shouldn't be between us ... time to simply be. But for now, there were more important things to take care of. Things like the truth of who I was. What I was. What I had to do.

It was time, as the book said, to *be.*

"And to move a fucking house," Edie agreed with gleeful satisfaction.

CHAPTER 29

As it turned out, deciding that I *would* move the house didn't mean that I *could*. At least, not right away. And certainly not as quickly as I'd thought. In fact, my choosing a path at last made pretty much no discernible difference whatsoever to our immediate circumstances, which was frustrating as blazes.

"Again," said Keven, her voice containing no inflection. A measure of her patience, or of her own frustration? It was hard to tell, since her face was carved of literal granite.

I balled my hands into fists at my sides, inhaled through flared nostrils, and gritted my teeth while I glared at her broken arm lying on the ground in front of the house. I counted to ten. Then twenty.

"I said—" Keven began.

"I heard you," I snapped, my gaze flicking to her and then back to the stone arm I'd been trying to move for more than an hour with my magick. "Just give me a goddamn minute."

I was ready to bodily pick up the arm and jam it into place on the gargoyle, but that would have defeated the purpose of this exercise. Well, half the purpose, anyway. Assuming I could pick it up in the first place, and that it would stay where I put it, Keven would at least have it back—but I would be no closer to being able to move an object with my magick, let alone the entire house that loomed behind me.

Keven cleared her throat, which I interpreted—likely correctly—as *you've already had an hour*, and my glower deepened.

I surveyed the arm. I knew what the problem was, of course. I just didn't know how to fix it. Because as much as I wanted to do this, wanted to believe that I could, there still existed a tiny nugget of doubt deep in my core. A whisper that belonged not to my Claire-voice or Edie or the ancestors, but to my past. To my upbringing, to my life with Jeff, to Paul—to everything I needed to leave behind if I was going to go through with this.

"*If?*" asked Edie. "*Maybe that's the real issue?*"

I shook my head. "No. I made my decision. I want to go through with this. I just need ..." I trailed off, not because of Keven looking askance at me, but because of the memories that surfaced suddenly, overshadowing everything else. Gutting me.

Bradyn, throwing his arms around my neck and clinging to me for dear life as his mother lay unconscious on the ground and monsters encroached on all sides. His voice wailing, "No, Grandma! No! Don't go!"

The effort it had taken for me to detach myself.

Natalie, pale and unmoving in the hospital bed, wires sprouting from her, monitors blinking and beeping around her.

"*Unfinished business,*" Edie said, and I heard the nod behind her voice. "*You need—*"

"Closure," I finished. "I need closure."

Because sometimes power was rooted not just in moving forward, but in letting go.

"Milady?" Keven asked behind me.

Something inside me shifted. Something deep, knowing, ancient. A shimmer began in the corners of my eyes and crept across my vision, as if gauzy, somewhat sparkly curtains had been drawn between me and the world. Except ...

Except it was more like a curtain had disappeared, letting me see what was really there. The energy of everything. The magick *in* everything. The entire world, from grass to bare earth to trees to sky ... all of it pulsated, moved as if it lived and breathed, and reached out to touch the energy that was everything else, including—

I looked down at the shimmer of my own hand, intermingling with the air around it. Me. I was a part of it. I was—

"Milady, perhaps we should try again later," Keven

suggested, "after you rest." Her voice remained neutral, but her weariness pushed against my back and settled across my shoulders, weighing me down. Weighing my heart down. So many unmet expectations ... so many worries.

And only one way to dispel them.

My gaze left my hand and traveled to Keven's—the one lying in the grass beside the footpath. It, too, shimmered with the energy that pulsated around it, touching the energies of the grass that cradled it, the air that passed along it. I held out my arm, hand upturned, feeling the throb and pulse of my own energy. My power.

"My magick," I murmured, equal parts thrilled, awed, and—yes, terrified—but mostly just ...

Be, said the book.

I am, I replied.

I watched the magick uncoil from my palm, from *me*, and twist through the air toward the stone arm. I felt it touch the granite's energy—its being—and begin to intermingle. I turned my hand over and, in my mind, curled my fingers around the rough stone, willing my magick to do the same, marveling at how solid the granite's energy felt in my grasp. I braced myself, exhaled a slow breath ... and lifted.

Sheer inertia resisted my will for a moment, then the limb twitched, twisted free of its resting place, and rose slowly into the air. One foot ... two feet ... three ... and then so high that I had to tip my head back to watch it. Giddiness welled up in me, a bubble of excitement and accomplishment that bordered on hysteria and wanted to burst from my throat in a manic giggle, but I made myself swallow it as the appendage wobbled precariously.

I stilled my thoughts and honed my focus. I had done more than my fair share of damage to Keven already, and I would *not* drop her arm now that I was on the verge of atonement for at least part of what I had inflicted upon her.

Inhale, I coached myself. *Exhale. Turn. Bring the arm with*

*you. Move it toward Keven. Lower. Closer. Her energy is reaching
for it. Wait ... just let them mingle ... feel that? They're joining.
Fusing. They're—*

One. They were one again.

I stared at the two-armed gargoyle in faint astonishment. I'd
done it. I'd put her back together again—or, at least, part of her.
I wasn't sure she'd ever be completely healed, because we'd lost
too many bits and pieces of her, beginning with the finger I'd
removed in the earliest of my magickal accidents. But this? This
was a start. A good start.

Keven stared at her returned hand for long seconds, as if not
quite believing her eyes. She flexed and closed her fingers, curled
and uncurled her elbow, lifted and lowered her shoulder. Then,
with an oblique look in my direction, raised her other hand to
the repaired arm, grasped it, and tried to pull it off.

Frankly, I wasn't sure who was more surprised that it stayed
attached—me or her.

"Or me," muttered Edie, heaving an undisguised sigh of
relief that should have been insulting, but I was too relieved
myself.

Keven's ponderous head swung in my direction, and she
studied me for long seconds, her gaze traveling over me from
head to toe and back again. "It seems, milady," she said quietly,
"that you are ready at last."

I drew myself tall. Squared my shoulders. Settled my feet
against the ground. I *was* ready, I thought.

For a lot of things. Starting with closure.

LUCAN INSISTED ON TRAVELING WITH ME TO THE HOSPITAL.
I didn't argue too strenuously, because I'd learned the hard way
that ley travel was a lot more pleasant with a magickal being to
shield me than it was when I attempted it on my own. Plus,

Keven pointed out that we didn't know yet if the ley might drain my powers again the way it had before, which didn't seem like an advisable risk, given what we were about to attempt when I finished here.

But I drew the line at letting the protector follow me inside.

"Milady," Lucan began, his voice a growl of irritation, likely at the prospect of yet another argument with me.

I held up a hand. "Not negotiable," I said. "We can't chance you drawing attention to us." I shuddered at the thought of the chaos that would transpire if anything happened that he deemed to be a threat, and he shifted to wolf form inside the building.

"And you think *that* won't draw attention?" Lucan raised an eyebrow and, arms crossed, looked pointedly at the cape I wore and staff I carried.

He had a point, but walking into the hospital with no outer garment at all in this weather would likely raise more questions than the cape would. I squinted against the wind-driven snow pellets trying to puncture my eyeballs and felt a twinge of guilt at leaving the shifter out here in the cold and dark at the end of the parking lot—but only a twinge.

Because he *was* a shifter, and if he got too cold, he could just take on his wolf form until I got back.

I, on the other hand, didn't have that luxury. I shivered and drew the edges of the cloak closer around me. "I'll have to take my chances," I told him, handing the staff to him for safe-keeping.

"I cannot protect you from here."

"I've already been to see Natalie once. If the Mages were watching her, they would have caught me then."

He scowled at my reasonableness. "I still don't like it."

"No, you just don't like losing," I said cheerfully. "I'll be fine, Lucan, I promise. I'll be in and out before you even know I'm gone. Keven said the potion she made is weak because she had so little to work with. It's going to take time, so it's not like Natalie will wake up so I can—" I broke off as my throat tightened. So I could what? Apologize? Say goodbye? Tell her I loved her and ask her to hug Bradyn for me? Suggest she leave my son?

All of the above?

I straightened my spine. "I'll be back soon," I finished, "and then we'll go."

I started toward the lighted entrance on the other side of the parking lot. Lucan's voice followed me.

"And that's the other thing," he called, "we're wasting time here! We should be gone already!"

This, from the man who hadn't wanted to attack Morok in the first place. I clutched the cape's hood closed at my chin, rolled my stinging eyeballs, and increased my pace through the snow. I knew Lucan didn't understand the delay. Now that he knew I'd mastered my magick at last, his need to attack Morok and find the others—especially Elysabeth, if she lived—drove him relentlessly. But it didn't change what *I* needed to do.

At least Keven had understood when I'd told her I had to come here first. She'd flexed and extended her arm as she'd listened to my explanation, continuing for a few moments more as she'd considered my words when I finished. And then she'd let her hand drop to her side, and she'd nodded.

"Yes," she'd said, ignoring Lucan's sputterings in the background. "Sometimes an ending is as powerful as a beginning. I will help you with yours."

An ending. I lingered on the word and its implications as I stepped through the automatic doors into the hospital. Is that what this would be? The last time I saw Natalie? My last chance to make amends for all I'd brought down on her and Paul and Bradyn? I set my jaw as I pushed back the hood of my cape and brushed the snow from my shoulders, then took a moment to orient myself. The last time I'd come, it had been through the back entrance with the help of Jeanne's staff pass. Then, I'd followed the main corridor and turned left to get to the ICU. Which meant that now, I would turn—

My gaze came to rest on a sign above the corridor entrance,

with "ICU" in bold green letters and a ninety-degree arrow pointing right. And , disappearing around the corner into that corridor, a man who stood head and shoulders above most others and carried himself with an unmistakable and all-too-familiar arrogance. My heart spiraled downward and landed with a thud in the vicinity of my toes.

"Fuckity, fuck fuck fuck," Edie murmured in my head.

I concurred. Because the last person I'd expected to run into —the last person on earth I needed to see right now—was my ex.

CHAPTER 30

THE INSTANT I WALKED INTO NATALIE'S ROOM, ALL THE months that had passed since my ex-husband's departure from our house and my life dropped away, and we fell into the old, familiar roles we'd perfected over a thirty-year marriage.

Or, at least, Jeff did.

As immaculately put together as ever in a dark gray suit, impeccable white shirt, and power-red tie, he stopped mid-sentence in whatever he'd been saying to Paul, and his gaze raked over me from head to toe. And then he bit out, "Jesus, Claire. What in the hell are you wearing?"

I, on the other hand, no longer fit my role. "Nice to see you, too," I replied, rolling my eyes at him instead of telling him to eff off as Edie was urging.

"*Wuss,*" my friend muttered.

But even that small show of defiance had made my ex blink in surprise. His brow furrowed, and his lips went tight. Actually, scratch that. His lips were always tight. With disapproval, annoyance, irritation, distaste ...

A hand seized my arm. Paul. I'd been so focused on Jeff that I hadn't noticed him coming around the bed where Natalie still lay, still unmoving, still hooked up to wires and monitors. I did notice, however, that my son's lips were as tight as his father's.

Oh, Paul.

"What do you think you're doing, coming here like this?" he growled, attempting to pull me back through the doorway. "I told you I never wanted to see you again. You have no business—"

I planted my feet firmly against the floor and leaned against the tug of his hand. He looked around at me in annoyance, and I shook my head at him. "Stop, Paul," I said. "Just ... stop."

To my surprise, he did. To my greater surprise, he blinked back a sudden welling of tears and gave a hard, audible swallow.

"I ..." he began thickly. He swallowed again, his hand slipped from its grip on my arm, and he swayed on his feet, his grief and despair rolling out from him like a physical force that buffeted against me. "She won't wake up, Mom," he whispered, his voice breaking. "They don't know what's wrong. Braden ... what am I going to do?"

And just like that, the grown man who was a father, husband, and successful businessman, the one who had ordered me out of his life with a bitterness and acrimony that would haunt me for the rest of my life, was nothing more than a lost little boy. My boy.

My heart broke all over again for all that I had wrought— no. All that Morok had wrought.

I pulled my son into my arms and hugged him tight, letting him sob into my shoulder, my grief matching his breath for breath, tear for tear. Grief for him, for Natalie, for Braden ... and for the countless other lives that I knew Morok had destroyed.

The fire within me surged and receded like another heartbeat, a greater one than mine. I would end Morok's earthly rampage, I promised those lives. No matter what it took.

Jeff's brusque voice suddenly inserted itself between us, along with his arm. "Of course she'll wake up," he said, prying Paul away from me. He stuffed a wad of tissue into our son's hand. "Now pull yourself together. You have to stay strong and have a little patience. And you"—he took hold of my arm the way Paul had done, but with a tighter grip—"have done enough damage. Paul asked you to leave, and—"

Paul blew his nose into the tissue and mumbled around it, "It's okay, Dad. Let her see Nat."

"No," Jeff said, still tugging on my arm. "You shouldn't have to deal with her after—"

"Lady Claire," a new, dangerously cold voice interrupted as

another hand covered Jeff's and pried it without effort from my arm, "is staying."

But I didn't need rescuing anymore. Not even from my past. "Lucan," I said. "I have this."

The amber gaze took a moment to leave my ex's crimson face and turn to me. It was another moment before the visibly furious shifter nodded his head and released his grip on Jeff.

"As you wish, milady," he said.

Jeff's face went from crimson to an interesting shade of purple, and he sputtered, "You—he—assault—*milady*?"

"Shut up, Jeff." I sighed with a weariness rooted in thirty years of listening to his tantrums and lectures and put-downs and—dear goddess, how had I put up with it all? Briefly, I wondered what would have happened if he hadn't left me. Would I still be with him, the way Jeanne was with Gilbert?

It was a sobering thought, but I shelved it for later as Jeff, who seemed to have a death wish, blithely ignored Lucan's presence—and his low, throaty growl—and thrust his face into mine, grating between clenched teeth, "*What* did you say to me?"

Jeff had never raised a physical hand to me, but this kind of intimidation was familiar—and still ugly. For an instant, my old insecurities flared, but then they settled back beneath my surface. Always a part of me, but no longer pertinent.

"Dad, for God's sake, back off," Paul snapped, but Jeff ignored him, too. So did I.

"I said," I grated, staring unflinchingly back at my bully, "shut up. And sit down."

I didn't wait for him to comply, because I knew he wouldn't. I would have to "help" him. *Air*, I thought. And with no effort beyond making the decision, I connected with that element and waved my hand, and a gust of wind—controlled and just strong enough—burst through the room and pushed Jeff backward and into a chair. Shock made his mouth hang open and a momentary apprehension flitted across his expression, then his fury returned, and he tried to surge up again.

It took even less effort to hold him there. And to have the wind snatch away his words as they emerged from his mouth, making his spittle fly back in his face and the tie he wore flap wildly over his shoulder.

"Jesus, Mom—what the hell—" Paul croaked. He put himself between me and the bed, his animosity toward me returning. His fear of me.

My window for helping Natalie was closing. I looked over at Lucan, and with his uncanny ability to know my thoughts, he closed the room door and leaned against it to prevent anyone else from entering unannounced. Medical staff would likely frown at my administration of Keven's potion to my daughter-in-law, especially when it started to glow.

I reached into the pocket at my hip and pulled out the tiny sachet. Keven's herbs had barely begun to sprout, and she'd been hard-pressed to gather enough to put any kind of potion together, never mind one that had to counter what she suspected was dark magick at work in Natalie.

"I wasn't with her when it happened," she'd said as she carefully combined the herbs she'd plucked from her new garden, *"but if she encountered a Mage, it is likely. This will bring her back, but it will take time."*

"How long?" I'd asked.

"Too long for you to remain to see her." The gargoyle had tied the sachet and handed it over to me with instructions on how much water to mix it with, and the incantation to repeat as I administered it. Then she'd patted me awkwardly and somewhat painfully on the shoulder. *"She will recover, milady. You have my word."*

Sachet in hand, I looked now at my next hurdle, Paul, and took a deep breath, ready to launch into an explanation, to beg him to let me give the potion to Nat, and to have Lucan hold him back if necessary.

He spoke before I could. "Is that for Natalie? Is it magic?"

The chair under Jeff bucked as he renewed his escape efforts. I met my son's gaze. "It is."

He clenched his fists at his sides, clearly struggling between what he perceived as impossible and his desperation to get his wife back. "Will it wake her?"

"Not right away," I said, "but yes. It will."

"And it won't hurt her?"

I let out an involuntary little hiss, and he shook his head. "I'm sorry. I shouldn't have asked that. I know ... I know you wouldn't hurt her. At least, not on purpose."

He still held me responsible. The knowledge was like a tiny knife slipping between my ribs, but at the same time, from his perspective, it was fair. Without responding, I indicated the woman in the bed behind him with my free hand.

"May I?"

There was a last hesitation, and then Paul stepped aside. Avoiding his chair-bound, visibly enraged father, he took up a position on the other side of the bed and watched as I tipped the herb sachet into an empty glass on the bedside table, poured exactly two fingers worth of water from the pitcher that was also there, and then swirled the contents together.

The herbs dissolved with a sizzle that was audible even over the steady beep of the monitor tracking Natalie's heartbeat, and a soft green glow enveloped the glass. Paul reached a hand out across the bed in a *wait* motion.

"You're sure about this," he said, his voice hoarse.

"I am."

His hand stayed, protectively hovering above his wife as he wrestled with himself. Then Lucan, still holding the door, cleared his throat.

"Someone wants in, milady," he said. "We need to hurry."

A banging on the door underscored his words and galvanized my son into making his decision. He pulled back his hand and nodded. "Do it," he said.

I leaned across the bed to gently pull Natalie's chin down.

Her lips parted, and I trickled a bit of the still-glowing liquid between her teeth, waiting to make sure her swallow reflex would kick in. It did, and I trickled some more as the banging at the door got louder and voices joined the demand for entry. Then, as the last of the potion disappeared into my daughter-in-law, panic gripped me. I'd forgotten the words Keven had given me, and without them—

"Let the light return and darkness depart," Edie's calm voice said, *"so you may be whole in your mind and know love in your heart."*

I almost sagged on top of Natalie, so great was my relief. "Thank you," I whispered, and then I repeated the words into Natalie's ear, putting heart and soul into their magick, their healing.

"Mr. Emerson!" a muffled voice reached through the crack where the door had edged open, despite Lucan's weight against it. "Mr. Emerson, what's going on in there? Open this door!"

"Milady," the shifter growled.

I looked over my shoulder at him. Nope. Make that snarled. Because his desire to shift into wolf form in the face of imminent threat was written in every line of his rigid body. I was out of time.

"Coming," I said. I pressed my lips to Natalie's cheek, set the glass on the table, and looked across the bed at my son. "I have to go. I don't know when—if—" I stopped, pulled together my unraveling emotions, and said, "She'll be fine. You'll be fine. But, Paul"—I nodded toward his father, fighting against the magick that held him in the chair and rendered him silent—"you're not him. For the sake of Natalie and Braden, do better. *Be* better."

"Mom, wait—"

But I didn't. I couldn't. I turned away from my son's extended hand and from his wife—and from the ugly rage that boiled in my ex—and met Lucan's gaze. "Open it," I said.

The door burst inward. A security guard tumbled to the floor, with a second nearly falling on top of him and a doctor and nurse staggering in their wake. In the same instant, I released the magick holding Jeff as he made another lunge. His momentum carried him up and out of the chair, arms pinwheeling, and he sprawled face first beside the guard on the floor.

In the ensuing tangle of limbs and flurry of demands to know what was going on, Lucan and I slipped quietly out the door and started down the corridor to the accompaniment of Jeff's enraged bellows—and, for me, Edie's chuckles.

"Don't you dare walk away like that, Claire Emerson! Get back here! Do you hear me?"

"Up yours, asshat," Edie muttered, and it was my turn to chuckle.

Lucan glanced down at me, an eyebrow quirked. "Milady?"

"It's nothing," I said. "Thank you for not interfering, by the way."

"There was no need," he said. "I would have interfered had you needed protection, but you did not."

I couldn't be sure, but I thought I detected a note of pride in his voice, and I smiled again. Closure *and* implied praise from Lucan? I'd take it. And then, still riding high on the closure part, I outright grinned as Paul's weary voice, raised above his father's, reached us just as Lucan pushed open the door at the end of the corridor.

"For chrissake, Dad, Mom is right. Shut up for a change, will you?"

"Huh," said Lucan, letting the door swing closed behind us. "There might be hope for that boy after all."

I'd take that, too.

I just wished I could be here to see it.

CHAPTER 31

I REACHED FOR MY HOOD AS WE STEPPED THROUGH THE sliding doors and into the snow again, then drew up short when I saw the vehicle that was pulled up to the curb before us. Jeanne, halfway out of the passenger seat, froze, stared back at me in equal surprise.

"Milady?" Lucan murmured beside me. His hand settled into the small of my back and nudged me forward enough that the doors could close again behind us, tension in his touch.

"It's all right, Jeanne is just ..." *Just a friend*, I'd been going to say, but was she anymore? On the other side of the car, Gilbert's scowling head popped up over the roof, and I scowled back. He was decidedly *not* a friend.

"I remember her," Lucan said. "And him." His hand didn't move.

"I've got this," I said, but I didn't feel nearly as confident as I hoped I sounded, and I was loath to move away from his warmth and strength. Saying goodbye to Natalie—along with my unexpected encounter with Paul and Jeff—would have been enough closure for me. Running into Gilbert, too? That just elevated the level of special.

"Jeanne." I stepped toward my former neighbor and maybe-friend for our usual exchange of hugs and cheek-busses, then hesitated, remembering how she'd sidestepped my embrace the last time I'd seen her. "Uh ..."

The brown eyes behind the red-framed glasses were guarded, but not hostile. "Claire," Jeanne replied. "You look—"

"You'll be late for your shift," Gilbert barked from across the car.

Jeanne pressed her lips together, then sighed. "He's right, actually," she said, with a little shrug of apology. She reached out and took my hand, pressing it between hers. "But I've been wanting to talk to you—about the last time I saw you. I said things I didn't—can we maybe get coffee this week? Do you have time?"

"I don't—I won't—" I shook my head and collected my words. "I'm sorry, but I'm leaving tonight, and I don't know if—when—I'll be—"

"Good riddance," snapped Gilbert. "Jeanne. Your shift."

"I'm fine, Gilbert," she retorted, rolling her eyes. She pulled me to one side with her, out of her husband's earshot. Her gaze searched mine and, despite our increased distance from the car, she dropped her voice to a murmur. "Something is happening, isn't it? It's that damned book …"

"The book has done what it needed to do," I said. "And you did what *you* needed to do."

"By putting you in danger?"

"By giving me what I needed to meet the danger I already faced."

"I'm sorry," she said. "For the things I said, and how I behaved. I was just—I'm not cut out for this kind of thing, Claire. I'm not brave like you. Or strong."

I snorted. "Are you kidding me? You're one of the strongest women I know, Jeanne Archambault! Look at what you do here" —I tilted my head toward the hospital beside us— "almost every day. Not to mention what you put up with at home." I winked to take some of the sting from my words, but I still meant them, because living with Gilbert required enormous strength, in my opinion. If only to keep from smothering him in his sleep.

Jeanne smiled sadly.

"Are you okay?" I asked. "Staying with him … is that what you still want?"

I braced for her anger, but she didn't take offense, only looked thoughtful for a moment, and then resigned as she once more stepped away from strength into the familiar. The comfortable.

"For the most part, yes," she said. "Although a holiday might be nice, one day."

We laughed the polite, slightly sad laugh of friends who knew too much about one another—and who knew when not to dig deeper—and then Jeanne pulled me in for a brisk hug.

"I really do have to get to work," she said. "And you—you'll be careful? We'll have that coffee when you come back."

"Of course," I lied, both about being careful and coming back, I suspected. I returned her squeeze, released her, and watched her discreetly wipe away her tears as she trudged across the sidewalk and into the brightly lit hospital interior. Tears for me, or for herself?

"Both," Edie said. *"Stupid woman."*

I didn't argue, not because I thought Jeanne was actually stupid, but because I knew Edie didn't think so, either. Slapping on the label was just a way to distance herself from our friend's pain—and our own helplessness.

"Milady." Lucan touched my elbow. "We should go."

"Yes," Gilbert sneered. "You should. And this time, you should stay gone, the way you said you would."

Goddess, but I detested the man. Shoulders rigid, I crossed the sidewalk to stand beside his car and stare across the roof at him. I remembered my desire to turn him into a cockroach if I ever got my magick back and wondered if such a thing would be possible now that I had.

"I'm open to finding out," said Edie, as Gilbert continued to spout off about my unwanted presence and Lucan began a silent seethe at my side.

I was open to finding out, too, but instead, I sighed. Whether or not I agreed with Jeanne's decision to remain with him, it was still her decision to make—and I was fairly sure altering her life without permission would constitute a use of power that the Morrigan would frown upon.

At least, permanently altering it would. But what if it was temporary? I stared past Gilbert's head to the crisscross of ley lines shimmering and shimmying across the parking lot as the tiny seed of an idea sprouted. Jeanne *had* said that a holiday would be nice ...

"Why, Claire," my inner friend said with delight, reading my thoughts even as they took shape. *"I didn't think you had it in you. Where are we thinking? Russia? China? The middle of the Sahara?"*

Her suggestions all held distinct appeal, but again, I wanted temporary. Something that would inconvenience the man, not render him dead.

Well ...

I brought my thoughts to heel and tuned out Edie's other suggestions of Mars or the moon as Gilbert blathered on in the face of my silent pondering of his fate. Somewhere distant, I mused, where he'd face questions and potential incarceration while his inexplicable appearance in the country was investigated, but not imprisonment in abysmal conditions. Somewhere ... neutral.

"Switzerland," Edie and I said together, although Lucan heard only my voice.

The shifter frowned down at me, distracted from his seething. "Pardon?"

"Switzerland," I said again, because what better country was there than the very epitome of the word *neutral*? I nodded satisfaction. It was perfect. I just had to figure out where to find a magical creature to—

I looked up at Lucan and raised an eyebrow in query. Puzzlement glimmered in the amber eyes. Then understanding. Then amusement.

"Switzerland," he echoed. "You're sure?"

"Quite."

A slow grin spread across his face behind the beard. "It will be my pleasure, milady," he said. "I'll be back shortly."

His gaze narrowed as he looked across the car to Gilbert, who had stopped talking to watch our discussion with something approaching caution. I decided I liked the expression a great deal more than his usual condescending one. Especially when Lucan vaulted easily across the car's hood to his side, and sheer panic took over.

Gilbert fumbled for his door handle, but it was too late. Lucan's strong arms encircled him, and before he could utter so much as a squawk of surprise, the shifter swept him into the nearest ley.

"Well," said Edie in my head. A single word, but it said so much more: w*ell done; I didn't think you had it in you; he had it coming; Siberia would have been better.*

"Well," I agreed, more than a little astounded by my request of Lucan. And a little disappointed that I couldn't have played a more active role in Gilbert's displacement. Ah well, at least he'd know that it had been my idea.

"You should probably park the car and take the keys to Jeanne," my friend nudged.

Park it, yes—and I did—but take the keys directly to Jeanne and have to explain why? Not a chance.

"Excuse me," I called out to a bearded nurse pushing an empty wheelchair through the doors marked "Emergency." "Do you know Jeanne Archambault?"

The nurse paused in the entry, and I joined him, slipping between the doors as they slid closed.

"It's a small hospital," he said. "Everyone knows everyone here. I think she just came in for a shift. Did you need to see her?"

I shook my head and held out the keys. "Can you just give her these for me? They're for her car. It's parked under the lamppost in the far corner of the lot."

"Sure," he said, taking the keys from me. "But I thought her husband was driving her in tonight."

He wasn't kidding that it was a small hospital.

"Change of plans," I said. Down one of the corridors, I spotted the security guards who had fallen into Natalie's room.

One was speaking into a cell phone, both wore determined expressions, and both had zeroed in on me. I scuttled for the sliding doors again, pausing long enough to add over my shoulder, "Can you give her a message for me, too? Tell her Claire said, 'Happy holidays.'"

"Happy—" He broke off, looking confused, and blinked at me. "As in Christmas?"

"As in she'll understand." At least, I hoped she would. I stepped out into the night again and started across the parking lot toward the ley line back to the Earth House. I hoped, too, that she'd use her holiday to reflect on whether the safety she claimed she wanted was worth the price she paid for it every day of her life.

But that was her battle, not mine.

Me? Now that I'd taken care of the closure I'd needed, I had an entire war to win. And this time, I was ready for it, because Keven had been right.

Endings were immensely powerful.

CHAPTER 32

"WE'RE READY WHEN YOU ARE," KEVEN SAID. SHE SOUNDED calm enough, but I suspected that if her knuckles could have turned white as she held the kitchen door frame, they would have.

For balance, she'd said. So that she wouldn't accidentally topple on top of me as the house landed wherever it was going to land. Or as hard as it was going to land. If it landed at all. Or took off in the first place.

Because we didn't know for sure. With no precedent, we didn't know anything at all. Just like we still didn't have much of a plan at all.

My gaze went to the ginger cat draped over the gargoyle's shoulder. Keven and I had both tried to remove him and put him out of the house, thinking that he would be better off staying behind. He had, after all, made the trip to Edie's once already, and if he found his way there again, I knew Jeanne would look after him. Gus, however, had his own ideas, and he had hissed at both of us and returned repeatedly to his perch, until we'd finally given up.

I had no idea if he would survive the trip through the ley, or what we might find at the other end, and my heart hurt when I thought of the danger I was about to put him in. But as I looked into the calm eyes that were an exact match to his ginger fur, he slow-blinked at me in cat language, seeming to tell me that he knew what was coming, and that he'd made a choice.

Intercepting our exchange, Keven took one hand from the door frame and placed it over the cat, who slow-blinked a second time, then closed his eyes in satisfaction. Keven nodded to me.

It was time, as Braden liked to misquote, to rock and roar.

Turning back to the worn, familiar table, I studied the pinch of short, salt-and-pepper hairs in the stone bowl before me. Kate's hair, retrieved from a brush in her house—the real Kate's house—by Lucan. Kate's, because the destruction wrought to the Earth house had been so complete that nothing of the Crones or their protectors had survived for Lucan's sensitive wolf-nose to find.

The hair's residual energy, a faint, barely there purplish glow, would, with my help, seek out its origins via another energy route—the ley lines. Then, in theory, the house—again with my help—would follow, and we would find the others and confront Morok at last. We hoped.

There was also a better-than-middling chance that we would land in the middle of an ambush, with every creature Morok controlled waiting for us, from shades to medusa to goliath. Or that we would simply be too late.

"We won't know until we try," Lucan said quietly, reading my mind. He stood on the other side of the kitchen from Keven, by the door that led to the garden, also holding onto the frame.

He was right, of course. We also didn't know if I could do this at all, if I tried. Which, when I thought about it, was probably why I hesitated. If I didn't try, I couldn't fail.

Trust, whispered the book on the table.

I downgraded my mental retort from "*fuck off*" to "*not helping.*" Then, because delaying was just making matters—or at least my nerves—worse, I stretched my hand out over the bowl, and summoned my intent. First, I bound myself to the house, rooting my feet to the stone of the floor as I had once done in the cellar—but on purpose this time. Then I turned my attention to the hair.

"Find her," I murmured to it, letting the shimmer of magick flow across my skin and drip from my fingertips into the bowl to mingle with that of Kate's hair.

"Slowly," Keven warned. "Too much, too fast, and you'll destroy it."

Lucan's gaze swung from me to her, and I sensed his puzzlement at the gargoyle's apparent interference with a Crone's magick. If he only knew. But I marched my thoughts away from the distraction and made myself focus on the hair … on the tiny hitch in its energy as my magick touched it … on the brightening of the shimmer around it as I fed—

A spark erupted in the bowl, and the hair fragments evaporated in a curl of smoke.

"Fuck," I said, staring at it in dismay. Then in horror. And then in plain annoyance, because seriously? I planted my hands on my hips, glared at the wisp that was all that remained of our plan, and reiterated, "Fuckity, fuck fuck *fuck*."

Could *nothing* about this magickal life of mine ever be easy? Just once? I was willing to take on the god of darkness and deceit himself, for goddess's sake. Willing to be a vessel for half of that same goddess's power. Willing to turn my back on my former life and sacrifice my entire—

The floor trembled beneath my feet. I glanced up, expecting to see Keven lumbering across the slate toward me. She hadn't moved. The floor trembled again. I looked down at my feet, still bound to the stone, and frowned. If Keven's footsteps weren't causing the vibration …

Something seized my wrist, and I jerked my attention up from the floor. There was nothing there—nothing I could see—but what felt like icy fingers held me fast, digging into my wrist, holding my arm outstretched. I couldn't pull away, my feet remained glued to the floor … and I didn't think this was how the plan was supposed to go.

"Um, Keven?" I croaked. And then I bellowed as the invisible hand holding mine tried to tear my arm from its socket and pain radiated through my shoulder and elbow. "Jesus Christ on a cracker!"

"Hold on!" the gargoyle shouted. "It's moving!"

I blinked back tears of pain. What was moving? The hand holding me? *No shit, Sher—*

I stopped in mid-sarcasm. Wait. She meant the house. The house was moving. It lurched and bucked beneath my fixed feet, throwing my body left, then right, then left again like a rag doll, albeit one with her arm in a vise. The tiny wisp of smoke that had risen from the burnt hair grew denser, darker, then billowed into a black cloud that filled the kitchen. Somewhere in its depths, Lucan coughed, but I could see neither him nor Keven. I tugged fruitlessly at my hand, one foot, the other foot. Nothing gave except for the ligaments popping in my shoulder.

Self-recriminations came fast and furious, delivered in my good old, reliable Claire-voice. *This was such a bad idea. A horrible idea. Why did you ever agree to—*

"Heads *up*," Edie interrupted the tirade. *"Something's coming."*

I peered over my shoulder at a ribbon of light undulating sideways through the smoke toward me, winking pale pink, then a deeper rose, then crimson. It behaved like a ley. But it didn't look like any that I'd seen before.

It wasn't much as far as distractions from being drawn and quartered went, but it let me tune out my former Claire. And then I realized that the ley wasn't moving toward us after all. *We* —me and the invisible whatever it was towing me—were moving toward *it* … and its hue was deepening with every inch closer that we got, until it was the color of thickened, drying blood.

All of my former-Claire's misgivings crashed in on me, and her voice shrieked at me to get away, to stop whatever this was before it was too late. Frankly, I was inclined to agree with her. But even as Edie snarled at her to shut up, it was already too late. The ley brushed against my bare arm, and I was sucked into a vortex.

The house attached to my feet followed.

CHAPTER 33

WE LANDED IN CHAOS, NOT ALL OF WHICH WAS CAUSED BY
me dropping a stone cottage into the middle of a city street.
Because that's where we were—and in a sizable city, judging
from the height of the buildings towering above me as I lay flat
on my back amid rubble and twisted metal. I blinked grit from
my eyes and spat it from my mouth as I stared upward.

Everything I thought I'd known about ley travel had been
thrown out the proverbial window on this trip. Without Lucan
to shield me in the circle of his arms, I'd expected to be disman-
tled atom-by-atom as I had been when I'd traveled alone before.
To be torn apart and dissolved in acid, to become my own
agony, and then to have the entire process reversed. I'd braced
myself for it.

What I hadn't braced for was absorbing an entire house, all
of its contents, and its three other occupants. For having to
expand to do so. For being stretched beyond all limits, and then
beyond imagination, and then beyond even that, until acid and
dismemberment would have been a blessing—all while spinning
through the vortex that was the path to Morok and who knew
what other horrors.

And then the spinning had stopped with a suddenness that
was the equivalent of smashing into a granite mountainside. The
house and its contents—including its occupants—had ripped
free of me, and I had slammed to the ground in a giant pile of
rubble and dust, with no idea where either Keven or Lucan were.

The other horrors, however, were more than evident.

Broken bricks, scraps of twisted metal, and shattered glass
littered the pavement around me—and judging by the lumps
digging into my spine, beneath me as well. I wondered if we'd
landed in a war zone, or at the very least, at the site of a bomb-

ing. Sounds bombarded me from all sides as voices shouted orders and instructions, others cried and called for help, and sirens wailed, their echo bouncing off buildings. Then a single, high-pitched shriek of terror pierced through the cacophony. More screams followed.

With good reason.

The bronze-colored building above me had begun shedding windows from its stepped facade in a random hail of giant, lethal glitter—and winged shapes poured from every opening they left behind. My jaw went slack, and my breath turned solid in my throat. Shades. Dozens of them. They screeched downward with outstretched talons and deadly, barbed wings to circle the heads of screaming pedestrians scrambling to find shelter.

The city didn't stand a chance against them. I rolled over and struggled to my hands and knees, and then—then, it got worse.

A gossamer-fine black filament landed on a broken brick beside my right hand and flared into white fire. Another followed, and another, and then they were everywhere, drifting through the air to land on every surface, each bursting into flame wherever they touched. The ones that dropped to the street flared harmlessly. The ones that landed on anything flammable, not so much.

An explosion rocked the street as a disabled vehicle halfway down the block turned into a fireball. A man ran from it, screeching and flailing at the inferno his hair and suit had become. I flung out a hand toward him, fingers tingling with magick, but he'd already fallen, his screams abruptly cut off, and I knew I was too late. At least for him.

My hand still extended, my gaze darted up, down, left, right. Where did I begin? Shades and glass continued to drop from the building, a visible cloud of fire pixies descended in their wake, and I still had no idea where—or *if*—Lucan and Keven were. Panic began a slow uncoiling in my chest. What if they hadn't made it through the ley with me? What if I'd dropped them somewhere along the way?

I finally had control of my magick, yes, but there were so many monsters, and I still had to find Morok, and—

A shadow loomed over me, and I flinched. Then a strong hand grasped me under the armpit, hauled me to my feet, and pulled me into an embrace with my face buried against a solid chest. A familiar, forest-y scent filled my nostrils, and my world rocked on its axis. Lucan. Lucan had made it after all, and with him—

A stone hand clamped onto my shoulder and spun me away from my moment of comfort, then turned me this way and that as its owner examined me for injury, batted away the incoming fire pixies, and muttered about how lucky I was to be alive.

Keven. She'd made it through the ley, too. A wave of relief and gratitude swamped me, doubled when I saw the grimy, indignant cat wrapped around her neck, and then faded as I saw past Gus to the Earth house—or what remained of it.

It sat crookedly, half sunk in the middle of the wide, four lane street, with the pavement buckled and broken around it. Its chimney was missing, along with most of its roof—and behind the gaping, ragged hole that had been its front entry, there was nothing. No staircase. No interior walls. Only a sense of despair and weariness that permeated the little that had survived. An uncertainty about its own future—and about mine.

I may have managed to bring the newly healed house with me, but my magick had turned it into a battered, empty shell. Not Morok's magick. Mine. Just like it had been my magick that had devastated the forest and destroyed the thousands of wards when I'd released it the first time.

Oh, I'd silenced Jeff and bound him to his chair at the hospital without killing anyone, but that magick had been small. Contained. What if the bigger magick, the stuff that required the full release of my powers, what if that would always be more than I could handle? What if I went up against Morok and made things worse instead of better? What if—

Keven suddenly pulled me hard against her, sheltering me

with her body as a pane of glass shattered against her back. My nose scraped against the granite of her shoulder, and the sting made my eyes water. It also stopped my pity-party thoughts in their tracks even as the chaos of a city under attack continued around us: sirens, screams and bellows, the shriek of incoming shades.

Because, like it or not, we three—me, Keven, and Lucan (with Gus as our mascot, bless him)—were the last resort here.

I was the last resort.

I closed my eyes and took a deep, steadying breath. I honestly had no freaking idea if I could do this, whatever "this" turned out to be, but I had to try. I *would* try. Keven put me away from her, her expression grim as she looked to Lucan.

"We're running out of time," she said. "You have to find Morok. Now."

"And where," he growled back, waving both hands at the street and all its buildings, "do you suggest we start looking?"

"You cannot sense your Crone?" she asked.

"I cannot." Lucan's voice was heavy.

I tried not to flinch at the implications behind that. It didn't mean she was dead, I assured myself, only that my presence still interfered with his sense of her. There was still a chance—there had to be a chance.

While gargoyle and shifter argued over where to look for the dark god, I looked up at the tower beside us. The structure seemed oddly familiar, but I couldn't place why. And while the windows had stopped falling from it, it continued to bleed shades and fire pixies. As if it were—

"The epicenter," I muttered.

My gaze trailed down the building's stepped facade, from the top floor to the brass and glass entrance a few dozen feet away, and then it stopped. I stared at the lettering on the polished marquee that proclaimed the building to be—

I blinked. Drummond Tower? Seriously? I craned my neck to the left, then the right, seeking confirmation and finding it in

LYDIA M. HAWKE

a lopsided street sign at the intersection. It read *Madison Av*, with an image of the Statue of Liberty beside the words. My jaw went slack.

Jesus Christ on a cracker. No wonder it seemed familiar.

Madison Avenue. I was on Madison Avenue ... in New York City.

I tried to adjust to the idea that I'd brought a house, a gargoyle, and a wolf-shifter with me through a ley line to freaking New York City—which was not, by the way, how I'd imagined eventually visiting here—and then to let it sink in that Morok's lair was *the* Drummond Tower on Fifth Avenue in that city.

I grabbed Lucan's arm, yanked him around, and pointed at the marquee. I was right. I knew I was right. Morok was here, in the landmark building owned by Ronald Drummond, a billionaire and former politician who had built his entire empire on lies and deceit, the poster-boy for the entire freaking patriarchy and —and I'd stake my life on this—very likely one of the god's Mages.

Lucan stared at the building name for a moment, and then his gaze met mine, grim agreement behind it.

Because it didn't get more appropriate than that.

178

CHAPTER 34

WHILE THE SHADES HAD SO FAR IGNORED US IN FAVOR OF easier prey, that changed when we stepped onto the sidewalk and headed toward the tower entry. In an instant, dozens of them veered away from their pedestrian prey and flapped in our direction. Morok may or may not have been expecting us, but neither was he taking any chances. Getting to him wouldn't be easy.

Keven swept Gus from her shoulder and dropped him on the sidewalk, then thrust me toward the entrance, keeping her shade-impervious bulk between me and the attacking horde. "Go!" she ordered. "I'll hold them off."

"What? No!" I caught at her hand, panic rising in me at the thought of leaving her behind. "What if—"

I'd been going to say *what if we need you*, but a hissing screech—no, many hissing screeches—cut across the sirens and shades and every other sound in the street, and the blood in my veins turned to ice water. My head jerked around as I sought the source. I found it a block away. A massive, serpentine shape slithering down the center of the street, sliding around and over the rubble, its many human heads waving in the air. Fangs stabbed at the unfortunate souls unable to move out of its path, lifting them and throwing them aside. The heads hiss-screeched again, reared back, and then zeroed in on—

Us. It had seen us.

The medusa slithered faster, crushing those in its way, its— their?—full attention on our little party.

Fucking hell.

Lucan morphed into his wolf form and sprang in front of me, his empty clothing settling in a heap on the concrete. Snarling and bristling, he leaned against my legs, forcing me back a step. I dodged him and grabbed again for Keven's hand, no longer concerned about needing her as much as needing to protect her.

"You have to come with us!"

She shook her head. "The house's magick is damaged. It's not strong enough," she said, disentangling herself from my fingers even as the wolf wedged himself between us. "I cannot move beyond this point."

Another screech from the medusa. The sound crawled down my spine and twisted through my belly. I shook my head—at it, at the idea of leaving the gargoyle to face it, at the thought of failing her yet again.

"I won't leave you here," I said. I'd seen firsthand how ineffective Nia's gargoyle had been against the serpent, and I knew Keven wouldn't be able to stop it. Was certain she wouldn't survive the attempt. "Not with that thing. Not alone."

"But you will," she said. Her calm, stoic stone gaze met mine, a very human understanding behind it. "You will, because you cannot save us all, Crone. We each have our part to play in this. Mine is to give you time to play yours, which you will do however you must. Now go."

Before I could object any more, she thrust the staff she'd pulled from the house's debris into my hand, then pushed me into the revolving door.

"However you must, milady," she repeated, and then she spun the door until I stood on the opposite side.

My last glimpse of her was as she turned to face the oncoming medusa, the ever loyal-to-her Gus standing with arched back and puffed tail at her feet.

I MIGHT HAVE GONE BACK TO HER—NO, I *WOULD* HAVE gone back to her—if Lucan hadn't burst through the door behind me, morphed back into naked-man-form, and seized my arm. He towed me toward a bank of elevators to the left in a huge entryway built of brass and marble and mirrors, which was just as gilded as the building's exterior and utterly deserted but for us. Then he pointed at the numbers above the elevators. Each elevator went to a different set of floors, and each had its own call button.

"Which one?" he demanded.

"I have no—" I paused. Wait. If Morok was here, he'd be in Drummond's apartment. And Drummond wouldn't live in just any apartment. He'd be in—

"The penthouse," Lucan and I said together, and as one, we turned toward the furthest elevator with the polished *Penthouse* proclamation above it. Before we'd taken more than a step toward it, however, the doors slid open.

With a screech that echoed through the deserted space, a shade burst from the interior and hurtled toward us. Lucan became wolf again and leaped for it, but his nails scrabbled on the polished marble and failed to find purchase, and his teeth snapped shut on air.

Instinctively, I slammed the end of my staff against the floor, held up my other hand, and summoned the power of Earth. A shimmering, almost invisible wall sprang up between me and the oncoming shade, too fast for the monster to slow or change direction. The foul creature slammed into the magick with a force that shattered it—the shade, not the magick wall—and a bloody mass of feathers and broken bones splattered six feet high and twice that wide.

As if in slow motion, blood and feathers slid down the wall and dripped into a black and red puddle on the floor, halfway between me and the elevator the shade had come from. A lifeless yellow eye settled into the center of the gore and stared up at me. I stared back, then lifted my hand again and stared at that, too.

In the distance, I registered the steady clack and hum of escalators, and the intermittent screech-hiss of the medusa as the sounds of the battle outside drifted through the slowly revolving door. My hand returned to my side, and my gaze dropped to the ooze on the white and gray marble, and something inside me broke loose and began a slow crumble. *I* had done that?

I knew the shade would have killed me if I hadn't killed it, but it didn't change that I *had* killed it. That I had, purposefully this time, raised my hands against another being and summoned the intent to destroy. That I would, before this was done, very likely need to do so again. And if it had been this hard to kill a monster, how would I—

Lucan's cold, wet nose nudged into my hand. I looked down into the amber eyes that warned me that we needed to move on, that told me he would stay in wolf form, that promised he would not be taken by surprise a second time. I clamped my teeth together against a plea that he take his human shape and hold me, knowing he could not. Would not.

Knowing it would be unfair of me to ask.

I dug my fingers into the thick, warm fur of his ruff, holding on as if to an anchor, and closed my eyes, searching within myself for reconciliation with my magick.

Through the revolving door came the boom of another explosion that made the marble shimmy beneath my feet. Then the wail of a siren. Then the angry bellow of Keven. The latter lanced me to my core. Keven. Beautiful, gruff, rough-hewn Keven, who had already given up all she was once, and who stood out there now, willing—expecting—to give up what she was now. Again.

I forced my eyes open. Then I lifted the end of my staff from the floor and my cloak from around my ankles, and I stepped around the remains of the shade to push the elevator call button.

Because yes, I had done that. And I would do it again.

However I must.

Because I must.

CHAPTER 35

IT WAS A TOSS-UP AS TO WHICH ONE OF US—ME OR LUCAN—was more tense when the elevator doors slid open onto the penthouse and silence greeted us. We waited for long seconds, Lucan barring my exit to prevent me from stepping out of the elevator (not on my immediate agenda), and me holding my staff in a hand that ached from its grip.

I stared out into the massive foyer, blinking at the sheer over-done opulence. This was a modern-day New York apartment? It looked more like someone's version of an overdone fantasy palace. Glitz didn't begin to cover it. Neither did gaudy, for that matter. It was ...

My gaze traveled over a sea of gold, along a marble floor and up marble pillars to the soaring, gilded ceiling. I blinked at a massive chandelier dripping with crystals. It was appalling, was what it was. And not as empty as it appeared.

Lucan's ruff lifted, and his lip curled in a silent snarl of warning as he looked up at me, and I nodded. I'd heard the chanting, too. I strained to listen, but the female voices were too muffled to identify. I could, however, tell that they came from above.

A staircase—marble, of course (how *was* the building standing up under all this weight?)—soared upward to our left, and I nudged Lucan's shoulder with my knee. Hackles raised, he padded toward it. I followed, my chest tightening with every step, until I struggled for enough oxygen to keep me upright.

We reached the foot of the wide, sweeping staircase. It stretched up to a second floor, and then beyond that to a third, and I had to tilt my head back to take in its full height. Its sheer audacity. Its—three looming wolves bounding toward us?

I whirled away, striking out with my staff as the first wolf launched at me from mid-staircase. Wood struck canine shoulder, wolf jaws closed on my cloak, I pulled, fabric tore, and—

"Enough!" a familiar voice roared.

The wolf holding my cloak released it so suddenly that I stumbled into the wall before Lucan's hand grasped my arm to steady me.

"Milady, are you hurt?" he demanded, channeling his inner Keven and turning me one way and then the other to examine me for injury.

I pushed his hands away. "I'm fine, but—" I stared past his bare shoulder at the man standing behind him at the foot of the staircase. The man who had shifted from wolf—not the one with strings of my cloak fabric hanging from its teeth—and roared at the others to cease and desist. Bearded like his brother beside me, one-armed, and looking as astounded at seeing us as I was at seeing him and the others.

"You're alive," he said, directing his words to Lucan rather than me. No great surprise there, because there was no great love lost between me and Bedivere after the near-death kitchen incident. "We thought—we were sure—why didn't you follow us?"

He shot me a suspicious, accusatory look as he asked the question, obviously suspecting I had somehow conspired to keep Lucan away from him and the others. Then his eyes narrowed at me.

"And you," he said, "Kate—Morok told us you were dead. He has your pendant."

"I—"

"There are only two ways a pendant can change hands," the burly protector continued, overriding me. "First, if a Crone dies. Second, if she gives it."

The wolf with the bits of my cloak in his mouth morphed into Yvain, who spat out the dark blue material and advanced toward me, hands curled into fists at his sides. "You *gave* him the pendant? Do you have any idea what you've—"

He stopped as Lucan inserted an arm between him and me.

"It's a long story," Lucan said, "and one we don't have time for now. Where are the Crones?"

"They're fine," said Bedivere. "We overpowered Morok, and they're raising their magick now to do the split."

"Overpowered?" I blurted. Whether my skepticism was in my voice or my expression, I didn't know, but none of the three protectors took it well.

The remaining wolf—Percival—snarled at me, and Bedivere's glower was enough to make me want to take a step—or ten—backward. I held my ground and hoped that my wiping of sweaty palms against my cloak was surreptitious enough that he wouldn't notice.

"You question the veracity of my words?" he demanded.

"I'm not questioning what you think happened," I said, "only—"

Bedivere's expression turned murderous. Okay, maybe I'd take one small step back. Just enough to pull myself together. I did, and then I took a deep breath and prepared to try again.

Lucan forestalled me. "The building is spewing out shades and fire pixies," he told his brother. "They're overrunning the city. And we left Kev—our gargoyle—battling the medusa on the street below. If Morok was truly out of commission, none of that would be happening."

"The medusa?" A flicker of uncertainty crossed Bedivere's face. "You're sure?"

"I've fought it often enough, so yes. I'm sure."

But Bedivere still shook his head. "Morok is down," he insisted. "It took all seven of us, and we waited days for the right opportunity, but he lowered his guard today. We attacked together and overpowered both him and his Mages. Lady Maureen imprisoned the Mages in a chamber she called a panic room, and the Crones have Morok bound and gagged in their circle. We left them there when we heard the elevator arrive."

I sidled around Lucan toward the stairs, but Bedivere intercepted me. "*Your* assistance," he said, "is not required."

"She's not here to help them, she's here to stop them," Lucan said.

Part of me wished I'd been the one to deliver the news that made Bedivere's jaw drop. A smarter part of me thanked the goddess Lucan had beaten me to it. Hastily, I returned to the safety of his protective wall as Bedivere's expression went from hostile to murderous, and he morphed from man to wolf and back three times as if trying to decide which form could do more damage. He settled into the one that could snarl intelligible words, albeit ones delivered with a spray of spittle that found its way to my cheek.

"She's *what*?"

Yvain moved forward to stand shoulder to shoulder with him. "Over my dead—" he began, but his words dropped off as the floor beneath our feet heaved, and its marble cracked in two with a resounding snap. Then the room—no, the entire building—tipped toward me and Lucan, pitching me against a pillar and sending Bedivere stumbling into me.

For a moment, I couldn't breathe. The shifter's weight crushed me, and my nose was squashed against the shoulder that held no arm. Then the room began to right itself, and Bedivere braced his one arm against the marble and pushed away, his brow knotted into a deep scowl as he widened his stance to find his balance. The swaying stopped, but the gallery of paintings on the wall along the staircase remained askew, and if Lucan was standing as straight as I was sure he was, the building had attained a serious left-leaning list.

But that was the least of our concerns.

"The chanting," I said, shushing Bedivere with a wave of my hand when he opened his mouth to speak. I looked past him to Lucan, a tiny hope sparking in me. Had we been wrong? Had the Crones truly overpowered Morok after all and achieved their purpose? "They've stopped chanting. Was that it? Was that the—"

I broke off as hundreds of ribbons glimmered into view

around us, their movements no longer graceful undulations, but spasmodic, convulsive twists and jerks. Ley lines—but not as they should be. These ones had ends. Severed, ragged ones that bled light onto the floor and squashed my newborn hope.

"That's not good," I whispered.

"No," Lucan agreed. "And neither is that." He pointed toward the living room to our left, with its bank of windows overlooking the city, and a sky that had turned to a dark, murky crimson—with a small, ragged black hole opening in it just outside the tower.

We moved as a group toward the gilt-and-glitz room with its leopard-print side chairs and cream leather sofa, drawn by the vista unfolding in the sky outside as the hole stretched one way, then another, growing larger. Growing closer. The air left me in a wheeze of shock and horror.

Dear goddess, he'd done it.

Percival morphed into human form beside me. "What *is* that?"

"It's the beginning of a portal," I croaked. I'd never seen one, but I knew. Knew, and felt the overwhelming despair of defeat. "Morok has taken the Crones' powers. We're too—"

A familiar, chilling shriek cut me off. The unmistakable scream of a former foe, hoarse and raw and filled with the unbearable mournfulness that I remembered from my first encounter with it. The sound came from the floor above us, reverberating through the apartment. It sliced through my heart and chilled me to my core, and I would have known it anywhere.

The goliath.

It was here.

One of the protectors—I couldn't tell which—snarled, and three of them became wolf again and raced toward the stairs and their Crones. Lucan, bless his heart, wavered, morphing half into his wolf before regaining his man form. He stood, seemingly frozen to the spot, the strain of wanting both to go to Elysabeth and to remain with me etched into every line of his body, every crease of his face. His bond to her was tearing him apart inside.

My bond to him was doing likewise to me.

Outside the window, the portal shrank and almost disappeared, then expanded again—but its outer edge was ragged, and its interior seemed ... murky. Perhaps it was supposed to be like that, or perhaps Morok hadn't yet succeeded, and we might still have a chance. *I* might have a chance.

I clenched my free hand into a fist, and with my other, I gripped my staff so hard it was a wonder it didn't become a part of me. I had sacrificed myself for Lucan once before. Could I again?

On the floor above us, it sounded as if a wrecking ball was smashing through the walls and windows. The goliath screamed again, and a wolf yelped. Lucan closed his eyes, his expression one of raw agony. I studied him for a moment, committing to memory every feature, every hair, every curve of muscle on his body. I thought about all we had been through together. All we had ignored between us. All we had avoided. For a single heartbeat, I allowed myself to imagine what might have been if Lucan had been allowed the power of choice, and then ...

Then I remembered what the others had sacrificed, too. Not just the Crones upstairs, but all the women who had come before them, who had served the goddess and done their level best to protect the world from Morok. The Crones, the midwitches and witches, the wise women of the world who had suffered at the hands of the patriarchy and yet fought on against the lies and deceit that tried to take away their power.

Power that I had now. In spades.

The wrecking ball upstairs sent a shower of plaster and gold leaf down on our heads. Snarls and yelps filtered down the stairs. The others needed Lucan, and we—no, *I*—had delayed long enough. I pulled back my shoulders and touched Lucan's arm. His amber eyes shot open, torment in their depths.

"Go," I told him, past the tightness in my throat. "Hold the goliath off as long as you can. I'll find Morok."

"Alone?"

"The Crones will be there," I reminded him. And, with luck, they might even still be alive, I thought. But I kept that part to myself, along with the possibility that I might not be able to let them continue living.

"However you must," Keven had said, and we had both known what she meant.

Lucan hesitated, and I was afraid he might argue, but then he nodded. He knew as well as I did who we were—what we were—and the part we played in the events that were unfolding. If anything, he knew even better than I did, because the last fifteen centuries of his life had been leading up to this moment.

Unexpectedly, he cupped my face in his hands and pressed a kiss against my forehead. In a gruff voice, he said, "Be careful," and—before I could react—morphed into his wolf.

I blinked after his disappearing form as he bolted up the stairs to join his fellow protectors, and my hand drifted up to the tingle on my forehead where his lips had touched. Then I glanced out the window, and my heart dropped to my toes.

I raced up the stairs in Lucan's wake.

CHAPTER 36

SHIT, SHIT, SHIT! I THOUGHT AS I HIKED MY CLOAK UP around my knees and took the stairs two at a time. A gargoyle-like shadow loomed on the wall beside me. I slipped and scraped my shin against a half-shattered marble tread, and my refrain changed to a verbal, "Fuckity, fuck fuck——"

A wolf sailed down the stairs to land in a heap beside me. It scrambled to its feet and returned whence it had come, sparing me not so much as a glance. Not Lucan. I blinked back tears of pain—how could shins be so damned painful, anyway?—and returned to pelting up the stairs, albeit with a limp this time.

I paused at the top to take stock. The four protectors had encircled the goliath, but they were not faring well. One's shoulder had been torn open, one's jaw was hanging unhinged, and all were bloodied, their sides heaving, staggering. And no wonder, because the goliath was as much of a monster as I remembered, with its stone gargoyle body covered in sparse patches of fur and its elongated muzzle, currently dripping with shifter blood. It was as much of a mountain as I remembered, too, its ears scraping the twelve-foot-high ceiling as it tipped its head back to scream again.

I cringed from the sound and the wrenching, soul-deep anguish it held—if, indeed, the creature even possessed a soul. *"An unfortunate merging of Merlin and Morgana's magick,"* Lucan had called it, *"Not quite wolf, and not quite gargoyle."*

I wondered whether there might once have been a man behind the wolf, but now wasn't the time to dwell on it. The shifters were doing as I had asked Lucan to do. They were holding the goliath off, and now—now, it was my turn to play my part.

"However you must," Keven's voice whispered again in my memory.

I did a quick scan of the upper hallway where we stood, and my gaze settled on the doorway beyond the goliath. There. The room on the other side would overlook the portal we'd seen from the window below, and Morok would be there.

Of course, the part about it being on the other side of the goliath was ... problematic.

I could have used magick. But summoning it would require an effort I preferred to reserve for Morok, given that I'd never thought to ask anyone if magick was a finite or a bottomless kind of thing. Did it get as tired as its practitioner did and require time to replenish itself?

So many questions and so little time to—

The goliath's head swiveled suddenly on its massive stone shoulders, and I froze as beady eyes fixed on me. For a second, we stared at one another—me and the monster created through no fault of its own—and then it roared in unmistakable, savage satisfaction, swatted aside the wolf standing between us, and lunged.

I'd lost count of the number of times Lucan had saved my life, and not just literally. The skills he'd taught me—the martial arts lessons with the staff that he'd subjected me to—had awakened in me instincts I'd never thought I possessed. Never imagined possible. Like the one that had me nosediving toward the floor even as the airborne wolf struck a wall with a sharp yelp.

Without conscious thought, I aimed myself at the gap between the goliath's legs and slid across the marble beneath it before it could slow its momentum, never mind change direction. I scrambled to my feet in front of the door, reached for the knob, threw every possible praise at the goddess when it turned in my hand, and slipped through to the other side. I slammed the heavy oak door shut on wolves and goliath alike, then instinctively sketched a sigil (something I hadn't known I knew) in the air. It flared with purple and blue light that spread out across the door, flared fuchsia, and sank into the wood.

To be honest, that last bit surprised the hell out of me, but only for a second, because whether I understood it or not, I was becoming accustomed to the *accept* part of the book that seemed to relate so closely to the *know*. And I was damned grateful for the knowing part, too, especially with the goliath throwing itself at the other side.

I took a step back as the door visibly shook in its frame under the assault. Whatever spell I'd cast, it wouldn't hold long.

I turned to face the room I'd slid into. It sat at the corner of the building, and its two interior walls were lined floor to ceiling with books. A cynical part of me snorted in surprise that Ronald Drummond would even bother to own a library, then I decided it was probably just for show, as so many other things in his life were.

The other two walls were all windows, of course, and I'd been right about the room overlooking the portal. And about Morok being here.

What I hadn't expected was to find him—still in Kate's body, of course—lying slumped in the middle of the Crones' circle. The women stood at the four compass points—north, south, east, and west— arms outstretched and eyes closed, their chant now just a murmur, which explained why we'd thought it had ended. So far into their trance were they that they seemed not to have noticed my entrance.

I hesitated, confusion obscuring the purpose I'd entered with. Had Bedivere been right? Had the Crones really managed to overpower Morok after all? But if that was the case—

I stumbled as a tremor began in the floor beneath my feet, grew to a shake, and became a sway that encompassed the entire building. The wall of windows cracked, a painting smashed to the hearth from above an ornate white-and-gold fireplace, books and knickknacks tumbled from shelves. Outside, beyond the portal, a building began a slow collapse, then another, then another, forever changing the skyline—and thousands of lives. A pall of smoke and dust rolled out over the city. The result of Morok opening the portal? Or—

The Crone's voices rose again in volume.

I whirled away from the devastation. "Stop!" I yelled. I launched myself at the circle. but succeeded only in winding myself. It was like trying to run through solid rock. I shouted and waved and danced a mad kind of jig, trying to get someone's attention: Nia, Maureen, Anne, Elysabeth. But none of them opened their eyes or seemed to know I was there. They were too far into their spell to see the devastation they were causing—and I was too late to stop them.

Or was I?

My hand found the pendant hanging from my neck. My fingers closed around it. An idea began a slow unfurling deep in my mind. I tried to turn away from it, because it was too awful to contemplate … but I had run out of options. It had come down to a simple choice: Did I let the Crones continue with their splitting of Morok's powers, which would destroy the entire world? Or did I not?

"However you must," said the memory of Keven's voice.

"Fuck," I whispered back. And then again, *"Fuck."*

My fingers tightened their hold on the pendant and the crystal at its center, and I turned my focus inward, to the slow build of my own power. My feet took root in the floor, and then in the building beneath, and then in Earth beneath that. Air swirled around me, expanding and contracting with each inhale and exhale. Water gathered in the walls and ceiling. Fire burned at my core.

I took my hand away from the pendant, letting my staff fall to the floor beside me, and blindly, instinctively, began to knit the elements together, my hands darting here and there to draw symbols in the air as I had seen Jeanne do. Ancient symbols, drawn from a place of knowing in me that I had never before visited.

"Goddess symbols," the ancestors' voices whispered.

Across the room, Nia opened their eyes and turned their head, a tiny frown of puzzlement between their brows as if they sensed something out of place. But they didn't look at me, they looked down. Looked at—

My gaze followed theirs and my heart kicked against my ribcage. My hands faltered in their air sketches. In the center of the Crones' circle, Morok had uncoiled from the floor. He rose to Kate's feet, stretched her arms wide, and laughed a tinkling laugh of pure, unadulterated mania. The Crones' voices dropped into silence, and the rest of them opened their eyes to stare at what Nia had already seen. Confusion gathered in their expressions as they glanced around at one another, and then looked back at the god spinning wildly, like a dervish, in their circle.

They took no notice of me at all. Belatedly, I realized that their circle didn't let them see what was outside its boundary. It did, however, let me see in. And what I saw made me go cold all the way down to my toes.

Morok was spinning so fast that he'd become the center of a vortex, and it was sucking in every atom of power that the Crones had raised, feeding it into him. The faster he spun, the more energy the vortex pulled from the circle; and the more energy it pulled, the faster he spun.

It was the epitome of a vicious cycle.

And now the Crones were raising their hands and sketching sigils of their own, and—

Shock held me immobile. We'd made no plan for this possibility, Keven and Lucan and I. I was supposed to stop Morok at the power level he already had, not after he'd absorbed the magick of the four Crones. Or, alternatively, to stop the Crones themselves from completing their split. But not this.

I wasn't prepared for any of this. I was so completely out of my depth that I didn't know where to even begin, and— and dear goddess, when had I become so arrogant that I thought for one second that I could—

"You're not arrogant," whispered Edie's voice, and I could have cried at the welcome familiarity. Might have done, if it had been only her voice. But as she continued speaking, other voices joined with hers.

"You are powerful," they said,

And still more. *"Know that, Claire Emerson. Know your power."*

Until they were a veritable chorus in my head, their reverberation vibrating through my chest, my heart, my core. Until my own voice joined with them.

"Accept the power. Trust it. Be *it."*

For one breath, one heartbeat, one last-ditch second, I resisted. I tried to believe that the voice was wrong. *Wanted* to believe it was wrong, because the alternative was too big. Too much. Too—

The battle I'd left outside the room smashed into the door, and I heard the wood crack.

"Fuck," I whispered. My staff leaped from the floor into my outstretched hand, and I brought it crashing down on the space between Maureen and Elysabeth. The force that met it jarred through my sixty-year-old shoulders and across my neck, and a hiss of pain escaped me. I was going to pay for that tomorrow— in spades.

If I survived that long.

I gritted my teeth and swung the staff again, this time aiming for a spot in midair that looked different, sparking slightly like a faulty electrical cord. The staff bit deep. Sparks exploded. A faint line appeared, running vertically from floor to ceiling, bleeding a pale violet light.

I forced my way through the split I'd made in the magick— not unlike what I imagined pushing through half-dried cement might be like—and grabbed Maureen's arm, bracing myself against the vortex's suction.

"Maureen!" I yelled over the howl of a wind I hadn't been able to hear from the outside. "You have to stop!"

Perplexed eyes turned on me. "Claire?" the Air Crone mouthed, her voice lost in the noise. "How——"

"No time!" I shook my head. "Morok is siphoning off your powers. He's already opened the——"

I got no further.

CHAPTER 37

THE VORTEX EXPANDED ABRUPTLY, SHOVING ME OUT OF THE circle, filling the room, and blowing out the entire wall of windows across from me. The howl of wind became a screech. The Crones kept their footing, but only just, their robes flapping around them as if they'd taken on lives of their own, the Crones' expressions masks of astonishment—then fear—then grim understanding. The building began a slow, inward dissolution, swallowing its own debris as the portal entered the room. It expanded. Yawned wide. Inch by inch, it moved toward the circle that still had Morok at its center.

The Crones fought back, their hands moving and darting before them, their mouths opening and closing on words I couldn't hear. Whether they were still trying to create a split or just trying to stop the god didn't matter. They were losing, and the more magick they raised, the more spiraled away from them and into Morok.

I grabbed for the pendant resting against my chest. It was time to bring to bear the full force of the power the Morrigan had given me. Time to end this. But even as I gathered my intention, Morok-Kate held a hand aloft at the center of the vortex, turned to face me—and laughed.

My concentration wavered, and then my blood turned to ice water in my veins as my gaze went to his upraised hand.

Was that a pendant dangling from his fingers? A Crone pendant? But how—? I tore my gaze away and glanced around the Crones' circle. I couldn't see their pendants, but if the women were working this kind of magick, they must have them. And if they had their pendants, and I had mine ...

I pulled my thoughts up short. Deceit, I reminded myself. Morok was the god of deceit. The pendant in Kate's hand was just an illusion, and he was trying to buy time. Trying to distract me. I firmed my stance and tightened my grip on my pendant, seeking its power. It eluded me as Morok-Kate laughed again.

Shit. I was letting him get to me. I turned my focus away from him, away from the other Crones, away from the advancing portal. I had to do this, and I had to do it *now*, before the portal reached the god who had opened it. I squeezed until the edges of the pewter frame around the crystal cut into my fingers and palm. I reached again for its power. The pendant—

The pendant crumbled in my grasp.

My focus and intention did likewise. I turned my fist over and unfolded my fingers. I blinked in bewilderment at the little pile of dust in my cupped palm. Had I squeezed too hard? But if Keven was right about it containing the Morrigan's power—half of it—that wouldn't be possible.

I gasped as cruel fingers seized my hand and turned it over to dump the dust on the floor. Morok-Kate stood inside the Crones' circle, one arm stretching through the wall formed by the vortex that still swirled. Kate's short salt-and-pepper hair did a manic dance in the wind.

"You seriously thought I'd let it be taken from me?" Morok sneered with her voice. "That I could be so weak?"

Still working through my bewilderment, I didn't know how to respond—or what to think. The pendant Gus had brought me was a fake? But that couldn't be, because I'd used its powers. Used it to rebuild the house, to put Jeff in his place, to heal Lucan, to bring the house and Keven and Lucan here, to seal the door against the goliath.

"You see?" Morok said, holding the pendant—*my* pendant— up again to twirl between us. "You're like all the rest of them, Claire Emerson, every witch that came before you, who thought they could stop me, because you have nothing. You *are* nothing. I was always going to win, and now I have."

The battle I'd left raging in the adjoining room crashed through the wall in a shower of plaster and splinters of gold-leaf molding. The goliath went down under the pile of wolf-shifters, but not even their teeth could penetrate the stone hide, and it shook them off and staggered to its feet, tilting its head back to roar in fury and its peculiar pain. So much pain.

Morok-Kate gave my hand a final, vicious squeeze and tossed it away from him like something distasteful.

"I win," he said again, "*Crone*."

Crone.

I knew Morok intended the word, filled with bitter invective, as an insult. A dismissal of me, of the ancestors who had come before me, and of the women whose powers he was stealing even as he spoke. And an unforgivable dismissal of the millions and millions of women around the globe whose very relevance had been stripped from them over the millennia by the lies he told and the deceits he wove.

Crone. My fingers clenched around the linden staff as the word settled into me. The dark god may have meant it as an insult, but I knew better. I knew the magick in the word. The power. I knew it. I accepted it. I trusted it. And now ...

Be, the book whispered to me.

And I was.

I drew myself up to my full height as the protectors fought fiercely to keep the goliath away from the circle containing their Crones. I planted my feet wide on the marble floor, barely noticing that, mere inches to my left, that same floor ended abruptly, with no wall to prevent a sixty-odd-story drop into a city under attack by monsters no human had ever seen before.

A new fire ignited in my core. Not one of magick and heat, but of cold fury, and my entire world slid into razor-sharp focus. I saw it all—and all at once. The Crones held captive by the god in their midst, dangling in the air at the edges of the circle they themselves had cast with the best of intentions. The pale purple light of their powers draining from them into the pendant Morok held. The disgusting, opulent display of wealth and power surrounding us, built on more lies and deceit and the backs of others. The city in flames at the foot of the building. The world beyond, which, if it survived, would continue to stagger for generations to come because of what Morok had whispered to it and what too many had believed—no, had been *willing* to believe.

Just as I had been willing to believe that my power lay only in the Morrigan's pendant. But it didn't. It couldn't have, because even without it, I had healed the house and Keven, brought them through the ley—

Understanding gelled. The ley lines. That was what had happened in them as I'd traveled alone in search of Lucan and the others. I hadn't been losing my magick; it had been changing as the power had moved from the pendant into me. The power had been *becoming* me—and I, it.

I just hadn't known how to recognize it at the time. I hadn't been ready.

But I was ready now. And I didn't just recognize it, I could *see* it, too, in the white light dancing across my skin and the sparks shooting outward to form an aura around me. White, the color of connection to something larger than me—to the Morrigan herself.

The vortex had slowed, moving sluggishly as it drew the last of the Crones' magick from them, and I lifted my gaze to the women hanging above the floor through no magick of their own. Their hands twitched limply at their sides.

Against all odds, the wolves had moved the goliath and their battle out of the room again, but it didn't matter, because Morok was nearly done. In a moment, he would have the Crones' full power—half of what had once belonged to the Morrigan.

Elysabeth's gaze met mine across the thinning vortex wall, her expression equal parts sad, defeated, and determined. We stared at one another for a moment and then she nodded her head. *"Do it,"* she mouthed. *"Stop us."*

However you must, Keven's voice reminded me.

I swallowed hard against the knife suddenly lodged in my

throat. Had it really come to this? Did four women really have to die to prevent another power-hungry asshole from trying to destroy the world? Four *more* women?

I stared at Elysabeth. At Maureen. At Nia. At Anne.

Then I lifted my chin and stood taller than I could ever remember feeling, and I reached deep into the new fire at my center. Reached for it, let it dance through my veins, and owned the fury that it fed in me. Because kill the ones who most deserved to live?

Fuck that shit.

CHAPTER 38

"ENOUGH!" I ROARED, AND THE FURY OF THE WORD drowned out the wind of the vortex and the sounds of battle between goliath and wolves alike. It reverberated through the remains of the room. It shook the crumbling floor. Because I wasn't just Claire anymore, and I wasn't just the Morrigan, either. I was *them*, too. I was the Crones who served her and all the others who had come before them through the millennia, and the ones who might have but never had the chance, and we were *done*.

We were also in trouble, because Morok-Kate whirled to face me before my voice had even died away, and a ball of crimson fire rolled toward me.

I had no time to brace, never mind deflect, and it hit me like a giant sledgehammer, separating me from my staff and slamming me backward into the bookcase-lined wall. Books rained down on my head and buried me beneath their weight, but they were nothing compared to the weight of my own magick turned on me, crushing every atom of air from my lungs.

"*Get up,*" a voice commanded.

I couldn't even whimper in response, let alone obey. My entire body was imploding, my bones felt like they were melting, and I couldn't separate pain from—

"*Get up!*" the voice said again, and a tiny, distant part of me frowned. Was that my—

"*Cheesy rice on a cracker, woman, get up and fight back, already!*"

It was. I blinked through the agony of melting. It was my Claire-voice. Actually advocating for me to fight and not to run away. It was a rather monumental moment, when I thought about it, but did it really have to take Morok nearly blasting me out of the building to get her on my side? I sucked in a tiny breath.

Me, and all of the women who were part of me.

My bones became solid again. I drew a deeper breath.

And now he'd gone back to his portal work. Turned his back on me—on *us*—as if we were of no consequence. As if we didn't exist, never mind matter. The prick.

"Right?" my Claire-voice almost squeaked in its indignation.

I scowled at Morok-Kate's back. At the salt-and-pepper hair. At the outstretched arms. At the power flowing toward them, each a distinct color as it drained from its owner. Bright blue from Nia, purple from Maureen, pale yellow from Elysabeth, and a deep, rich orange from Anne. The absolute *prick*.

I shoved aside the book under my hand and braced my palm against the floor. Gritting my teeth, I pushed upward from beneath the many tomes and staggered to my feet, then stood swaying as the books fell away from me and dropped over the edge of the disappearing floor. I wasn't just running out of time; I was running out of building.

The portal had reached the circle and hovered now at its edge. Its perimeter seethed with deep, blood-red flames tinged with black; its center remained murky and dense. It was twice the size that it had been outside the window. And, inside the circle, the Crones' powers danced together in a swirling rainbow. They merged easily with one another, forming new colors, then separated again, but despite the grim effort etched in every line of Morok-Kate's body, they refused to enter the pendant—*my* pendant—held aloft in his hand.

He didn't seem to notice that I'd stood again, so focused was he on his purpose. He had clearly dismissed me as a threat. There would be no better time to strike than now, but if I was wrong … if he sensed my magick again …

I wouldn't get another chance.

The hole forming between worlds writhed and twisted, flames bleeding from its border, its center notably less dense.

Morok was gaining control. I still had no idea what I was going to do, but I raised shaking hands and focused on his Kate-back. Maybe if I summoned everything I had, if I hit him with all I could muster, then—

A new idea occurred to me. At first, I thrust it out of my mind as quickly as it had entered, because it was an awful idea, rife with the potential for utter disaster, and desperate even for me.

And then … then, in almost the same instant, I let it back in again, breathed through it, and let it settle into my core. Because, truth be told, going up against Morok was equally rife with risk.

And sometimes the most desperate ideas—like opening portals instead of closing them—were all that you had.

As plans went, it wasn't much of one. In part because I had no time to refine it, but mostly because of its glaring issues.

The first issue was timing. If this was going to work, I had to take the pendant back from Morok before he went through the portal. No pendant, no Crone powers, no escape. He would be trapped in Camlann for eternity. With it, however, I had no doubt that he would follow through on his threat to collect all of his powers from all of the splinters that had been created, and then return here to destroy the world in its entirety. Because, prick.

So, yes, timing was everything, and I didn't have a great track record where that was concerned. I'd underestimated Morok the last time I'd tried to outmaneuver him, which was how he'd gotten hold of my pendant in the first place. I absolutely could not underestimate him now.

The second issue was what I would do with the pendant if

—*when*—I got it. It contained almost all the powers raised by the Crones—which was half the powers of the Morrigan herself —and I had no idea how to disperse those powers, or if I needed to, or what it would do to the world if I did.

Or if I even could.

And third ... third, how in hell did one go about opening a portal?

In the end, I relied on instinct and brute force. I rooted myself to Earth and pulled Fire from my core, and Air and Water from the room around me, and then I wove them together with the ancient symbols whispered to me by all those who had gone before. My hands flew through the air before me, weaving and knotting and stitching, and with each sigil they created, the elements grew stronger and the magick in me expanded. Slowly, I formed a sphere before me, solid and ephemeral at the same time. I cradled it in my palms, hardly daring to breathe lest it fly apart or dissolve—or, goddess forbid, I dropped it.

It was ... exquisite. It contained every color that ever existed—and no color at all. It was translucent, and it was opaque. As luminous as dawn and as dark as the darkest night. It was everything I possessed, everything I was, and it was ready.

I raised my gaze from it toward the portal. It was ready, but was I?

Just then, a wolf slid past my feet toward the drop into the city, fifty stories below. Its nails scrabbled desperately, futilely, for a hold, and piercing blue eyes—Yvain's eyes—met mine as it began to slip over the edge. I jerked a hand away from the sphere and beckoned to my staff. With the speed of a whip, the linden limb shot out a tendril that wrapped around the wolf's shoulders and lifted it back onto solid floor, then released it and recoiled again. It moved so fast that I almost couldn't follow its path. So fast, that I almost missed its significance. Its importance. The role that it could play.

And then I knew how I was going to make my plan work, and that I, too, was ready. I was more than ready.

Yvain limped past me—the battle with the goliath had returned to the room again—and, sphere before me, I walked toward the circle. Purpose marked my every footfall. Determination, every thud of my heart in my chest.

When I reached the staff, I didn't pause, didn't hesitate. I stretched out a hand above it, and the limb flew up from the floor and into my grasp. My fingers closed over the smooth, familiar shape, and I continued forward with it. Me and my linden—given to me by Keven and carved for me by Lucan—together again.

The circle tried to resist me when I reached it. I pushed through. The vortex tried to throw me out. My hair and cloak whipped wildly about in its wind, but I didn't give so much as an inch. I stepped between Nia and Maureen into the circle's center, and then stopped behind Morok.

As if they had been waiting for me, for this moment, the Crones' powers wound around one another, coiled tighter and tighter, and slipped into the pendant the god held in Kate's outstretched hand.

"Now!" shouted the voices of a thousand ancestors.

I obeyed without thought, without hesitation. I threw my hands wide, releasing the sphere from my left and the staff from my right. One end of the staff slammed into the marble floor, shattering it, piercing it. Standing rooted and upright like the tree it had once been, it lashed out with a tendril as it had to Yvain, but this time, the tendril wrapped around Morok's wrist and with its tip, pried the pendant from Kate's unprepared fingers.

Before the dark god could react, the sphere of magick flew into the heart of the unopened portal and exploded in a blinding, dizzying flash of light. My eyelids slammed shut against it, and sparks went off behind my eyeballs.

"You!" Kate's voice hissed.

I forced my eyes open, blinking away the spots dancing across my vision. Her face was inches from mine, and she—no, Morok—was livid. I wanted to quail from the absolute, utter hatred behind those eyes, but I didn't. Timing was everything, I reminded myself—and so was the element of surprise.

"Me," I agreed. I grabbed hold of Kate's shirt front and pulled the dark god closer. "And *I* win, asshat."

I shoved as hard as I could. Caught off guard, Morok stumbled backward. Surprise flared in his expression—and then realization as he understood what was happening. He flung out a hand as he fell toward the open portal, grabbing for the pendant held by the staff. His fingers—Kate's fingers—caught in the chain, slowing his fall. Then the pendant tore free from the tendril.

Morok stumbled, caught his balance, and slowly straightened to Kate's full height in front of the open portal.

Half a dozen feet separated us.

It might as well have been the breadth of the universe.

I had failed. I had failed, and now Morok had the pendant, half the Morrigan's power, and an open portal to absolute destruction. I watched him hold the pendant up in triumph, letting it dangle from Kate's fingers and twirl on its chain. With her other hand, he reached out and scooped a handful of red flames from the portal's edge, and then, with a single, invective-filled, "*Bitch*," he drew back Kate's arm to launch the magick at me.

I made no move to protect myself. There was no point. We had lost. I, the Crones, the Morrigan. The thousands who had come before—

A blur of gray shot past me.

"Lucan, no!" I lunged after him, but I was too late. Lucan's wolf left the floor, fangs flashing white, aimed at Kate's throat. Time stood still. The world dropped into slow motion.

Lucan's front paws hit Morok square in the chest. The god grunted at the impact, and surprise bloomed across his expression. His arms flew up and forward as Lucan's weight carried him backward into the portal. It began to close.

Instinctively, desperately, I threw myself after them.

I didn't know what my intent was. I didn't want to go through the portal myself, and I knew I wasn't strong enough to pull Lucan back, even if I could have grabbed hold of him, and—

My fingers brushed against pewter and crystal as what felt like a block of concrete slammed into my ribs. At the last instant, as my feet left the floor, my hand clamped shut, and then—

Then I was sprawled on the floor, and the goliath was disappearing into the shrinking portal, and the portal screamed—or maybe the goliath did—and brilliant, crimson fire flared, and ...

It was gone.

CHAPTER 39

My horror was instantaneous. My grief, absolute.

I stared at the emptiness. I had done it. I had opened the portal, and Morok had gone through, and now he was forever trapped in the Camlann splinter, where his diminished powers would make it impossible for him to open any other portal.

And I'd trapped Lucan with him.

I wanted to dissolve into the grief. To let it pull me under. To lose myself in its profoundness. I wanted to *be* it, because right then, in that moment, I didn't know how to be anything else.

But I could not, because I was still something more. Something other. I was mother, grandmother, friend, Crone ... and right now—I looked down at my clenched hand—right now, I held a veritable ticking bomb.

The pendant I had snatched back from Morok bucked and burned in my grasp, searing my palm. The magick it contained, taken from the Crones, surged against its confines, demanding release. It was all I could do to hold onto it—and the Crones who might have known what to do to keep it from blowing up in all our faces were slumped in little, semiconscious piles on the floor.

Or what remained of the floor. Because that was bucking, too, and disintegrating more with every undulation that marble was never meant to endure. Great chunks of the penthouse had fallen into the city below, including the better part of the panic room that had been revealed behind one of the bookcases by the collapse—along with its Mage occupants, it appeared.

I didn't know how the building was still standing. I knew only that Lucan was gone, and—

Hard fingers closed over my wrist and yanked me to my feet.

I looked up into a naked Bedivere's fierce scowl. He nodded at my fist.

"Can you control it?"

"I …" I trailed off and shrugged, a pitiful lift of my exhausted shoulders. "I don't know."

His mouth tightened behind his beard. I would get no sympathy from him. "Try," he said. "We need to get the Crones out of here. The building is coming down."

As if to underline his words, a steel beam dropped from the gaping hole in the ceiling, landed in the middle of what had been the Crones' circle, and began to melt into a puddle. Another, still above us, dripped molten metal onto Bedivere's bare shoulder. He let go of my wrist to sweep it away and, without so much as an acknowledgment of his charred flesh, added, "You can help Elysabeth."

"But—"

He cut me off. "The leys out of here are broken. There are three protectors and four Crones. If you don't help her, she will die."

I watched him join Yvain and Percival to clear the opening where they and the goliath had smashed through the wall. I was fairly sure we were *all* going to die, but yes. Yes, I suppose we should at least try to get out. Lucan would have wanted —

I closed my eyes against a fresh stab of grief and the tears that wanted to follow. The scorching pendant settled into an ominous pulsing in my hand, each throb more intense than the last.

Enough. My roared word returned to whisper through my mind, but it carried no power anymore—only weariness. Defeat. Because dear goddess, hadn't I done enough? Given enough? How much more could the Morrigan possibly want from—

The sudden rush of wings filled the air, and I ducked as a crow flew past my cheek, so close that its feathers brushed my skin. Dozens more followed, a black cloud swirling above the fallen women. As one, the three protectors shifted into wolf form and crouched, snarling, over their respective Crones—and then, just as swiftly, each shifted back into man form and dropped to one knee before the woman who emerged from the cloud.

No, not the woman. The goddess.

The Morrigan.

As before, she was dressed in a long gown of what looked like black feathers, but I knew it to be actual crows that clung to her.

As before, she held herself regally, haughtily—every inch a goddess even without her powers.

Unlike before, I felt no fear. No intimidation. Not even a hint of a tremble, except in the hand holding the pendant, which I was sure had welded itself to my palm by now. That trembled a *lot*, mostly with the effort of holding that much power together.

The Morrigan looked down her beak-like nose at me, black eyes glittering. "You defeated him," she rasped. "You did well."

"Did I?" Bitterness laced my voice, and I felt Bedivere's narrow gaze on me. I gestured at the crumbling building, at the open wall overlooking the city that had learned today about magick—and suffered mightily for it—at the Crones who tried and failed to rise before the goddess they served. At a world that no longer contained Lucan.

"The cost ..." I trailed off, unable to put the losses into words.

A crow-clad shoulder lifted carelessly. "It would have been greater had you failed."

Which I might still do, if I didn't safely disperse the power trying to crawl out of the pendant and along my skin. Grimly, I tightened my hold yet again—and then I understood the Morrigan's presence.

"You've come for this." Gritting my teeth against muscles screaming with tension and fatigue, I lifted my shaking arm and extended my pendant-holding hand toward her. I didn't open my hand—in part because I was afraid the power would escape, but mostly because I was pretty sure my fingers had seized shut.

The Morrigan inclined her head. "You may bring it to me."

Oh, I may, may I?

I didn't suppose one should snort at a goddess, but the sound escaped before I could catch it back. All three protectors' heads whipped around at my disrespect, and a scowling Yvain half rose from bended knee. He subsided again, head bowed, when the Morrigan's gaze swiveled in his direction. I wondered if I should apologize for insulting her, and then decided I really didn't care. I'd had my fill of gods and goddesses and the wars they waged with humans as their pawns, and if she chose to smite me, or whatever goddesses did to their underlings, so be it.

The Morrigan held out her hand. I stared at it, mulled over the wisdom of refusing, then stepped forward. Because whether I liked it or not, she was still a goddess. And because I wanted to be rid of the damned pendant.

Thin fingers wrapped around mine, talon-like and leathery, their nails pointed, black, and curved. My own fingers resisted for a moment—I was right about them having seized up—but they were no match for the ones prying at them. The pendant left my grasp, and the energy it contained rolled outward like a wave.

I flinched, expecting the worst. A shudder ran through the building—through the very air itself—and the protectors threw themselves over their Crones to shelter them from falling debris. All but Elysabeth, of course, who had no more protector. I took an instinctive step in her direction, but the falling debris stopped, and she seemed to have escaped the worst of it, and the wave of power—

I turned back to the Morrigan, who studied the pendant she held. The pendant of the Fifth Crone—my pendant—which now contained the powers Morok had taken from the Crones—the ones the Morrigan had split between the four pendants of Earth, Air, Fire, and Water.

But not the ones that had become a part of me.

The crystal in its center pulsated with a soft, mauve glow, and as I watched, even that died away, until it sat inert in the goddess's open palm. I held my breath and waited for her reaction.

"Well," she said. She looked from it to me, her head cocked to one side like that of one of the birds she resembled, her gaze curious. Thoughtful. Measuring. As if she could see through me to the power itself. "Well," she said again. "I did not foresee this occurrence."

I held my hands up and out to my sides, palms open and facing her. "It wasn't intentional," I assured her. "I didn't mean—"

She silenced me with a gesture. "If I thought you meant to, you would be dead already."

Already. Did that mean there was still a chance? I swallowed and continued holding my arms out. I sensed movement from the protectors and/or their Crones, but I didn't dare take my eyes from the Morrigan. I might have half her power, but she had the other half back, and she knew far better than I how to wield it.

The silence between us grew. I worked up the nerve to break it.

"What do we do?" I asked. "You can take them back from me, right?"

"Not while you live, no." She continued to study me, her gaze traveling from head to toe and back again. Then, at last, she shrugged again, with both shoulders this time. "It is what it is," she said, as if rendering judgment.

Which she was, in a manner of speaking.

I dropped my arms, quivering from the strain of holding them out, back to my sides. "Wait. You mean, I'm to keep them? Your powers?"

"I see no other way. They have become you, and you have

become them. I will not destroy you to take them back. I will wait until you die."

She said it so matter-of-factly that I couldn't even be upset by the morbidity of the declaration. I could, however, be surprised. And I was.

"You would do that for me?" I blinked at her. "You would wait that long?"

"I have been without the greatest part of my powers for centuries," she said. "A few years more will not matter."

I tried not to think too much about what her definition of a "few" was. And I was far too exhausted to decide how I felt about retaining half the powers of a goddess, right now. I mean, on one hand, the idea was life-changing, but on the other hand, my life had already changed so much that I wasn't sure it would make a difference anymore. I shelved the conundrum for later contemplation.

"Say thank you," Edie hissed in my ear.

"Thank you," I said. *I think.* A new question occurred to me. "Um … am I allowed to use them?"

The Morrigan stared at me, then tipped her head back and laughed with a rusty sound that made me wonder how often, if ever, she made it, and—were her black eyes actually twinkling at me?

"I should think your companions would be glad if you did," she replied. "As would the city dwellers, to have you move the house out of their midst. The ley lines are regenerating."

Good point—and good to know. But I still had questions. "What about after that?" I asked.

The goddess regarded me for another long moment. Then her thin lips curved beneath her beak-like nose, and she repeated the words she'd used when I had refused the Cup of Power she'd offered me at our first meeting.

"You'll do," she said. And with that, her gown exploded into an outward rush of wings, I ducked, and she was gone.

CHAPTER 40

THERE WAS NO FANFARE IN OUR RETURN TO THE CLEARING outside Confluence. No sense of triumph or victory. No sense of anything, really, except overwhelming loss. At least, that was the case for me. I didn't know how the others felt.

After opening a portal and defeating Morok, returning what was left of the house and its occupants to the clearing outside Confluence had been, magickly speaking, almost an easy task for me. But the Crones had been barely conscious, and their protectors injured, and the moment we'd arrived, Keven—who had blessedly survived the medusa's attack—had thrown herself into healing them.

She'd confined them to the shattered sitting room at first, then moved them upstairs when the house had healed enough to provide sparse second-floor rooms on the day after our arrival. Since then, she'd lumbered up and down the rickety stairs countless times, with Gus following like a silent orange shadow in her wake, but I hadn't ventured that far. Partly because Keven preferred that her patients, especially the Crones, stay quiet, but mostly because ... well. Because.

I looked up from the table as heavy footsteps heralded Keven's return to the kitchen. Sure enough, Gus was at her heels. Half of one ear was missing, he had a gash healing above one eye, and a patch of fur had been scraped from his shoulder, but —miraculously, given the monster he and Keven had gone up against—he had survived. My gaze went back to the newspaper that Percival, the least damaged of the protectors, had stolen from someone's porch that morning,

Pictures of the destruction we'd left behind in New York City dominated the front page even now, four days after our return. We had defeated Morok and his monsters, yes, but the city had suffered enormously, and the repercussions were being felt around the world.

Magical creatures, as it turned out, couldn't be captured in photos or video, and any footage of the attack showed nothing more than the devastation being wreaked—buildings collapsing, people dropping to the ground, spontaneous fires breaking out, explosions. Despite the inevitable rumors of alien attack, most governments and politicians were blaming the devastation on terrorists from just about every country and faction in the world, and the resulting saber rattling was downright terrifying.

Which meant, essentially, that even with Morok gone, little had changed.

"It will," Keven assured me, as I muttered as much and set aside the paper.

I scowled. Because things might change here, perhaps, but what about in Camlann? What would life be like there for Lucan, consigned for eternity to the same splinter as the dark god and the goliath that had gone through the portal after them? I shuddered at the thought. Goddess, what a mess I'd made—

"Ahem." Edie cleared her throat in my head. *"Who made?"*

I sighed. This not taking responsibility for the entire world was tough, but Edie was right. "Morok," I murmured, and it was as much a reminder to myself as a response to her. "Morok made the mess, not me."

Keven looked sideways at me as she set a cup of tea on the table, but she'd become used to my random mutterings to my invisible friend, and she didn't comment. I glanced at the murky yellow liquid in the cup and wondered what the brew was this time. The gargoyle kept changing it in her attempts to heal me of what she called my melancholy, and I kept dutifully drinking it and assuring her it was helping. I didn't have the heart to tell her that I didn't think one *could* heal from this kind of heartache. Certainly not in the span of a few days. Not even with half the powers of a goddess coursing through one's body.

Keven tapped a stone finger on the newspaper. "It will take

time," she said, "but without Morok's influence, the truth will emerge. All the truths will. In time."

I changed the subject. "How are the others today?"

Keven grunted and shuffled back to the wood stove and the various steaming pots on top of it. I'd managed to land the house back on its foundation without destroying the herb garden she'd replanted, and she'd been able to harvest enough to begin healing the others. But with the house also healing (again) and unable to lend its magick, it was a slow process.

"You could go and see for yourself," Edie suggested, her voice a little on the tart side. Probably because it was the umpteenth time she'd made the suggestion.

No one asked you, I growled back in my head. Also for the umpteenth time. But at least I remembered to use my "inside" voice for a change.

"They're getting better," Keven answered my question. "They're asking for you."

And I preferred to continue avoiding them. I buried my nose in my cup and sipped the musky-smelling tea, then made a face at the sour aftertaste. I was nowhere near ready to rehash the tale of what had happened, or to explain how I'd come to lose Elysabeth's protector and gain half the Morrigan's powers. I hadn't even told Keven about that last part, although I suspected one of the remaining shifters might have done, because they'd overheard the exchange between me and the goddess, and Keven kept giving me long, speculative looks when she thought my attention was elsewhere.

I had the impression that she wanted to tell me something, but … well, frankly, I didn't want to hear it. I didn't want …

Fuck, I didn't even know what I didn't want.

"Maybe—" began Edie.

I gagged down the rest of the tea and slammed the empty cup on the table, cutting off the rest of her words, because I didn't want those, either. Keven sent me another of her looks as I pushed the bench back from the table, wood screeching against flagstone, but she said nothing as I snatched my cloak from the hook beside the door to the hallway.

Outside the kitchen, I paused to swing the cloak around my shoulders and let my eyes adjust to the sudden dimness. Then I stomped down the dark, narrow corridor that quite matched my dark, narrow mood.

I closed my eyes at the thought and stopped walking, then rested my hand on a rough wall to steady myself. What was wrong with me? I should be celebrating, not wallowing. I'd just done the impossible, for goddess's sake. I'd learned to control the power of the Morrigan, I'd defeated Morok, I'd moved a *house*—twice—and I'd even saved the Crones I was supposed to have sacrificed. And before any of that had even happened, I'd already stood up to my ex and begun healing the rift between me and Paul.

"And don't forget that you also sent Gilbert to freaking Switzerland," Edie added.

But not even the thought of Jeanne's husband having to explain his passport-less presence in a foreign country was enough to make me smile.

Edie sighed. *"Claire—"*

"Don't," I said. "Just don't."

So of course she did.

"You did everything you could, my friend. Lucan is not your fault."

No, but he was absolutely my loss.

My throat went tight, and tears burned behind my eyes. That, I thought, was the real reason I didn't want to see any of the Crones. Worse, they would want to celebrate my victory, and I didn't think I could bear that. Not yet. Not when victory felt so very hollow.

The corridor walls closed in on me, and my tears escaped. Fiercely, I swiped them from my cheeks. I hadn't cried yet, and I wasn't going to start now. I didn't dare, because I was afraid I might not be able to stop. I gritted my teeth, and the dull ache that I'd been carrying in my temples since waking that morning became a steady thump.

A walk. That's what I needed. Fresh air and exercise. And out of this freaking house.

"No offense," I told the corridor. The house didn't respond.

I started forward again, my entire being focused on the front door outlined by daylight creeping in around the edges of its ill-fitting frame. One more thing the house hadn't yet fixed.

"It has no reason to heal," Keven had said yesterday, when I'd asked why it was taking so long this time. *"It has lost its heart."*

"Because Elysabeth is no longer Crone?" I'd asked. But the gargoyle had merely given me one of her looks, grunted a non-response, and turned back to her cooking.

Ever helpful, was Keven.

I reached for the door handle. The sound of a throat being cleared stopped me. I didn't have to look back to know that it had come from the foot of the stairs—and from Bedivere. For an instant, I considered pretending I hadn't heard and continuing on my way, but Bedivere wasn't the sort to be ignored, and it would be easier just to see what he wanted. I let go of the handle and turned.

"Running away?" the burly shifter asked, resting his only hand, clumsily bandaged by Keven's thick, stone fingers, on the ramshackle railing.

"I need some air," I said. "I'm just going for a—"

"You shouldn't be out alone."

Before I could form an objection, Bedivere had limped down the last couple of stairs and crossed the tiny foyer that, like the rest of the house, had yet to grow to its former grand size. He stopped beside me and waited.

I dug deep for politeness. It was hard to find, especially where Bedivere was concerned. "Thank you, but I don't want—"

"Let me rephrase. You're not going out alone." He reached past me with his bandaged hand and twisted the door handle. If the action caused pain, his face didn't show it. And his gaze never left mine.

"Morok is gone," I reminded him.

"His Mages are not. And with no wards to protect the house or at least give us warning ..." He trailed off, leaving the admonition unfinished. Because that's what it was. An admonition. A pointing out of yet another failure on my part.

When I'd returned the house to the clearing, Keven had suggested that I call the wards, too. I hadn't seen the point, and at the time, I hadn't had the energy. I still didn't. But I didn't have it in me to argue with the shifter, either—especially when his next words floored me.

"Besides, milady, I need to speak with you."

I stared at him, astonishment warring with curiosity and then with more astonishment. I wasn't sure what surprised me more, the fact that Bedivere wanted to speak with me, that he'd sounded almost civil, or that he'd just addressed me as—

The full impact of his words sank in, and it was my turn to narrow my gaze. Bedivere wanted to speak with me? The very idea sent a chill through me, and running away suddenly seemed like a viable option. Curiosity, however, got the upper hand. I had no doubt that I wouldn't like what he had to say—let's face it, I never much liked anything Bedivere had to say—but I wanted to at least know what it was.

I squared my shoulders and nodded. "Fine," I agreed.

He inclined his head and held the door wider. I stepped past him and out onto the wide flagstone that served as a porch, and—

The blast of magick came out of nowhere. It hit my left side and threw me a dozen feet through the air. I landed hard on the semi-frozen ground of the clearing, grunting as the wind was knocked from my lungs. A second blast hit before I could catch my breath. The third, I managed to deflect with a flick of my wrist as my magick and survival instinct surged together. And the fourth ...

By the fourth, I had regained my feet, rooted myself in the Earth, and gathered the elements to me, almost without conscious thought, moving with the certainty of power. The power of magick. The knowledge of a goddess.

I conjured the same shimmering wall that I had against the shade that had come out of the elevator. It blocked the roiling mass of dark red, black, and burnt orange coming at me and threw it back at its sender, many times magnified. Two men flew backward under its impact and landed at the edge of the forest. One did not rise. The other regained his feet swiftly, and his hands began a dance in the air as he drew sigils to summon a hex. Dark sigils that seethed with menace and a thirst for power.

I scowled and checked my connection to Earth. It was solid. Whatever he threw at me, I could repel it. I could hold him off forever, if I needed to. But I didn't want to. This was supposed to have stopped with Morok. Did his followers not understand that their god was no more? That he wasn't coming back?

Another sphere of crackling power rolled toward me, and I parried it. The Mage facing off against me scowled, and his hands sketched faster.

"You can't win," I called across the clearing. "He's gone."

"But we're not!" he shouted back.

I fielded another blast, this time a fire ball, and sent it into the ground at the Mage's feet. He did an awkward jig to stamp out the flames in the dry grass.

"For goddess's sake," I snapped. "Enough. Morok lost. Like it or not, that means you've lost, too, and—"

Before I could finish, a blur of gray shot through the doorway and across the clearing. The Mage threw his hands up defensively, but it was too late. Crimson spurted like a fountain from him, and he crumpled onto the frost-covered grass, the magick he'd gathered again exploding in a harmless shower of sparks and sizzles.

The wolf that had torn out his throat continued on to his companion. A shriek sliced through the late-autumn stillness and then, abruptly, was cut off. I stared at the fallen men in shock. Horror. Utter disbelief.

The wolf morphed back into a naked Bedivere, who spat out a mouthful of blood as he stalked away from the fallen Mages and back toward the house. Toward me. He stopped when he reached the flagstone porch, and his gaze traveled my length from head to foot and back again. I hadn't released the magick I'd gathered yet, and I was glad of its distraction as it rippled over me, making my skin tingle.

I gestured vaguely at the fallen Mages and then let my hand settle to my side again. It clenched into a fist. "Why?" I whispered.

"They were here to kill you." He shrugged. "They wouldn't have stopped until they did."

"But we didn't have to kill *them*," I said. "I was managing—"

"No. You were delaying the inevitable. And you talk too much."

"He has a point," the always-supportive Edie chimed in.

"I …" I trailed off, because I didn't have a reply.

Bedivere grunted. "You don't like to kill, do you?"

The question startled me and made me profoundly uncomfortable at the same time. Because I *had* killed—far too many times. "I'm not a sociopath," I snapped, "so no. I don't *like* killing, and I find it disturbing that you do!"

"I'm not a sociopath, either. I'm a protector. And I protected you." Seeming to have deemed the matter settled, he leaned down to scoop up the clothes lying abandoned in the doorway by his transformation. Then he straightened and added, "But if you're going to go after Lucan, I can't be there, which means you'll have to toughen up. You'll need to be faster. And you can't hesitate. You'll need to kill, swiftly and without thinking, or you'll never make it. Do you understand?"

The ground felt like it had dropped out from under my feet, and I shifted my stance to keep from falling over in shock.

"Wait," I croaked as he turned his back on me. "If I'm going to *what*, now?"

But my words dropped into nothingness as the shifter disappeared into the house. I gaped after him, the magick still crackling across my skin, and tried to stitch together coherent thought.

"Did he just say … " Edie's voice trailed off into uncertainty.

"No." I shook my head. "He couldn't have. I heard him wrong."

"But we both heard him," she said.

I shook my head again, then remembered at last to release the magic. It slid away from me like a whisper of silk. Numbly, I lifted my cloak clear of my ankles and stepped over the threshold, back into the house I'd just been so desperate to leave.

I stood in the open doorway and stared up the staircase to the floor where the Crones and protectors were. Where Bedivere had most likely gone.

"We both heard him wrong," I told Edie. "We must have. It's the only explanation, because otherwise …" I trailed off, unable to finish.

"But what if we didn't?" my friend asked.

Lucan, my heart answered.

ALSO BY

The Crone Wars

Becoming Crone

A Gathering of Crones

Game of Crones

Crone Unleashed

(release August 15, 2023)

Once, there was power in her magick. Now, she must find magick in her power.

Claire Emerson has lost her magick—and with it, her place among the Crones. It should spell the end of her involvement in their centuries-old war against the dark god, Morok, but it can't. Because Claire knows something the others don't—Morok has become an imposter in the Crones' midst, and their destruction is imminent.

To stop the dark god's nefarious plan, Claire will have to find her missing powers. But neither she nor her allies have a clue where to start —and that's the easy part. The hard part? Getting past Morok's monsters in time to rescue the Crones. Especially when she comes face to face with Morok himself.

Will Claire's powers be enough to defeat a god and save her companions—and the world?

The Grigori Legacy

Sins of the Angels (Grigori Legacy book 1)

Sins of the Son (Grigori Legacy book 2)

Sins of the Lost (Grigori Legacy book 3)

Sins of the Warrior (Grigori Legacy book 4)

Other Books by Linda Poitevin

The Ever After Romance Collection

Gwynneth Ever After

Forever After

Forever Grace

Always and Forever

Abigail Always

Shadow of Doubt

ACKNOWLEDGEMENTS

Writing a book is never entirely a solo journey, even when you're an indie author.

First, inspiration needs to come from somewhere (thank you, Claire Faguy!), and then you need people to listen to you moan and complain when the writing gets tough (my husband Pat puts up with the bulk of that), as well as someone to remind you that yes, you really can do this (looking at you, Marie Bilodeau).

Then, when the actual writing is done, you still need to turn it into an actual book with things like a cover from the always fantastic Deranged Doctor Design, and stellar editing, provided again by my amazing friend Laura Paquet (who went above and beyond this time by letting me turn in the final chapter a full week after the rest of the book because life).

I'd also like to thank Claude Cadieux, who provided me with the locating spell that Claire uses in the story. I've seen the power of this one for myself, and you should definitely make a note of it!

And last but far from least, a special mention to the fantastic people who have emailed me and/or followed me on Facebook*. You guys have been *so* excited and enthusiastic about Claire, and I cannot begin to tell you how much that has helped me stay on track. This book? It's for all of you. Love you guys!

*If you're on Facebook, too, you can find me at facebook.com/LindaPoitevin

ABOUT THE AUTHOR

Lydia M. Hawke is a pseudonym used by me, Linda Poitevin, for my urban fantasy books. Together, we are the author of books that range from supernatural suspense thrillers to contemporary romances and romantic suspense.

Originally from beautiful British Columbia, I moved to Canada's capital region of Ottawa-Gatineau more than thirty years ago with the love of my life. Which means I've been married most of my life now, and I've spent most of it here. Wow. Anyway, when I'm not plotting the world's downfall or next great love story, I'm also a wife, mom, grandma, friend, walker of a Giant Dog, keeper of many cats, and an avid gardener and food preserver. My next great ambition in life (other than writing the next book, of course) is to have an urban chicken coop. Yes, seriously...because chickens.

You can find me hanging out on Facebook at facebook.com/LindaPoitevin, and on my website at LydiaHawkeBooks.com, where you can also join my newsletter for updates on new books (and a free story!)

I love to hear from readers and can be reached at lydia@lydiahawkebooks.com. And yes, I answer all my emails!

9 781989 457108